## Praise for Lynda Aicher's
*Energen series*

"...Aicher introduces some intriguing concepts to the ever-growing paranormal/romance field."
~ *Library Journal on* The Dragon Stirs

"The world building...is fantastic; a mix of myth, mystery and reality, historic and yet modern at the same time."
~ *Long and Short Reviews on* The Dragon Stirs

"Lots of plot twists and turns, really interesting special effects and intensely erotic suspense...If you like fantasy, adventure and romance don't miss out on *The Dragon Stirs*!"
~ *Sizzling Hot Book Reviews on* The Dragon Stirs

"I was smitten with this book from the first chapter and couldn't put it down. The descriptive prose drew me into this alternate world view of Earth and left me reaching for more."
~ *Sensual Reads on* Stone of Ascension

# Look for these titles by
# *Lynda Aicher*

*Now Available:*

*Energen*
The Dragon Stirs
Stone of Ascension

# Stone of Ascension

*Lynda Aicher*

Samhain Publishing, Ltd.
11821 Mason Montgomery Road, 4B
Cincinnati, OH 45249
www.samhainpublishing.com

Stone of Ascension
Copyright © 2013 by Lynda Aicher
Print ISBN: 978-1-61921-366-1
Digital ISBN: 978-1-60928-876-1

Editing by Christa Desir
Cover by Angela Waters

This book is a work of fiction. The names, characters, places, and incidents are products of the writer's imagination or have been used fictitiously and are not to be construed as real. Any resemblance to persons, living or dead, actual events, locale or organizations is entirely coincidental.

All Rights Are Reserved. No part of this book may be used or reproduced in any manner whatsoever without written permission, except in the case of brief quotations embodied in critical articles and reviews.

First Samhain Publishing, Ltd. electronic publication: September 2012
First Samhain Publishing, Ltd. print publication: August 2013

# Dedication

The path to publication is never as solitary as the illusion of writing makes it out to be. For me, there were many people who helped along the way.

This includes my awesome and supportive critique partners Sue, Jennifer and Paula. Thank you for your time, feedback and insights into every aspect of this story. You girls are the best.

My beta readers Lori, Valarie and Corey whose thorough reads spotted the story holes with ruthless honesty that only made the book better. I'm still amazed at your willingness to help an unknown who invaded your book club. And to Cindy for being my cheerleader the whole way.

Most of all to my family. From my parents who never doubted my dreams and were there to pick me up every time I tried and failed. To my husband and children who live with a distracted, grumpy writer but still dance around the kitchen with me when I succeed. Never forget, I will be there for you too.

# Prologue

He prowled restlessly. Anxious. Agitated. Back and forth. End to end. Over and over. Endlessly repeated after a thousand years of rest.

The flames danced around him. Taunting, biting, stroking. The heat at once pleasant and painful. A kiss and a slap. A caress and a jab.

The bars were weakening. The time was coming. His time was almost here.

Again.

His long, coarse hairs brushed against the icy metal. His scaled, spiked tail slammed against the black bars of entrapment, the whine of the failing metal music to his ears.

Soon.

The humans were finally succumbing to the dark. To the anger. To the charms of the Oppressor.

But there was still one who could guarantee his victory. Or hinder it. One who owned the key to all that would come.

Fire roared from his mouth. The flames soared between the thin spaces of the bars—the only part of him permitted to escape. For now.

Soon. His day was almost here.

The Year of the Dragon had arrived. This time, he would be freed.

# Chapter One

Amber Morningstar flinched, an automatic reflex at the sudden pop of yet another firecracker as it echoed through the night. She released her breath and forced her muscles to relax. Not an easy task given the mob of people that clogged the street and sidewalks.

Pushing back the niggling apprehension, she scanned the people again, looking for a familiar face. *Anything* familiar would be nice at that moment. Instead, she saw nothing but the continuing sea of bodies that pushed and shoved at each other in the excitement of the Chinese New Year celebration.

A fresh blast of icy air whipped down the street, gusting harshly and taking biting nips from her exposed skin. Awnings and flags fought back against the might of the elements, flapping and snapping in resistance. Amber stifled the shiver that encased her and shoved her nose into the warmth of her coat collar.

Taking her first trip to New York City in January was not the most logical move. It had sounded exciting when her friend, Kayla, had suggested the trip. The desire to come, to experience something new and different, had outweighed all the practical arguments against it.

Her Aunt Beverly had even gone so far as to expressly forbid her from making the trip.

A twinge of guilt rippled through her at that thought. At twenty-three years old, Amber could walk away from her aunt, live her own life like most grown woman did. But obligation was not easily pushed aside. Aunt Bev was her only family, and she couldn't abandon her.

So, for the sake of peace, she often found herself bowing to the desires of her aging, overprotective aunt. Desires that had limited Amber's life experiences to the stifling perimeter of her aunt's antique shop and the Wampanoag Indian Tribe of Gay Head. Any associations outside that closed circle were harshly discouraged. Growing up had been an exercise in isolation and detachment. She'd even forgone the college experience, taking online courses to earn a business degree.

But there was more to life, and she itched with the desire to experience it. The pull to come on the trip, the longing for an adventure, had been so strong she'd left a note on the counter back in Newport and came to New York City anyway.

Now she was alone, without her phone and with no way to find her friends.

The low chatter of multiple dialects and languages blended together forming an incoherent cadence of sound, making her feel even more isolated and alone. Needing out of the crowd, she let the bodies push her to the relative safety found between a fresh fish stand and a display of knock-off designer perfumes. The two scents clashed with each other in a combination that she registered as uniquely Chinatown.

"You try?" The sharp question was followed by a persistent shove of a bottle of perfume at Amber. The small Asian woman holding the offering looked at her with expectation, her smile full of hope for a sale.

Amber shook her head. "No, thank you."

The woman turned away, her face immediately flaccid as she hunted up her next customer. Amber shoved her hands into her pockets and tucked her nose farther into her coat collar in an inadequate attempt to dilute the rank fish smell.

Once again, she scanned the people in hopes of finding her friends. Her eyes caught and held on the sharp profile of a man, his tall frame allowing his shoulders and head to tower over the crowd. She blinked, her breath hitched.

It couldn't be him.

The ambient glow of the street lights and Chinese lanterns cast a valley of shadows over his face before he turned away, preventing her from verifying what she saw.

Pulled by an undefined force, she took a step to follow him before she jerked back and came to her senses. What was she doing? It couldn't be him, she repeated to herself. She shook away the thought as delusional thinking on her part.

Her pulse returned to normal as she chided herself for her foolishness. Her secret infatuation was getting out of hand. Three years of admiring Damian Aeros from afar was now causing her to wish him up in unlikely places. A childish act on her part.

"Hey, Amber." A deep voice cut through the dull clamor of the crowd. Amber jerked her head toward the sound and smiled in relief as she spotted a familiar face from their group.

"Nate," she answered, stepping forward to meet him. "I'm so glad to see you." Her anxiety eased, and she relaxed for the first time in over an hour. As mutual members of the Wampanoag Indian Tribe, she and Nate had known each other for years.

"What happened to you?" Nate inquired as he dropped his arm around her shoulders and propelled her down the street with the flow of the people. "Kayla's frantic looking for you. She has us all out hunting you down."

"I got distracted by a dragon dance." She shot him an apologetic expression and hoped Kayla wasn't too worried. "It was stupid of me to get so caught up in the performance."

But the stunning colors, the macabre face of the dragon, the intoxicating lure of the drum beats had almost hypnotized her into forgetting everything but the dance. The dragon had been so intriguing, both beautiful and frightening. Each side had pulled at her until she'd felt lost in the complexity of emotions the mythical creature had stirred within her. Even now, the distant, rhythmic beat of drums pulled at her.

Called to her.

Another chill raked her, and Nate pulled her snug to his solid frame. "Are you okay?" His breath was warm and his voice vibrated against her ear, sending small tingles down her spine as he leaned in to be heard over the noise.

"Yes." She ducked her head to hide the burning flush that raced over her cheeks. Having him this close was suddenly more disturbing than being alone in the crowd. Like most other things in her life, her experience with the opposite sex was embarrassingly limited.

She cleared her throat and tried to ease away from his side. "We should give Kayla a call. Do you have your phone? I left mine at the hotel."

"Sure," Nate agreed as he steered her to the side and ducked into a small alley. He backed her against the wall and briskly rubbed his hands over her arms. "There. It's a little quieter and warmer here."

Nate wedged his body close, forcing her to look up to see his face. A smile curved over his firm lips, but seemed to stop before it reached the cool depths of his brown eyes. The hard angles of his cheeks and square chin stood out under his dark skin, clearly identifying his Native American heritage.

"Better?"

She nodded, unable to answer over the lump of nerves forming in her throat. Nate brushed the errant strands of his black hair out of his eyes. He dropped his hand and rubbed the callused tips of his exposed fingers over her icy cheek. He continued the motion, pushing her hair back to tuck it behind her ear.

Amber inhaled, startled by the light touch and intimate gesture. Nate was attractive, but like most members of the tribe, he'd basically avoided her before this. She thrust her fists deeper into the pockets of her coat and tried to process his actions. What game was he playing?

She wet her dry lips and straightened her back. "So were you going to call Kayla?"

"I can take care of you. There's nothing to be worried about," Nate's deep voice soothed as he slid to the side, blocking her view of the alley entrance.

The sound of Irish bagpipes started in the distance and seemed strangely out of place amidst the Chinese lanterns, paper dragons and lingering scent of raw fish. As out of place as Nate's interest in her. Self-doubt riddled through her, encouraged by years of loneliness.

"Maybe we should just head to the hotel," Amber said as she made an attempt to slide past the solid wall of Nate and into the relative safety of the crowd.

"Why? The night's still young," Nate insisted, blocking her way. "It's the Year of the Dragon. Time to get wild and have some fun. Time to try something new." His voice lowered in time with his subtle forward movements that once again brought her back against the bricks.

She swallowed thickly when he braced his hands on the wall and leaned toward her. Her muscles tensed in a mix of anticipation and trepidation. She had a sudden interest in the worn, cracked details of his leather jacket, her gaze darting everywhere but to his.

"Look at me, Amber." His warm breath brushed across her cheek, his husky voice an accelerant to her racing heart.

Closing her eyes, Amber gathered her courage. Why did he make her so nervous?

"Do you know how beautiful you are?"

Nate's words made her lips curl up in a sarcastic smile, the dreaded heat flushing her cheeks again. Beautiful was not a description usually applied to her. Shy. Quiet. Reserved. Those were the adjectives strangers placed with her name. Bastard, whore's daughter, and slut's reject were the ones she'd grown up with.

The slight pressure of his finger on the underside of her chin had her lifting her head to meet his gaze. His eyes were hooded, heated and should have seared the chill straight out of her bones.

"You have the most amazing eyes...pools of deep gold, like your name," Nate murmured, scanning her face. "There's a sense of innocence about you that clashes against the haunting pull of your heritage." He moved his hand up to cup her cheek. "You remind me of a treasured Indian princess. One who holds herself aloof, but secretly longs to play."

Her heart thumped wildly as his lips moved toward her own dry ones. Each vertebra was pressed to the hard bricks and her fists stretched the fabric of her pockets, her fingernails gouging into the tender flesh of her palms.

"Do you want to play, Amber?" The words were smooth as silk, yet husky. Not really a question at all. Her gut clenched in expectation edged with snippets of angst.

She watched his eyelids close right before the warm flesh of his lips met hers. She followed his lead and closed her eyes, making a cautious decision to let the moment happen. His touch was hard, almost demanding as his lips brushed hers. His tongue ran a line over her bottom lip before it thrust between her lips and into her mouth.

Startled, she flinched, gasped and he plunged his tongue in farther. His mouth was hot, his tongue everywhere, his lips hard and bruising. She pulled back in surprised resistance. His hand snaked behind her head to stop her retreat and slam her against his solid length. Off balance, she jerked her hands out of her pockets to push at the cold leather of his coat.

This was *not* what she wanted.

Her stomach curled in disgust. The kiss was hard, brutal and felt almost punishing. The kiss was all about Nate. What he wanted. What he could take.

Nate stepped forward and sandwiched her against the wall. Wanting out, Amber shoved at his chest to pull away from his embrace. He wasn't having it. Instead of backing away, his hand tightened, holding her head in place.

Panic quickly overrode every other sensation. The many lectures she'd received from her aunt on the dangers of men and the indiscretions of women ran through her mind as she pounded against the solid mass of Nate's chest.

He didn't move.

She tried to twist her head away only to have his lips grind against hers. Her mouth felt violated, her lips battered.

What had she gotten herself into? She knew Nate. He was supposed to be safe. Someone the tribe respected.

But he obviously didn't respect her.

"Come on, Amber," Nate breathed against her mouth. "Loosen up." His mouth crushed back onto hers before she could even take a breath, let alone respond.

Frantic now, she pounded at his chest as she tried to wiggle away. Date rape screamed through her mind. *No.* She blinked back tears and scrambled to remember her self-defense skills. She wouldn't be a victim.

Not like her mother.

Nate forced her legs apart, thrusting the hard ridge of his thigh against her sex, sending her heart into her throat. His hand found its way under her clothes, his fingers cold against the warmth of her bared stomach. He jerked at the snap of her jeans, forcing his hand down where it shouldn't be. Where she didn't want it. Ever.

"Come on, Amber. I know you want it," Nate panted. "Just like your mother."

"No! *Stop.* Get. Off. Me."

Challenge gleamed in his eyes. "I bet your mom said that before she fucked every guy in the tribe. Don't whores run in the family?"

"*No.*" Desperate, she pushed, punched, tried to kick—anything to get away. Anything to stop the nightmare. His fingers reached the edge of her panties and her tears finally fell. Mortification banked her, sinking hard against her shielded virtue.

How could he do this to her? He wasn't a stranger. He wasn't some random guy. He was Nate.

Nate—who was no different from everyone else in the tribe who equated her mother's actions to her. Damn them. *All* of them.

His fingers descended further, brushing her pubic hair, clawing downward despite her protests.

"Nate, *stop*. I don't want this." Not this. Never this. Reaching up, she grabbed a fistfull of his hair and pulled. Hard.

"You *bitch*," Nate snarled, grabbing at her hand. "You're going to pay for that."

"I said *no*," Amber insisted right before she slammed the heel of her other hand against his nose. The sharp, backward snap of his head was satisfying until his hand closed around her throat.

"That's going to cost you." His fist tightened on her neck, choking off her air. Frantic, she grabbed at his wrist, the need for air her new priority. She scratched at his hand and kicked out her feet, desperate to break free. To get away from him.

Suddenly, she was falling forward, Nate's weight yanked from her, her pleas answered. A hand grabbed her arm, stopping her face-plant on the cement and whipped her around until her back was braced against the opposite wall.

Her hands were splayed flat on the hard brick behind her, her chest gasping for breath as she scrambled to process what had happened. Her relief at being freed was quickly doused by rank terror.

Nate was sprawled face down and unmoving in the dirty grime of the alley. Crouched over him was an Asian man dressed in all black except for a white cloth woven through the belt loops on his pants. His face was focused, his arm raised and ready to strike.

The grip on her arm tightened when she tried to run. A second Asian man, dressed identically to the one standing over Nate, held her in place.

"What do you want?" she rasped, struggling to get free of the hold on her arm, but her captor was not letting go. She opened her mouth to scream only to have his large hand clamp it closed before any sound came out.

Fear froze her in place. Her eyes bulged in a panicked search for escape. There were people, thousands of them, wandering by just feet away on the sidewalk, and not one knew she needed help.

"Do not move, child." The raspy voice drifted up from the darkened depths of the alley, his Asian accent heavy in the crisp words. "You must stay away from the dragon."

Amber stared into the darkness, searching for the man behind the disembodied voice, dreading what would happen next. Just how bad would the situation get? Did she just go from date rape to gang rape? Trembling at the thought, she squeezed her eyes shut and sent up a silent prayer for anything but that.

"You need not be afraid of us," the ancient voice soothed.

Her eyes flew open to see a third man standing directly before her. Where had he come from? How did he move so fast?

A gust of wind bellowed down the alley, blowing the ends of his long silver mustache against his white silk robe. He was an older Asian man with a face that matched the voice and deep, coal eyes that made her feel as if he could see clear to her soul.

"We are not the enemy of the Marked One." He smiled, the action deepening the lines that sprouted from the corners of his eyes.

She shook her head in denial and pressed into the bricks, attempting in vain to disappear.

The ancient man tilted closer, leaning heavily on a long, wooden staff. One of his wrinkled hands snapped out, moving way too fast for a man of his age, to clamp across her forehead. His palm was startlingly hot against her cold skin. His eyes narrowed to tiny gashes then, just as quickly, his hand returned to his staff. "You don't know yet, but you will soon."

In a flash he was standing over Nate. "You must stay away from the dragon." He reached down and yanked off one of Nate's fingerless gloves. He raised the bare hand for her to see the intricately etched red-and-gold dragon tattooed on the back. "The mark of the dragon is evil. You must stay away from all who wear the dragon on their hand."

In a blink, the man was once again standing before her. He removed a small, carved box from the depths of his robe and shoved it at her. "You must take this, child. It belongs to you. But do not touch it until you are in the safety of the circle."

Amber took the box hoping it would make the man go away. A smile whipped across the old man's face. He inclined his head, and the man holding her arm immediately released her.

"Now run, child." His demand left no room for questions. "Go home. Leave this town. Tonight."

Startled and baffled at all that had happened, Amber didn't move. Her chest heaved and her throat ached as jagged breaths of air were forced out. Her fingers were clenched around the odd little box, frozen in place by cold and fear. She stared at the strange man like he was a figment of her imagination. Maybe he was.

A low moan emanated from Nate as he stirred on the ground. The three men quickly faded away from her into the darkness.

"I said run!" The ancient man roared, pointing to the open end of the alley.

Amber jumped, then took off in a flight of pure panic. She clutched the box to her chest and barreled into the crowded street, straight into a rock-hard chest. Stumbling back, she ignored the sudden tingling that raced over her skin and bolted around the form that held the lingering scent of pine. She tore through the people, ignoring the shouts of anger. Her only thought was to flee.

To do as the man said and run.

Her focus narrowed to a pinpoint, eyeing the most direct path through the slow-moving people. Her nimble frame gave her an advantage and for once, her above average height was welcomed. The frigid air froze her lungs with each panting breath as sweat raced down her back. Red and gold lights lit up the area, the eerie sound of bagpipes still whining in the distance making the entire situation seem ever more foreign. Wrong.

How was this happening to her?

Her heart continued to race, fueled by panic, fear and the overriding sense that her life depended on her getting out of the city. Of getting away from all that was different and back to her quiet routine. Life with her overbearing aunt suddenly felt like a safe haven and not the prison she'd so recently thought it to be.

She halted, breathing deep, trying to get her bearings. She needed a cab. The hairs on the back of her neck prickled and itched in a feeling so strange she gasped, shuddered and protectively tucked the little box into her inside coat pocket.

Out of nowhere, the head of a large, open-mouthed dragon bounded out of an alley. A scream tore from her throat. The dragon head whipped around, the empty black eyes bearing down on her. The red fringe of hair surrounding its face snapped wildly in the wind. The pointed white teeth glistened in the sharp lights that flared in the night. Irrational thoughts of death by dragon swarmed her brain and stunned her heart.

The rhythmic, clanging crash of cymbals bounded into the silence, and the giant head swiveled away to lead the long, golden body into the street.

Not real. Her heart restarted. Her mind reeled. Of course it was fake. It was just another dragon dance, a part of the celebration. Like the firecrackers.

Tears threatened before she swallowed and quickly blinked them away.

Dashing past the dragon procession, Amber pushed her way out of Chinatown to the busy street of Broadway. There had to be a cab there. Had to be.

The wind pummeled her chest, forcing her to lean into the biting current to stay upright. She stood on the edge of the curb, frantically searching for an available taxi.

A hard yank on her arm pulled her around as the pent-up fear finally left her in a silent shriek of pure terror.

# Chapter Two

"*Amber.*" She heard her name shouted over the din of the receding dragon procession and her own frozen mind. "Amber, what's wrong? Are you okay?"

A sharp shake snapped Amber back. "Kayla," she practically sobbed. Relief doused her, making her muscles limp as she embraced her friend.

Kayla returned the desperate hug, and Amber worked to stifle her ragged breath and regain her composure. She was safe. The thought repeated in her mind, enabling her to slow her breathing. She pulled back and caught the questioning look Cara made to Stacy. The two women were also members of their tribe and part of the group that had come to New York City.

"What happened?" Kayla questioned, keeping a tight hold of Amber's hand. "What's wrong?" Her knowing gaze searched Amber's face.

"Nothing. I'm fine," Amber stammered as she flattened her expression and gave her friend's hand a tight squeeze. She pushed back the mortification that filled her at the thought of what almost happened. Of what Nate had done to her. She couldn't think of it right then or she'd crumble. "I just got a little overwhelmed by the crowd."

Kayla's eyes narrowed, doubt lining her features.

"Really, I'm fine," Amber said, trying to reassure both her friend and herself. She forced a tight smile before she pulled her hand out of Kayla's grasp. The gentle touch made her lie feel worse. "I'm just happy to find you." That was the truth.

"Where'd you go?" Cara asked. "Everyone's been looking for you."

"It doesn't matter," Kayla cut in. "We have to leave."

"What do you mean leave?" Amber looked between the other women, trying to piece together the conversation. The fact that it was exactly what she wanted only made her more nervous. How could it be that easy?

"Grandfather called and said we needed to leave the city and return home tonight." Kayla's voice had lowered to a soft, hollow echo that sent chills of foreboding over Amber's skin. Chills that reminded her of the exact same words the old Asian man in the alley had told her. "Or more specifically, to get *you* out of the city."

"What? W...why would he say that?" Amber stuttered in shock. Did the shaman know what happened to her? About the box? Nate? Her stomach churned in a state of denial.

"You know how grandfather works. *Why* isn't a question he answers," Kayla said before she moved to the curb and scanned the street, her face a study of concentration as she peered into the maze of advancing cars and took charge of the situation.

The very fact that the shaman had ordered them home only increased Amber's anxiety. The respected elder never gave out unjustified demands.

And no one, absolutely no one, questioned him.

The shaman had an uncanny ability to sense...things. To know details about people or events that most people wouldn't know.

Amber licked her lips, unable to stop the quick look over her shoulder. She pulled the zipper closed on her coat, a stealth move to keep the box hidden. She wasn't prepared to share the events of the evening with the other women. They had no reason to believe her, and she had no desire to relive what Nate had done to her.

Or share the box.

"Why did you disappear?" Cara asked, stepping up beside Amber. "You really upset Kayla."

"And now we have to leave," Stacy mumbled, the younger woman looking away in annoyance. "Your mother might have been the tribe whore, but at least she knew how to have fun."

"*Stacy,*" Cara reprimanded. "That was uncalled for."

Shame—unwanted, underserved—shivered through Amber. Refusing to show how much the words hurt, she lifted her chin. Her mother's past was not hers.

"Then stay. I'm not making you leave," she replied as calmly as possible.

"Kayla won't allow it. The guys get to stay, but we have to go home," Stacy said, tipping her head at their unofficial leader. Like her grandfather, Kayla's quiet authority combined with her legacy granted respect that few within the tribe questioned.

"Here's a taxi. Let's go," Kayla yelled back to them, checking her watch. "If we hurry, we can get our stuff and catch the last train home."

Amber waited until the women moved forward before she sucked in a deep, shaky breath and followed them. The wind pounded her, a hard sideswipe that circled and pushed before it shoved her toward the open door of the taxi. Again, that eerie chill drifted over the back of her neck, and she tucked her arm tight against the lump in her coat.

Someone was there. Watching her. She knew this even though she couldn't see them. Logic dictated that was impossible. That she shouldn't know this. That is was a product of her wild imagination.

Every other instinct told her it was fact.

Did they want her? The box? Both?

Why?

Her breath hung in her chest until the doors slammed shut and the cab pulled away from the curb. She could handle the enemy next to her. The one she knew. The one she had long ago learned to battle.

It was the unknown malice that prowled the shadows and vibrated in the air that tightened her stomach in barely contained panic.

She needed to get home. Where she would be safe.

Where the box would be safe.

She didn't question the odd thought. She just knew it to be true.

The Year of the Dragon was not a year for her to celebrate.

The yellow cab eased away from the curb, quickly lost in obscurity as it blended with the many taxis that filled the streets of Manhattan.

But he still knew exactly which car she was in.

Just like he always knew precisely where she stood within the crowd, no matter the size or location, at every rally he'd been forced to attend over the last three years.

For some unknown reason, he always knew where she was.

Even if he didn't know *who* she was.

He could have found out. He had the connections and status to make it happen. But what was the point? He couldn't approach her. Be a part of her life or bring her into his when nothing could come of it but pain. His. Hers. Both. Yet, he still looked for her. Sensed her before he even saw her. Was drawn to her in a way that held no logic. So he resisted. As he knew he must. Then why was he here in Chinatown?

The energy had pulled at him until he'd given in. Even though he didn't trust it. Didn't dare believe in the energy. Not anymore. Not since it had so brutally betrayed him long ago.

And then he'd known. Instantly.

It was the Year of the Dragon and she shouldn't be here. Nowhere near such danger. Evil she couldn't comprehend, but had unknowingly faced earlier.

His fists tightened into hard clamps of suppressed anger as he thought of how close she'd come to being harmed. Of the sinister look that had glinted in the enemy's eyes before he'd dissipated out of the alley like a coward. The Shifter had run instead of facing him, an Energen who could fight on his level.

As rival factions of the Energy races, the two species had been mortal enemies since life began. Their battle established over the most devastating force on earth.

Energy.

Silent, invisible, intangible. Long before the humans even realized what it was, Energens and Shifters had fought for control of the energy. One to balance it, the other to own it.

But why the woman? What interest was she to the Shifter?

He closed his eyes and inhaled, letting the scent of cinnamon flood his mind. A memory of her, not the current surroundings. He vibrated with the energy, the rush of power and sensation that had ignited when she'd crashed into him as she fled the alley. Her touch, as brief as it was, had flashed like fire and ice in his system.

Was she part of a plan? An enticing lure meant to trap him? But by whom? And for what reason?

He felt the energy expand behind him, a brief ripple of warning that had him spinning around in defense. What he saw was not what he expected.

"No," the man said. "I usually am not."

"Who are you?" he demanded, ready for battle. Then he registered what the man had done, that he'd read his mind. His eyes narrowed, his distrust heightened. "You are an Ancient with the power of Spirit. Why are you here?"

The old Asian man tilted his head, sending the long, white ends of his mustache swaying. "To remind you, Damianos Aeros, disgraced heir to the House of Air, of the prophecies of old."

"Prophecies mean nothing to me," Damian bit out.

"But they should, when they are about you."

"*Impossible.*"

The Ancient continued as if Damian hadn't spoken. His calm demeanor and soft voice added power to the words he recited. "A thousand years of exile, a thousand years of rebirth. Taken down in shame to rise in glory. At his side a virgin bride, the hidden bird to bind his soul. To this end, the world will flow. Without the rise, the world will fall. One of light, one of dark. Two to wield all five. Circles will rise and must hold strong. Together the two will lead us all."

Then he was gone.

Damian cursed, frustration forcing him to kick the metal trash can that stood beside him. The resounding clang echoed down the alley, but did nothing to settle the unrest that stirred within him.

Reaching deep, he buried the emotions, shook off the insidious desire that threatened to pull him under. A thousand years he'd been away. Pushed away from all that was his. Stripped of everything he'd known because of the energy. Because of the lies.

But still, he hungered to return to his world. His family. Despite how impossible that was. How futile his wishes were. Dreams that were nothing but empty longing that raked him in the darkest of nights.

No. His life was far from the Energen world. A life he'd built on his own knowledge and determination. One filled with success and respect, even if it was only from the humans.

He took a quick look around then dissipated out of the alley, heading for home.

This was not his battle. Not anymore.

# Chapter Three

The sun was breaking over the horizon as Amber turned the key and dragged her bag into the antique shop in Newport, Rhode Island. Her shoulders sagged with relief the instant the lock clicked into place.

The train ride home had been long and strained. The rest of the women had all dozed off either to avoid talking to her or to simply catch some sleep. In truth, she had been thankful that they'd slept since she couldn't. Her mind had been too wired, replaying the events of the night.

Absently she rubbed her tender neck. The mental image of Nate's hand circling it flashed hard and fast in her mind. She winced and swallowed the bile that burned the back of her throat. Nate had tried to rape her. Had hurt her and threatened her life. Hate, pure and rancid, boiled in her. He'd made her feel so helpless. She was ashamed and disgusted but at whom? Herself or him?

God, she should have listened to her aunt. She should have stayed in Newport and never gone to New York. The wild ramblings of her Aunt Bev crept into her thoughts. The constant lectures about how Amber was special. About how she must stay pure and that destiny had a plan for her. And what was that? For her to live a solitary existence caring for her aging aunt and a second-rate antique shop?

The daring trip to the city had been just that. Daring. A walk on the wild side. And look where it had gotten her. She felt the tears rising and blinked them back.

It was too much to process right then. If she let the emotions out, they'd take her down and she couldn't let that happen. Not now. Not ever. She had to keep moving.

Catching a quick look at the clock, Amber left her bag by the door and moved into the shop. Her aunt would be awake soon, and there would be hell to pay for her little adventure to the city.

With shaking hands, she removed the wooden box from her pocket and set it on the cluttered counter at the back of the shop. She stared at it with a mixture of hatred and longing. The box was relatively small, about the size of a deck of cards, but in the shape of a diamond and around two inches deep. The exterior wood was intricately carved in curling designs and curious shapes. The workmanship was exquisite and had the antique dealer in her awed and impressed by the technique, style and simple uniqueness.

The woman in her saw nothing but an ugly reminder of last night's events.

The clashing feelings of desire and revulsion knotted the muscles in her gut. It was only a box, she reminded herself. But her skin crawled with the falseness of her conviction.

The pull to open the box was startling. It smoothed over her in a wave of longing. Her fingers flexed in nervous anticipation. But what was it? What if it was something bad?

Still, after all that had happened, she had to know.

There was a tiny gold twist-lock on one side that was daring her to turn it. Open the box and look inside. See the gift. It was hers.

In a flash, Amber snapped her hand out to twist the lock and flip open the lid. The air sparked with electricity, and the dank surroundings of the shop suddenly vibrated with expectation.

Nestled within the box among the folds of royal purple velvet was the most beautiful stone Amber had ever seen. Diamond in shape, it was a strange mixture of white, violet and gold that shimmered and glowed like it was lit from within. The colors moved, blending to varying shades before her eyes.

And it called to her.

Her fingers tingled and her mind fuzzed.

She had to touch it. Take it and claim it as her own. Something so beautiful couldn't be evil. Numbly, she reached out to reverently caress the smooth surface of the stone.

Pain. Fierce, searing, blinding tore up her hand, burning a path of scorching agony.

Gasping, Amber jerked her fingers away, but the pain continued. She snapped the lid closed. What the hell was that? She stared at her palm, but saw no damage, not even a burn mark. Was this the punishment she got for going against her aunt's wishes? For wanting something more in her life?

Tears stung her eyes as she sniffed back her frustration. She needed to get rid of the box. Put the whole stupid night behind her. But her heart clenched and balked at the thought.

She couldn't get rid of it.

The slight creak of the floorboards overhead spurred Amber into motion. Her aunt was awake.

Shaking her hand in an attempt to relieve the odd soreness that remained, she looked around for a place to hide the box. The urgency to stash it away increased with each squeak and groan on the stairs as her aunt descended to the shop.

Spotting an old sewing trunk in the corner, Amber rushed to stow the box inside. She didn't question her actions or why she had to hide the stone. She just did.

Throwing some old blankets over the box, she closed the trunk then pushed it back behind a tall china cabinet, stacking random objects and trinkets on top of it.

"Amber, is that you?" Her aunt's firm, flat voice drifted through the shop. Crap.

"Yes, Aunt Bev. It's me."

Silently, she moved back to the counter, stiffening her back for the confrontation to come. She wiped her damp palms on her jeans, took a deep breath and froze.

On the back of her hand along with the lingering sting of pain was an elegantly sketched tattoo of a white bird rising in flight.

*No way.*

Hastily she rubbed at the image, frantic to remove it. It stayed. How?

No way. No, no, no. *No.*

She scratched at the etching, prepared to gouge the image off her skin. Anything to get it off. Anything to make it go away. To make it *all* go away.

Her skin turned red with welts that marred the thin flesh on the back of her hand. But the bird stayed unscathed.

It was beautiful in its simplicity. Haunting with its stark color. And taunting her mercilessly with its refusal to disappear.

Aunt Bev stepped into the room. A deep frown creased her forehead and matched the curve of her thin lips. Amber shoved her shaking hands into her coat pockets and tried to still her quaking nerves.

The old, pink bathrobe was cinched around her aunt's plump girth like a protective shield. The slightly bed-messed silver hair did not deter from the overall aura of superiority that always emanated from her aunt. Technically, she was Amber's great aunt, but since Aunt Bev was Amber's only living relative, the distinction never mattered.

"So you're back." The icy chill of the words matched the hard look of disapproval that sparked from her deep brown eyes. "I hope your little trip was worth the worry you caused me."

Amber bit down on her bottom lip, letting her aunt's anger pool around her. Any reply would be wrong.

Her aunt stepped forward until she stood a mere foot away, completely invading Amber's personal space in a practiced move of intimidation. Amber held her ground. At five foot ten, Amber was taller than her aunt. The fact her aunt had to look up to meet Amber's eyes was an advantage she secretly relished.

"Your foolishness could have cost you everything." Flames of determination flashed in her aunt's eyes, her face a hard mask of controlled fury. "You have no idea the evil you play with. I have tried desperately to keep you protected. To keep you safe. I have given up everything for you. Yet you still resist me. I thought you were better than your mother. I *raised* you to be better."

Shame—her own this time—clogged her throat. She had disappointed her aunt, the one person in the world who actually loved her. "I'm sorry you feel that way. I didn't mean to cause you worry."

Which was true. Her aunt might be overbearing and protective, but she always meant well. When Amber had found herself alone in the world at the age of nine after her mother was murdered, it was Aunt Bev who had taken her in without question. Despite her aunt's many faults, Amber had never doubted the love she felt from her adopted parent.

Aunt Bev's gaze searched Amber's face before the stiffness slowly left her body. Her voice softened, the concern now evident in the faint curl of her lips. "Are you okay, Amber?" She reached out to cup Amber's cheek. "When Joseph called looking for you, I panicked."

Amber swallowed and forced her voice to stay even. "The shaman called here looking for me?"

"Yes. He said it was important that you get home." Her eyes drilled into Amber, putting an edge on the low currents of her voice. "Why?"

"I don't know," she hedged, ignoring the sudden burning pain on the back of her hand. She could tell her aunt didn't believe her. But she couldn't tell her what had happened.

Her aunt turned back toward the stairs. Her voice drifted quietly through the room. "I love you, Amber. I've always tried to do what was right for you. I've tried to do my role as Joseph ordered when he brought you to my door. But, more than that, I've guarded and protected you. Kept you safe—as I was told to do. I've..." Her breath hitched, her shoulders stiffened then relaxed, before she continued. "It is time for *you* to keep yourself safe. The time is coming when your life will be in your hands alone. I can only hope that you are prepared for it. That you make the right choices...that you can handle it."

"What are you talking about?" Amber stared dumbfounded at her aunt's back. "Protected me from what?" The questions tumbled through her brain, the confusion causing her thoughts to scramble in a futile attempt to understand what her aunt was saying. Her fingers itched to reach out and touch her aunt. To reassure and comfort her, but the burn on the back of her hand reminded Amber she couldn't.

"There's no need for you to protect me anymore, Aunt Bev. I appreciate all that you've done for me. I love you, but I'm old enough to take care of myself. That's why I went on the trip to New York even though you told me not to. It wasn't defiance that made me go, but a desire to expand, to explore the world and try new things. And nothing happened. Everything's fine. I'm back safe and sound."

Her aunt sighed, a big breath filled with more than just air. "You can lie to me, but I hope you don't lie to yourself."

Thankful her aunt couldn't see the flush that heated her cheeks, Amber fumbled for words, looking for solidity in her suddenly tumbling world. What was going on?

"I don't understand what you mean," she finally mumbled.

"And that may be my greatest failure," Aunt Bev whispered before she shuffled away.

She gaped at her aunt's retreating back until it disappeared around the corner. The stairs creaked as she made her way back to their apartment. Amber ached to go after her and ease the rift between them, but now wasn't the time.

The burning sting on her hand began to fade with her aunt's retreat. She pulled a shaky hand from her pocket to stare again at the mysterious bird scored into her skin.

*How? Why?* What in the hell was happening to her life? *To her?*

Her eyes were pulled to the corner where the sewing trunk sat. Her fingers absently rubbed the mark on her hand, and she was surprised at how smooth the surface felt. They were linked—the stone and the mark—that was obvious. It wasn't logical. It was too weird and unbelievable.

And *definitely* not meant for her.

Maybe it was all a mistake. And maybe there really wasn't a bird branded into the back of her hand. Her gaze drifted down to stare at the proof that it wasn't all a dream or mistake.

The bird *was* on her hand.

Her chest constricted as an overwhelming feeling of doom settled in for a long, unwanted visit. She could no longer deny that somehow she was getting the adventure she so foolishly wanted.

Now, if she could only give it back.

# Chapter Four

*Eight weeks later*

Amber stared at the gathering crowd from the safety of her car. It was a dank, cold morning that threatened snow and had most people, smart people, huddled warmly in their homes. Exactly where she wanted to be. Instead, she sat soaking up the last bit of heat and forestalling the inevitable.

She spotted Kayla weaving her way through the group of people, chatting with some, smiling at others, comfortable in her surroundings. There were a number of members from the Indian tribe attending the mayor's speech. All coordinated by Kayla in protest of the wind turbines that were being erected in Nantucket Sound.

In the eight weeks since the awful trip to New York City, Amber had managed to evade and dodge Kayla's repeated attempts to contact her. Avoidance was her primary objective. Denial her mantra. The longer she could ignore everything—pretend nothing was different, nothing had changed—the better. She hadn't touched the deceptive little box since she'd stuffed it in the sewing trunk, had blatantly ignored the bird mark, and had sighed in relief when the shaman had remained quiet—when *everything* had remained quiet and normal.

Which made her think that maybe she really was being paranoid. Even if there was an unwanted bird etched onto her hand. She needed to get out, and the rally seemed like the perfect way to mingle without having to answer questions. There would be too many people around for a deep conversation.

At least, that was her plan.

Amber glanced at the clock on the car's dashboard then took one last look through the crowd. No Nate. She still wasn't ready to face him. Her stomach curled just thinking about him.

Biting the bullet, she opened the door and exited into the frosty air that gusted off the water. It was a stupid place to hold a rally, but then she suspected the mayor's publicity committee had hoped March would roll out like a lamb instead of the lion it was.

She quickly crossed the street, tucking her head against the wind as she followed the small path through the park to the assembly area. The back of her hand prickled beneath her glove, reminding her why she had been avoiding everyone.

The mark wasn't easy to hide.

Make-up, which seemed to fade quickly, extra-long sleeves and fingerless gloves had worked so far in keeping her dirty little secret hidden. Her aunt had remained silent and distant since her quiet outpouring of...what? Guilt? Anger? Resentment? Amber still wasn't sure what it had been, but she'd left it alone, uncertain how to bridge the rift that had opened between them.

Kayla, however, was more persistent, and Amber hadn't been ready before now to dodge her questions about New York, Nate or her new fashion choices.

The snow crunched beneath her boots, the low chatter of the assembling crowd growing louder but indistinguishable over the harsh brush of the wind. Amber kept her head down, her shoulders hunched against the cold that attempted to sneak around the collar of her coat.

Her mind was busy rehearsing her words to Kayla, silently orchestrating the meeting, preparing herself to deflect any questions and act casual. The hard smack of wool against her forehead jolted her out of her thoughts right before her nose met the same unmoving wall.

She jerked back in surprise. The bird mark burned under her glove, matching the odd sensation that scorched through her. Amber stared at the black wool as she caught a whiff of pine scent and realized she'd just rammed into someone.

"I'm so sorry. I wasn't looking..." The quick, embarrassed apology that tumbled off her lips died when the person turned to reveal the deep, crystal blue eyes of the man she'd just plowed into. Her breath caught.

Damian Aeros. This time, she wasn't imagining him.

"No problem." His deep voice glided through the air in rich baritone notes. "Are you okay?"

He looked her over while she struggled to find her voice. "I'm fine. I'm sorry. I didn't see you." The jumbled garble of statements came out sounding just as flustered as she felt. Great. She took a deep breath and tried again. "I'm the one who ran into you. Are you okay?"

A slight smile curved over his firm lips and lifted the hard set of his features. "I'm fine."

"I should watch where I'm walking," she said in a lame attempt to hold a conversation. He was even more attractive up close, and her tongue suddenly felt thick and foreign in her mouth. "Then maybe I wouldn't crash into innocent people."

"An incident that has allowed me to finally meet you," he said smoothly. A light danced in his eyes as they held hers. The blue depths entranced her and reminded her of the sky just before sunrise when the purity of color was at its deepest.

Heat flushed through her. What did he mean, finally meet her? She felt her cheeks burning and knew the blush was giving away her secrets. She smiled and hunted her blank mind for a witty reply.

A punishing gust of wind pummeled her back in a surprise attack that forced her forward to within inches of his chest. He flicked his hands up to catch her arms, holding her steady. The tattoo seared and fluttered under her skin as a staggering flash of sensation consumed her.

Her eyes widened as his face hardened.

"What..." Her words trailed off under his rigid gaze.

He dropped his hold on her arms and stepped back. His lips thinned removing the warmth from his expression.

"Excuse me," he snapped, before turning away to move toward the stage.

What was that about? Amber shook off the sense of loss, and absently rubbed the tingling from her fingers as she watched him greet the mayor and shake hands with others assembled near the base of the platform. He radiated power, from the expensive cut of the black wool trench coat that accentuated his tall frame and the broad breadth of his shoulders to the crisply folded violet silk scarf that was wrapped around his neck and tucked neatly into the collar of his coat. The unique color added to the pure sense of unchallenged male that emanated from him.

She shoved her shaking hands in her pockets and turned away, dismissing the lingering tingle that raked her body as nerves.

Damian Aeros, CEO of a global wind turbine company. Of course it was nerves that had her acting so foolish. The strange feeling of rightness that had overcome her when the wind had pushed her toward his chest was silly and stupid. It was nothing but wishful thinking once again and wrong on so many levels.

The thought of Kayla's reaction to her blunder made Amber smile when she finally reached her friend's side. At least she had something to distract Kayla with.

"Hey, guess who I just plowed into, literally?" Amber interjected before Kayla could start asking questions. "Mr. Aeros himself."

Kayla laughed. "Good move. I wish I could have seen it." She cocked a smile at Amber. "In fact, I wish I'd thought of it myself. Did you give him a good kick too?" Her laughter bubbled over and infected Amber.

"No. It was embarrassing. Really," Amber said, shaking her head. There was no way Kayla could know about her hidden fascination with the CEO. Kayla saw him as the ultimate villain and held him personally responsible for the wind turbines being erected in the pristine waters of the Sound.

A sharp, piercing squeal reverberated from the speaker, causing everyone to cringe. Kayla shot Amber an assessing look before the mayor's political advisor stepped up to the microphone and began to speak.

"Don't think this gets you off the hook. We still need to talk," Kayla leaned in to tell her.

"About what?" Amber played the stupidity card.

"Why you've been avoiding me for two months."

"I haven't been avoiding you," Amber insisted, but she couldn't meet her friend's eyes. "I've just been busy."

Kayla gave her a dubious look. They both knew that Amber's life wasn't that busy. Kayla softened. "I just want to be sure you're okay. I was worried about you after New York."

Now the guilt kicked in. Why was everyone so worried about her lately?

"Nothing happened," Amber deflected again. "I'm fine. Really. Aunt Bev was a little mad, but we both knew that was going to happen. Did your grandfather ever tell you why he ordered us home?"

"No, of course not. You know his eccentric crypticness. He only reveals what he thinks you *need* to know. Evidently, the why of leaving New York is something we don't *need* to know." She gave a shrug of dismissal and held Amber's gaze. "Do you know why?"

Yeah, she'd walked right into that one.

Amber smiled and blatantly ignored her friend's question. "So what were the chances of me running over the head honcho like that out of all the people here?"

Kayla's eyes narrowed, but once again, she let Amber do the duck and dive. A reprieve Amber feared wouldn't last for long.

"About as probable as the wind turbines all magically tumbling into the ocean," Kayla countered.

"Or the sun suddenly appearing to warm us the hell up." Amber chuckled, waving her hand dismissively at the cloud-drenched sky. The laughter died from her lips when the clouds separated in an unnatural move. The golden rays of the sun rained down on the small gathering, making it seem like Amber's action had parted the clouds.

Kayla stared at the sky in stunned amazement. "Yeah, maybe," she mumbled, all amusement gone, the lame attempt at a lighter mood wiped out by the eeriness of the moment. She looked to Amber, her soft voice raspy in a way that had the damn hairs rising on Amber's neck once again. "And maybe there's a reason why you ran into Damian Aeros."

# Chapter Five

He stood still and rigid. Waiting. Observing. Assessing.

Patience. Damian Aeros was tempered with it—a thousand years' worth of finely cultured patience. The kind that enabled him to stand stoic and placid as the overly boisterous voice droned on, trying to entice the gathered crowd.

The harsh wind snapped over the podium, ripping at the papers and compelling the esteemed mayor of Newport, Rhode Island to clutch at the fragile pieces in a frantic attempt to maintain control. The mayor's voice faltered as the wind rushed against the microphone, forcing its own harsh voice to roar over the speakers in a glaring demand for attention.

But Damian's focus wasn't on the words of the mayor. No, his concentration was centered on the tall, raven-haired beauty bunched in the middle of the small crowd.

The one he always found. She was striking in her simplicity—make-up free, lips naturally red, cheeks rosy from the cold. Her long, unbound hair glimmered like silk in the light and flowed around her head like waves of dark water. She appeared distant, almost lost, clearly not focused on the mayor's words as her gaze veered off to stare at the turbulent waves on the Sound.

What was she thinking about? Why did he care?

His fingers tingled with the faint, lingering energy that had shot through him when he'd touched her. An innocent collision followed by a reflexive action meant to keep her from tumbling against him again. But the jarring rush of feeling that had flashed through him had been anything but innocent.

Who was she?

A person's energy signature usually made it easy to tell if they belonged to the Energy races. But hers had been jumbled, a mixture of signals that, although predominantly human, had also hinted at something more.

She was a mystery. One that only intrigued him more each time he saw her, even though it shouldn't.

"To further elaborate on the advantages of Nantucket Wind, I'd like to introduce the founder and CEO of Aeros Wind Turbines, Damian Aeros." The mayor's loud, booming voice broke into Damian's thoughts and brought him back to the task at hand.

Damian stepped up to the podium under a smattering of polite applause. His company, the one he'd started and built from the ground up, was in the middle of a never-ending project to erect wind turbines in Nantucket Sound. Although environmentally advantageous, they were touted as a visual eyesore by coastal purists.

This was yet another in hundreds of such events organized in a lame attempt to garner support for the politically unpopular project. The company publicist insisted he attend these events. So once again he was freezing his nuts off on a Saturday morning, smiling politely to the crowd as they waited for one more preplanned speech.

Only this morning, his pinpoint focus was distracted by her.

For five years, he'd listened to the protests and offered nods of understanding and statements of acquiescence that eased minds and curdled his stomach. But ultimately it was worth it. The turbines were going up, and it was one small, positive thing he could still do to honor the balance of the energy and protect the very people who protested Nantucket Wind's existence.

Today, he was tired of pretending. Throwing off the planned, canned speech filled with platitudes and politically correct words, Damian let his real thoughts be heard.

"Most of you here today are protesting the wind turbines simply because you can see them. That's it. Even though the turbines will be over six miles away from the nearest island town and closer to ten miles away from the mainland, you don't want to look at them. You would rather slowly kill the earth with the continual use of non-renewable resources than look at a few swinging blades on the distant horizon."

Short-sighted fools.

With effort, he hid his impatience. He let the grumbling die down, although most of the crowd appeared too shocked or frozen to react.

"And let me tell you why Nantucket Wind is vital to our local economy," the mayor bellowed, interrupting him and subtly trying to brush Damian aside in a blatant attempt to smooth over the damage his brief speech might have caused.

"But what about our rights?" a feminine voice called out from the crowd. "What about our views on what is sacred and our ability to practice our spiritual beliefs?" Damian's gaze darted through the crowd, picking out the dark-haired woman who'd posed the question. "Why doesn't anyone care about them?"

The portly mayor stumbled to answer the question from the female. Damian recognized the questioner immediately. She'd been one of the most vocal in the Native American protest of the wind turbines and was just one of the many local tribe members there today.

Damian spoke over the fumbling mayor, his clear voice cutting off the other man. "I understand that the local Native American tribes are upset because the wind turbines are going to hinder the unobstructed easterly view that you require for a spiritual ceremony. I appreciate the tribe's needs and beliefs, but unfortunately, some things are bigger than any one group's wants. This is one of them."

Usually, he wouldn't come right out and say that, but today, he felt the change in the air. The time for patient pretense had passed.

The mayor immediately jumped back in and tried to once again control the microphone. Damian didn't fight him. He'd made his point.

Another bite of wind gusted off the icy waters, blasting the frozen crowd with a punishing reminder that there were far better things to be doing that morning. Damian took a step back, curled his fingers tight and burrowed them deep into the pockets of his wool trench coat. The temptation to up the punishment and assist the wind in its unrelenting torture itched over his fingers. It practically begged for him to do it, whispering its seductive voice, urging him to give in.

It would be so simple to use his powers, his affiliation with the air, to increase the wind's strength. To pummel the crowd until they retreated. Tempting, but not possible. Going down the path of punishing the innocent would go against everything he'd been striving to prove for the last millennium.

The sudden pull of being stared at in a deliberate, penetrating way simmered over his senses. His attention snapped back to the crowd to find a set of dark golden eyes boldly locked onto his. Like always, they were stunning in their clarity, and mysterious in their depth.

They belonged to her. At that precise moment, with their eyes held—his attention solely on her—the air pummeled the crowd. It whipped around the beauty, swirling her hair in black, silk ribbons around her body. She blinked and looked away before pulling her gloved hand out of her pocket to clear the hair away from her face. He was captivated by the simplicity of her actions, the graceful movement of her arm as she tried to capture and tame the errant strands.

Apparently frustrated at her lack of success, she yanked off a glove, baring her fingers to the bitter elements and furrowed her brow as she continued to swipe at the mass of black. The winter headband she wore did little to control the waist-long hair against the force of the wind.

The flash of white amidst the sea of black grabbed his attention. His eyes narrowed in focus as his stomach tightened then churned in slow, dreaded anticipation.

It could be nothing. Instinct, honed and cultivated along with his patience, told him it was more. She was more.

Her hand flashed then held as she worked a piece of hair from the clutches of her lips, offering him a clear view of the mark on the back of her now gloveless hand.

A white bird rising in flight.

He inhaled sharply, his breath held, incapable of moving through his lungs. A millennium of pain and betrayal, of soul-wrenching longing pierced through his heart.

The wind died a sudden, startling death, and the abrupt shift caused his senses to rise in warning. It was her. It explained so much. The Marked One had finally been found.

By him.

The sudden stillness that dropped over the crowd after the relentless pounding by the wind was far more chilling than the air itself. Amber got her hair under control and quickly put her glove back on. An unexplained need to leave urged her to hurry.

The mayor was still slinging his propaganda to the gathered group, but she couldn't care less. She stole a quick look out of the corner of her eye, but it only confirmed what she already felt.

His focus was still on her.

What had compelled her to stare so boldly at the handsome CEO? She'd been startled when he'd caught and held her gaze. Even more amazed when she'd brazenly met his challenge. For that's what it'd felt like—a dare to look away.

Of course, she'd lost. But for that brief moment when she had ventured to play, the intensity had been startling. It was as if he could see into the very heart of who she was...and he wanted to know more.

Now he wouldn't look away.

She stifled a shiver as she remembered the last time a man had looked at her like that. It had been almost two months since Nate had attacked her, but the events were still fresh in her mind. She had been duped by a man she thought she knew. So naïve that she hadn't heeded the danger signs until it was almost too late.

Lesson learned. She might be naïve, but she wasn't stupid.

And this man, with his hard, chiseled features and stoic mask of authority was stroking every warning instinct she had, despite the way her stomach fluttered when she looked at him.

Maybe because of it.

She leaned closer to Kayla. "I have to go."

Her friend shot her a look. "Why? You said you would be here to support us."

"I know," she hedged. "I did, but I really need to go. I told Aunt Bev I would be back by noon to open the shop." It wasn't a straight lie. She had promised to open the shop, just not by noon.

"Do you need help today?" Kayla raised her eyebrow in question, the look one of sleek sophistication.

"No. Thanks. It'll be slow with the weather like this." Amber caught her hair in her grip as the wind started up again, the brief respite from its torment over. "I can handle it on my own. Aunt Bev will be back from the reservation by late afternoon anyway." She'd made the day trip to Martha's Vineyard for a tribal council meeting. Although the majority of the tribe members lived off the reservation, the council meetings were still held on the island.

"Okay." Kayla licked her lips and shook her own hair away from her face. "Thanks for coming today. I know it's basically a lost cause, but it's still worth fighting for our beliefs."

Amber looked away, unable to meet the fiery resolve that flashed in her friend's eyes. It was hard to see her dedication and commitment to a community that had always regarded Amber with wary distance. She often wondered why Kayla was so kind to her when most tribe members were not. But then she didn't want to question one of the few friends she had.

And Kayla had never given her a reason to doubt the truth of her friendship.

Amber stole another quick look at the stage and stiffened as she once again caught the hard-edged gaze of the CEO. He was *still* staring at her. Not Kayla. *Her.*

Why? Because she ran into him earlier?

His stare drilled into her like a slam to her chest. His firm, square jaw was tilted upward in a position that forced him to look down on her. It was nerve-wracking. Her stomach knotted as her body flushed with sudden warmth.

But she didn't look away. She straightened her spine and narrowed her eyes to meet his taunt with a dare of her own. She would not cower. Never again.

"Are you okay?"

The sudden question yanked Amber's attention back to her friend. "Oh, sorry," she mumbled, shaking her head to clear her thoughts but unable to resist another darting glance at Damian Aeros. "I'm fine."

Kayla, always perceptive, didn't miss the action nor, apparently, the sharp focus of the man on stage. "What's going on?" Her brow creased in concern as she leaned toward Amber. "Why is he staring at you?"

"He's not." Her quick denial only confirmed that he was and that Amber knew what Kayla was talking about. *Damn.* "I don't know. I've got to go anyway."

She pulled away and pushed through the small crowd before Kayla could question her further. She could feel his eyes on her as she weaved through the people and made her way to the edge of the gathering. How do you *feel* someone looking at you? But she could tell, without looking, that he watched her retreat.

Her heart accelerated with each step closer to escape. Her breath quickened as the panic increased. The back of her hand itched and burned where the strange brand had appeared. That was how she thought of it. She felt branded. Forced to wear a symbol she didn't want. Could not remove or escape. And she still had no idea what it meant. Why she had it. *How* she got it.

Now it stung as if in warning.

Tears burned in the corners of her eyes, the weight of the last two months pressing down on her. She blinked rapidly to clear the nuisance as she finally broke free of the bodies and rushed across the park to her car. Her hands shook and she fumbled the keys before she was safely encased in the confines of her car.

*Damn it.* She swiped hastily at the tears, hating what they represented, cursing her own inability to control them. They were her bane, her body's betrayal of every emotion she felt.

Happy, sad, worried, scared, embarrassed—they all manifested as tears, much to her humiliation. To the world, tears were a blatant symbol of weakness. She hated that perception. Hated that they only reinforced what people already thought of her.

She took a shaky breath in a failed attempt to calm herself and slow her racing heart. She started the car and prepared to bolt back to the safety of the antique shop. She looked out the side window to check for cars and stopped dead.

He was there—watching her. A silent sentry on the far edge of the park. And behind him, Kayla stood calmly taking him in, assessing his actions and maybe even Amber's.

What in the hell was going on?

He started to move toward her, his eyes never straying. Kayla flanked him, keeping her distance, but not losing ground. The game of cat and mouse ensued, leaving Amber to feel like the cheese bait.

The unfamiliar urge to confront him boiled up and spiked her temper. He had no right to stalk her, to make her doubt herself and run.

A quick tap of a horn jerked her attention back to the road. Behind her a car waited with its blinker on, eager for her spot. Jerking her car into drive, she pulled out, casting a quick glance across the park.

Damian had halted his pursuit, but still watched as she drove away. Why? Even as she asked, she was certain it was a question she didn't want answered.

# Chapter Six

Amber closed her eyes, leaned her forehead on the cold wood of the door and inhaled the comforting scents of wood polish and age that assailed her upon entering the backdoor of the antique shop. The smells were a part of her life and brought with them simplicity and routine.

But no matter how safe she felt at that moment, it was time she stopped ignoring events and looked at them for what they were. Related or not, there were too many things piling up for her to continue in her blissful haze of self-denial.

Something was happening.

She might have felt excluded from her tribe for most of her life, but that hadn't stopped the Native American beliefs from becoming ingrained within her. There was more at play in this world than what could be seen. Joseph and his mystical knowledge of events was proof of that.

Good or bad, it was time Amber prepared herself for whatever was to come. She needed all the facts to do that, and she was certain her aunt had them or at least knew who did.

Acceptance was the first step in moving forward. So forward she would go—just as soon as she could move. A small, mirthless laugh puffed from her chest at the contradiction. Having the will did not bring with it the courage.

Right. She licked her lips, straightened her back and exhaled. Despite the whacked-out events around her, she still needed to open the shop and take care of the responsibilities of the day.

Never ask why, always ask what. Her aunt's mantra echoed through her thoughts almost as if Aunt Bev stood behind her and whispered the words in her ear. A shudder snaked down Amber's spine, enticing her to call out. "Aunt Bev, you here?"

Silence. She was still alone.

Amber pushed away from the door and moved down the short hallway to the small office, removing her winter outerwear and hanging her coat on the hooks lining the wall. Rubbing her hands together, she moved to the thermostat and nudged the heat up a tad. Her aunt would probably have a small cow at the extra two degrees of warmth, but to heck with it. Bravery came in small steps, and she would consider this her first one.

She flicked on the light and turned toward the desk to grab the front door keys. Shock froze her in place, comprehension registering as her mind processed the state of the office. It was destroyed. The usually ordered space was now a jumbled mess of tossed papers, broken objects and emptied file drawers. Even the safe had been pried open, the contents emptied onto the floor. Clearly ransacked by someone in a hunt for what?

Panic followed quickly on the heels of the numbed shock. Pinpricks of needles shimmered over her skin, igniting her heart rate and engulfing her in a cold, damp sweat. Her mouth was suddenly parched as her brain fuzzed to one, and only one, thought.

The stone.

Amber tore from the office, careening into the shop, heedless to any danger that might still remain. All thoughts of personal safety, of calling the cops or exiting the building were obliterated by the overriding need to get to the stone.

To ensure its safety and hold it so no one else would ever get it.

Some small part of her brain recognized the insanity of her actions and thoughts. But it wasn't enough to stop her. Driven by a craze that defied explanation, Amber barreled through the disaster field of the shop. Heedless of the broken glass, blocked aisles or shattered objects that littered her path. Her only thought was to find the stone.

Insane.

She reached the back corner where the sewing trunk sat overturned and open, the top tray tossed to the side, the antique quilts tumbling from the depths. Dropping to her knees, she dove into the contents. Her fingernails scraped over the hard wood of the trunk, her knuckles banging against the sides in her frantic search for her hidden box.

It had to be there.

She couldn't process the overriding need that assailed her. The bird mark burned, and sweat beaded on her forehead and raced in rivulets down her chest.

The box wasn't there. *No.* It had to be there. It couldn't be gone. *It was hers.* She was unwilling to accept defeat. Not that fast.

Amber clenched her teeth in determination and tore into the quilts, grabbing and patting madly at each one. Where was it? She would know if it was gone, wouldn't she? Some unfounded intuition within her said she would. That she would feel the loss.

It was that vital to her.

Finally, her hand hit upon something solid within the folds of a quilt. She stilled, hoped, then dove blindly through the mass of painstakingly hand-stitched squares, careless of the fragility of the cloth, mindless to everything but reaching the object within.

The sensitive skin of her fingertips brushed over the etched wood before she grabbed the small box in her hand. Relief, like nothing she'd ever felt before, rushed through in a raw waterfall of emotion. The burning on her hand instantly cooled, and her panic descended in a crescendo of stark, jagged breaths.

It was there. Still hers.

Slowly, almost afraid to be wrong, she pulled the box from beneath the material. She flipped the lock, springing the lid open to see the stone glistening within the folds of the violet cloth. Visual confirmation set loose a swarm of butterflies to flutter wildly within her chest.

She snapped the lid closed and rested back on her heels, her fingers gliding gently over the carvings in reverent wonder. The air in the shop hung heavy, expectation and anticipation all jumbled into one tense ball of sensation. The energy was almost tangible, enticing her to claim what was hers.

To possess what she so desperately wanted.

She clenched the box to her chest that heaved with anxious gulps of stale air. *Mine.* Yes, she would claim it. It was too hard to ignore and deny. The contents of the beautiful little box belonged to her.

She pushed to her feet and crunched over the broken glass on shaky legs to reach the back counter. Using her arm, she brushed the pens, paper and random objects out of the way, uncaring of where they landed. She set the box down in the newly cleared spot and simply stared at it. How did it hold so much power over her?

Power?

Yes, power. That's exactly what it was. There was no other word to describe the control it seemed to have imposed on her since the moment the box had been shoved into her hands.

Amber lifted her gaze from the box to survey the room, which she had ignored up till now. Quick, analytical eyes took in every detail of the shambled destruction. The beloved Edwardian writing desk sitting tilted on its side. The treasured, Noritake crystal serving pieces shattered in their case and scattered across the floor. Even the enormous grandfather clock that had honored the back wall with its grace and strength since the shop opened was lying face down in a pile of splintered wood.

Nothing had escaped the wrath of the assailant. Every piece of furniture was broken, every mirror cracked, every fragile piece of glass shattered. Pictures were torn from the walls and savagely cut apart. Clouds of fluff billowed around the room, ripped from chair cushions and decorative pillows.

Clearly, the intent had been destruction, not theft. The formally cozy, welcoming shop now felt cold and violated.

Much like herself.

Biting down on her bottom lip, Amber gathered her courage and opened the box once again.

The stone glimmered in stunning shades of violet that randomly reminded her of the crisp, silk scarf that had encased the neck of her CEO. But the colors evolved, moved and changed, ascending upon each other—violet, amethyst, purple, gold—drawing her into the stone's depths as it sparkled with an unnatural light that defied logic.

And it called to her. Whispered enchantments. Promises. Beckoning her to claim it. The air sparked with electricity, snapping with small pops of static as it charged around her. The odd occurrence only registered in Amber's peripheral awareness as her sole focus now was the stone and her need to possess it.

Her heart raced, and her breath stilled. The stone was reaching out to her like physical fingers pulling her closer.

Closer.

Urging her to touch it until she had to comply. She wanted to comply. She was incapable of resisting. She reached her hand out, following the call of the stone. Everything in her demanded she make it hers.

Her hand hovered over the shining gem. The air held its breath, and her pulse slowed before her fingers drifted down to cover the stone.

A bolt of searing hot force shot through Amber's hand, up her arm and through her body like a jolt of lightning signing a note of pure power. She lifted the stone out of the case to reveal that it was attached to a long, gold chain made of tiny, delicate links. It pulsed in her palm in sync with her heartbeat, sending waves of scorching energy with each repeated throb.

She stared in wonder at the breathtaking brilliance she held captive. The stone was amazing. It was pure beauty, warmth and brilliance all in one.

*It was hers.*

A sudden chill ran up her spine and Amber jerked out of her trance with a sense of danger. But from where and why? The shadows in the room appeared to grow longer, darker, closer. The air felt tight, crushing her like a physical weight.

She shoved away from the counter and pressed against the wall. The energy in the room crackled with expectation. She scanned the area searching for what, she didn't know.

Suddenly, the air shifted and pushed against her in a quick gush of force.

"What in the...?" Her words died out as the figure formed before her. Where there was once just space, a man now stood. Solid and strong. Six foot six inches of pure testosterone. And not just any man.

It was *her* CEO. The man who stole her breath, hunted her with his eyes and made her heart race.

Without a thought, Amber launched herself at the form. It had to be a figment of her imagination. Gorgeous men did not form out of thin air.

She slammed into the wall that was the man's chest, igniting a fire inside her and knocking the wind out of her for the second time that day.

*Damn. He was real.*

She scrambled away, confused and terrified. The sound of the air rushing through her nostrils in short, panicked puffs and the sharp bite of her teeth on her lips told her she was awake. This wasn't a dream.

The man commanded attention from his solid, stiff shoulders down to his firm, wide-spread stance. He was still dressed in the black wool trench coat and slacks he had worn to the rally, complete with the violet silk scarf tucked neatly into the folds of his coat. Like always, he reeked of authority.

He was a man who was used to being obeyed.

His deep blue eyes penetrated her with precision and calculation. He scanned her from toe to head and back down, a perusal that left her skin tingling under his gaze. His assessment halted to focus on the fist that had a death grip on the stone.

He stepped forward and grabbed her wrist in one lightning-quick motion. His fingers clamped around the fragile bones, firm, but not painful. The restraint only underlined his strength. Amber yanked on her arm to pull it out of his grasp, but he held firm.

"*No.*" He couldn't have it. It belonged to *her.*

Heat seared through the thin layer of her shirt where his long, strong fingers circled her wrist. The bird mark tingled with an awareness that was almost welcoming. It didn't burn like she'd become accustomed to. Instead it rippled with warm, soothing waves of...longing.

"Let me go," Amber demanded. "What do you want?"

She watched, entrapped both physically and mentally by the man before her. His focus was on her hand, not the object she held within it. He didn't lift his head or meet her eyes. Instead, he slowly reached out his other hand and pushed up the material of her shirt, revealing the stark, white bird etched into her skin.

His breath hitched, and his hand stilled a moment before his fingertips brushed lightly across the surface of her skin in an elegant caress over the bird. The touch left a trail of heat, the warmth reaching deep into her body. She was certain her imagination was running crazy because it felt like the bird shuddered in delight. The sensation rebounded within her. She bit down on her tongue to hold back the startled gasp that threatened to betray her.

"You are the Marked One," his deep voice murmured, an edge of awe mingled with the words. His fingers still stroked the bird in seemingly absent wonder.

"What?" she croaked. Amber cleared her throat and tried again, desperate to sound coherent and unafraid. The energy poured out of the stone and swirled around them in hot, vibrating waves. "What do you want? Why are you here?"

"You are the Marked One." His voice was stronger, more insistent.

Her breath stuck in her lungs as her mind flashed back to the alley. To the exact words the Asian said before he gave her the stone: *We are not the enemy of the Marked One.*

"What are you talking about?" What the hell was the 'Marked One'?

He jerked his head up, his eyes locking with hers to silently convey the importance of his next statement. "The one who bears the mark of the white bird will have the power to change the world."

She broke eye contact and looked down at the bird etched on her skin. Despite the profound statement just made by the overwhelming man before her, relief flooded her system.

He didn't want the stone. It was still hers.

She was the one.

This woman who pulled at him. Who enticed and lured him like no other.

She was the one who could save him. The one who could return everything he had lost. His family, his status, his community and most of all, respect from the people who really mattered—the Energens.

Excitement whipped through him, awakened from a long, dormant absence, forcing Damian to call on the patience that had served him so well. He had to temper the anticipation with the calm, icy reality of all that must be done. He studied his lost beauty, ignoring the heat that radiated up his arm from her wrist and the energy that was attempting to suck him in, closer to her.

Her gaze lifted from her hand to stare at him in defiant resignation. Her chin was tilted up, showing off her strong jaw and graceful neck. But it was her eyes that captured him, as they always did. They were a stunning shade of hazel and gold rimmed with long, dark lashes. He felt like he was staring at a pair of precious jewels that currently sparked with shock, fear and a touch of strength. Her eyes were a deadly weapon she wielded without knowledge.

His body responded immediately, tightening and rippling with the energy that pulled at him. He was instantly in tune with her like he'd known her forever.

As if she belonged to him.

Impossible.

Stifling the strange notion, he focused on the task. "You called me here. Why?"

"I what?" the beauty sputtered, then her eyes narrowed and her back stiffened. "I did not call you here." She paused as if a thought just took hold. "How *did* you get here?"

Her voice held strong even as she jerked on the arm he held hostage. There was no pretense that she didn't recognize him. No shock of amazement or fainting that might consume a weaker woman. Giving her a brief explanation could go a long way in gaining her trust.

A trust that would get him what he needed.

"The energy called me here. To you. You bear the sign of the Marked One." His fingers skimmed over the mark of the bird once again. "The sign to all in the Energy races that the Great War is coming." There, done. "Now, you must come with me."

Shock flashed across her face, her golden eyes sparking with irritation. "Do I look crazy to you?"

His gut clenched, desire pulling hot against the pooling energy that built in his system. No. Crazy was definitely *not* how he would describe her.

He raised an eyebrow. "So it's common for strange men to appear before you out of thin air?" Her suddenly still, pale face brought a small quirk of satisfaction as the question hit its mark. "I was called here for a reason. How did you do it?"

"I didn't do anything."

The ring of truth in her voice gave him pause. Was it possible she really didn't know what was going on? Was she that innocent, that unaware of what she was? "You did something. The energy was clear, pure—stronger than any I've ever felt. It still is."

Her fist clenched around an object in her hand. Damian flipped her wrist to see what she held. He inhaled sharply in stunned silence when he saw the stone gripped tightly within her grasp.

"Where did you get that?"

Once again she pulled on her arm. "It's mine," she stated almost desperately. "It's just a stone."

He chuckled softly. "Wrong. I think we both know it's more than just a stone. Its beauty alone screams of power and reverence. And if that wasn't enough, the energy it emanates is unlike anything I've ever felt." He twisted her wrist from side to side to get a better look at the object. Oddly, he had no desire to take it from her.

The stone appeared almost fluid, churning in varying shades of violet, white and gold that continually climbed over each other in a persistent struggle for dominance. More importantly, it hummed with power. Old, ancient, enchanted. It was strength in its purest form.

It was a power that would be sought by many. Just like the Marked One would be.

With reluctance, he let go of her wrist and instantly felt the missing connection. His fingers stung like they had fallen asleep and were trying to reawaken. But then he realized his entire body felt that way. His blood pumped and hummed with renewed vitality.

The urgency pushed at him. They needed to move before others arrived. He picked up the small wooden box that sat open on the counter, extracting the simple gold circle that rested within it before closing and pocketing the box.

Damian stepped forward and pulled her into his embrace before she could protest.

"It's time to go."

The simple words were the only warning she received before he dissipated out of the small shop with his beauty clamped firmly in his arms.

# Chapter Seven

Amber felt oddly free and light. She held on to Damian like he was her lifeline. Hell, he *was* her lifeline. Letting go was not an option.

In a flash of light, the world solidified, and her feet landed on solid ground. Her arms continued to grip the strong body in front of her. Within his sheltering hold, the energy—that fiery sensation that burned and tingled as it raced through her whenever he touched her—encased her.

For just a moment, she embraced that elusive feeling of being protected and safe. Slowly, her stomach settled and her mind responded to the surroundings.

It was *freezing*.

A cold wind pummeled them in its furry and blew through the thin layer of her cotton shirt like it was tissue paper. She shivered and fought the disturbing desire to stay huddled against the large frame that was providing the only source of warmth. But sanity snapped back into place.

Amber pushed hard upon the solid chest in front of her and stepped out of his arms. Instantly, she felt the sudden emptiness as the fire ceased. She was aware that he let her go. He might be the executive of some big company, but the solid muscle under his expensive clothing was proof that he was no pencil-pushing figurehead.

She wrapped her arms around herself in an attempt to retain the receding heat and block the icy wind. She shivered again and shoved her clenched fists under her armpits to keep them from becoming popsicles.

He stood there guarded and silent—watching her.

"Where are we?" Her anger quickly pushed back the rising panic and overtook the original shock that had numbed her.

He reached up and extracted the violet scarf from around his neck. "North Dakota."

"What?" Her mouth hung open in disbelief. Her misfiring brain cells held her in place as she tried to process his words. Slowly, Amber turned her head and took stock of her surroundings.

They were standing on the front porch of an old farmhouse in the middle of nowhere, North Dakota, if she was to believe him. There was nothing but drifting snow banks and open fields broken up by the occasional tree line as far as she could see. It was harsh, brutal and eerily empty.

Taking advantage of her frozen astonishment, Damian stepped forward and wrapped his scarf around her neck. With surprising tenderness, he carefully pulled the length of her hair out from under the scarf so the soft material was tucked against the skin of her neck.

"Why did you bring me here?" she asked numbly. She would ignore the question of how for the moment. There was only so much information she could process at one time.

Damian stared at the nondescript wooden door of the farmhouse. "This is the eastern entrance to my..." He bit back his words, a brief flash of pain crossing his face. "The enclave."

"Here? In the middle of nowhere, North Dakota?" She whipped out her arm and motioned at the barren landscape to emphasize her point.

His lips curled in a quirk of humor. "Yeah, doesn't seem like a very smart choice." He scanned the empty, cold land, a blank look holding his face. "When we first came to this land, it was wild and free, nothing but open space. Two thousand years ago, the entire continent was unclaimed. The location was chosen because of what it provided."

She stifled a shiver. When he didn't continue, she prompted, "And?"

He looked back at her. "And it suited our needs. Here," he said, removing his long, wool coat and holding it open for her.

She lifted an eyebrow, doubting his sudden kindness.

"You're freezing." He lifted the coat slightly. "Please, put this on. It is not my intent to freeze you to death."

Reluctant to trust his motivation, she was too logical to stand there shivering when a warm, winter coat was being offered. She turned and quickly shoved her arms into the waiting coat and tightened it around her. Instantly the shaking in her limbs stilled. His lingering warmth surrounded her and brought with it the faint hint of pine that she was beginning to associate with him.

Once again, he gently, almost reverently, pulled her long hair out from where it was trapped between the coat and her back letting it run through his fingers until it hung free. The soft caress sent whispers of pleasure coursing over her scalp and down her spine.

Unnerved by his kindness, she jerked away from his touch and spun back around, eyeing him warily. He shoved his hands into the pockets of his pants, but otherwise showed no outward effect of being exposed to the cold weather. Evidently, the black wool suit jacket was warmer than it looked.

"Where did you get the stone?" he demanded softly.

She hesitated, her fist clenching tighter around the object in question, before admitting, "It was given to me."

"By whom?"

"Does it matter? It's mine," she reasserted.

"Yes, it matters."

She remained silent since divulging all of her secrets didn't seem smart. After a second, he sighed.

"We need to contain the energy before it calls more—" He paused abruptly and looked around. He reached into his pocket and extended the gold ring that he'd pulled from the box earlier. "Here."

Her confusion must have shown on her face. He pointed to the chain dangling below her fist that clenched the stone. "Put it on."

"What?"

"The stone is attached to a chain. Put it on."

"Why?" Her eyes narrowed, her suspicion rising.

"To keep it safe."

With slow, hesitant movements, she grasped the chain then lifted it over her head, the whole time keeping her gaze firmly on him. When the chain was around her neck, she reached back to lift her hair out from under the links then adjusted the scarf until the chain rested gently against her neck, the stone nestled between the rounded swell of her breasts.

She stiffened, retreating a step as he approached. "What are you doing?" Her hand went protectively over the stone.

He extended the ring again. "I believe this will snap in place around the stone and contain the energy. I don't want the stone. But others will. We need to stop the energy broadcast that the stone is emanating, and the circle should do that."

She had no idea what he was talking about, but she understood one important fact—he didn't want the stone.

Again, relief swamped her. Did she trust him? Did she have a choice?

Her hand shook as she stretched it out to snatch the offered ring. What did he mean by "contain the energy"? She fumbled with the chain, lifting it from her chest to eye the stone. The chain was attached to a corner of the stone by a small loop so it hung suspended in the diamond shape.

She lifted her gaze, unclear on what he wanted her to do. Damian reached out, extracted the ring from her grip, and then carefully set the circle around the stone where it rested in her palm.

Within seconds, the sensations died—the heightened awareness, the insistent vibration that rubbed imperceptibly over the hairs on her skin, the weighted denseness in the air that surrounded them were all gone.

Amazing.

"You felt that?" Damian held her gaze. "That was the energy. Now, pinch the ring into the small clasps on the corners of the stone to hold it in place." A spark of stinging flames shot up her arm at the simple brush of his fingers over her palm. She flinched at the strange sensation and the quick withdrawal of his hand indicated he'd felt it too. Was that the energy? The odd feeling ignited a longing within her that was unfounded and unfamiliar.

She snapped the ring into place and let the stone fall back to her chest. It looked stunning, the violet diamond mounted within the simple gold ring resting against the navy cotton of her shirt.

"Now, your name."

"Why?" She buttoned the coat then crossed her arms tightly over her chest.

"So I can stop thinking of you as the lost beauty."

His admission stunned her. She took a step back. Her instant denial was no doubt a result of the last time someone had called her beautiful. Nate. And look where trusting had gotten her then.

She cautiously assessed him. Like always, his clothing was impeccable and cut to accentuate his strength. The crisp white shirt under his dark suit appeared even whiter beside the golden tones of his skin, and the royal violet tie was knotted to perfection. Everything about him spoke of power. Despite all that had happened, he still drew her in, pulled at her until she couldn't help but wonder what it would be like to be protected by him. To be held and cherished by a man so totally in control.

"Amber." The small concession was given as a challenge. She lifted her chin and waited.

He gave a slight nod in acceptance. "Amber. How appropriate."

"Why?"

"Your name is very powerful," he answered. "Amber—the blood of trees. It is formed from nature to shield and protect against infection, to give a tree a chance to heal as it restores itself from the inside out. It is the color of liquid sunshine, yellow for the midday sun and orange for the fiery sunset. It is alive, still and active. It is the balance that harmonizes yin and yang, as well as the past, present and future. It has the power to change negative energy into positive energy. But most importantly, it provides protection. Something you are now in need of."

Her lips thinned. "I don't need protection."

"Oh, you need more protection than you can imagine."

Her panic flared, but she tried to control it. It was a pointless endeavor, but she would contain it—there was no way she would let him see it. This was all too extreme and beyond real. Every fiber of her body rejected the crushing feeling of being trapped and forced into something she wanted no part of.

A chill that had nothing to do with the weather snaked over her. She exhaled, trying to maintain her calm and gather her wits. There had to be some logic in this. But there had been no logic to any of the things that had happened to her since New York City. Why should this be any different?

"How did we get here? No, wait." She held up her hand to stop his answer. "I don't want to know. Just take me home. I don't care where we are or how we got here. Just take me home."

"I can't do that."

"Obviously you can since you brought us here. What you're saying is you won't."

She turned away and paced to the end of the narrow front porch. Her boots thumped against the worn planks of wood. The barren landscape that greeted her off the back and side of the house offered no escape and did nothing to ease her tension. She turned back to him.

"If there's some big enclave here, where are you hiding it?"

"The energy field that circles our lands presents the illusion of what you would expect to see. The energy repels normal humans from investigating further and also prohibits anyone from entering who doesn't have permission."

She swallowed. Energy fields? "All right. I know who you are, but maybe I should ask *what* you are."

Sighing, he extracted his hand from a pocket and rubbed it over the back of his neck. The first sign of frustration she'd seen from him. He returned his hand to his pocket and met her eyes.

"I'm an Energen. We are an evolved branch of homo sapiens and have been here since life began."

He looked completely serious, but Amber was having a very hard time keeping a straight face. "Okay, I'll play—evolved how?"

"By evolved, I mean we have the ability to control the energy and elements of the earth."

This time, she did laugh. She scuffed her foot over the wisps of snow that had collected on the porch. "Really? You expect me to believe that?"

Her laughter did not spread to him. He continued to look at her with a straight face. "Can you find another explanation for how we arrived here?"

Her laughter died. Damn. "How'd you do that?" Guess it was time to tackle that question.

Now he smiled. "Energy. Simply put, I broke down the energy within us and then used the energy around us to move us here."

Big damn. As advanced as humans might be, she'd not heard of any human traveling through the air via molecular disintegration as of yet.

"So, what—you're an alien?" Seemed like the next logical thing to assume. As if aliens were logical.

"No." He shook his head patiently. "I'm just as human as you are."

He certainly looked human. But still, it was a little too extreme to easily process. Even with her exposure to the tribe shaman and his seemingly mystical abilities, jumping into the realm of foreign species with unnatural powers was an entirely different thing.

But then, she apparently had a tattoo permanently etched onto her hand because she'd touched a stone.

"Why am I here? What do you want with me?" Edging down her panic, she tried to focus on the facts. Stepping over to a window, she peered inside, but could see nothing through the white-backed curtain that blocked the view. She gave up and looked back to Damian.

His night-sky eyes stared into hers, making her feel exposed and emotionally vulnerable. "I told you. You are the

Marked One." He tilted his head, indicating her hand, which was hidden under the length of his coat sleeve. "There are prophecies going back thousands of years predicting your appearance. Telling of how you will have the power to influence the fate of the world. How you and you alone can turn the tide between good and evil. You, Amber, are now the most important person in my world. In the world of my people. It is my duty to bring you in."

*What?* "Oh, no, no, no. That *cannot* be true. I am *not* that girl," Amber denied as she edged toward the stairs. "Believe me. I'm not the adventure girl who's going to change the world. Attending protest rallies is about as daring as I get. So you can take me home, and I'll forget this ever happened."

The stoic look on his face told her Damian wasn't buying it. She wet her lips, then darted down the short flight of steps and sprinted through the narrow path into the snow. She had no idea where she was going, but getting away was imperative. The need to escape pressed on her, propelling her legs until she dropped with a jolt, sunk thigh deep into a snowdrift.

"There's nowhere to run."

His cool voice chiseled at her nerves. Releasing a frustrated sigh, she leaned back and yanked on her leg until it emerged from the depths of the snow. "Yeah, well, I'm not going to stand here and wait for you to drag me off to my death." She straightened and turned back to the house only to find him standing directly in front of her. Damn, he was quiet.

"I'm not going to kill you." Amusement flickered over his face as he watched her shake and stomp the snow off her leg. "Or, as you say, drag you to your death. But I do need to turn you in."

She froze. "What do you mean, turn me in?" What in the hell was he talking about? Panic edged back in to take an icy hold on her remaining calm.

He looked away to stare across the frozen field. The wind gusted up, pummeling them both as they stood open and exposed to the elements.

"It's for your own protection."

63

The way he refused to look at her had Amber doubting the truth of his last statement. She grabbed at her hair, the wind forcing it to dance and fly in wild streams around her head and over her face. Silently cursing, she tried to rein in the strands. This was one of those days where she wished she had the courage to just cut it all off.

She jumped when his hands brushed against her head to control the wild mass of flying hair. A spark that she now associated with pure energy raced along her scalp and down her back, warming her entire body. It edged back the panic and shot spears of longing straight to her core. How did he do that?

"There," he said once she had the mass clamped tightly in her hands. He stood so close she had to tilt her head back to look at him. His hands still rested on her head, entwined within her hair. He looked down at her with an intensity that had her blood suddenly boiling. This man, this stranger, affected her in a way that he shouldn't. In a way that should have her running away scared instead of slowing leaning forward, pulled in by his touch and the unchecked desire that was evident in his eyes.

Abruptly, he pulled away. "Come back to the porch. At least it offers some break from the wind." He turned and walked toward the house without waiting to see if she followed. His assumption of her obedience irritated her, but there was nowhere to run. There were no tracks in the snow or even a plowed driveway to indicate that anyone had been at the farmhouse since the snow began last fall.

The house itself was well kept, with pale yellow paint, white trim and the broad white porch that stretched across the front of the two-story structure. Curtains hung closed over every window, and empty clay flower pots were tucked into the corners of the porch, waiting for spring to arrive. There was no hint of neglect, but it felt absolutely deserted.

Once again, logic won out over stubbornness. It was stupid, and cold, to stand out in the wind. And she wasn't really scared of him. By him. Maybe it was because she'd watched him for so long that it felt like she knew him. Despite the oddity of what was happening and the exceedingly strange and unbelievable events that had been thrust upon her, the man himself did not inspire fear.

Now the events themselves, those were another thing.

She discounted the strange feelings left by his touch and followed him up the steps, lifting the hem of his coat to keep from tripping. She looked around and waited for him to say something.

He didn't.

"So why do you think I'm this so-called Marked One?" she finally put out there as she took the time to roll up the sleeves of his coat. Questions were way preferred to the uncomfortable silence that threatened to pull away the false calm she presented.

"Because you are. The mark on the back of your hand—the white bird rising—is a rare and unique symbol that will only appear on the one who has the strength to control its power."

Reflex had her tucking her exposed hands into the deep pockets of his coat.

"You're wrong," she bluffed. "I picked out the design and had the tattoo put on at a tattoo parlor. I'm not this Marked One." Amber willed back the blush that would give her away.

"No. I'm not wrong." His gaze held hers. "You are the Marked One. The energy tells me so. It screams of power, of vitality, of ancient ways that will be called to use with your arrival."

So much for lying. Amber struggled for another answer. "Then there must be a mistake. Wrong place, wrong time, wrong girl. That kind of thing happens all the time."

He shook his head, denying her doubt. "We have waited thousands of years for your appearance. There is no mistake. No accident. No wrong girl. You, Amber, you *are* the one."

Before she could fire off another denial, the door to the house swung open, eerily silent. Absent was the squeaky hinges or click of the door latch that usually accompanied the action.

Damian stepped between her and the man who had appeared in the doorway. Damian's entire body became a mass of tightly held muscle. His hands were out of his pockets and clenched at his sides. He pulled his shoulders back, straightening his spine until every last inch of his imposing height was displayed.

He was primed and ready for something.

She snuck a quick peek from behind Damian to look at the new arrival. He was slightly taller than Damian, dressed entirely in black that matched the midnight black hair that brushed his cheekbones and the onyx depths of his eyes. The bulk of his finely toned muscles was clearly outlined under the thin cotton of the short sleeve shirt and impressed upon Amber that he could kick some serious ass.

Like Damian, the man exuded authority as if he was born with it. He owned it. Demanded it. And currently challenged Damian with it. Thankfully, Damian didn't appear to be intimidated by him or the look he was giving them.

"Damian." The man's deep voice rumbled across the short distance between them. His face remained impassive. The man might be considered handsome if his chiseled features didn't look like they were cut out of stone.

"Xander." Damian's voice held zero emotion.

The man crossed his arms over his broad chest. "What do you want?"

Damian's back straightened even more, if that was possible. For some unexplainable reason, Amber reached out and rested her hand on his back. The heat, the vitality that sailed up her arm made her breath hitch. His muscles contracted at her touch.

Did he feel it too? That odd power that sizzled between them whenever they touched?

The stone burned against her chest, sending its own waves of energy spiraling through her. A strange sense of urgency had her reaching under the coat with her free hand to slip the stone under her shirt.

No one else needed to see it. Needed to know she had it.

The overwhelming claim to ownership came barreling back to her. Damian had proven himself a non-threat to the stone, so her defenses had gone down. But this new guy, he screamed threat.

"I've brought the Marked One." Damian's voice matched the elements, icy and cold. His words sounded hollow. But there was no doubt he fully intended to turn her over to this man. Still, she couldn't muster the desire to pull her hand away from his back.

Like the stone, he belonged to her.

Hissing as if she'd been burned, Amber jerked her hand at the strange thought. She quickly stepped away, retreating from him. Her movements brought her into full view of the imposing man in the door. He assessed her with expressionless eyes before turning his attention back to Damian.

"I need proof."

"You'll get it when I see the council."

"This is all a big mistake," Amber jumped in, unwilling to go along with whatever plans they were making. "If I could use a phone, I can make a call and be on my way." As impressed as she was with her ability to keep her voice normal, her small speck of self-importance was smacked back down when both men looked at her, then dismissed her.

"I can't trust you, Damian." There was just a hint of sadness in the man's voice.

Damian inclined his head. "Accepted. You can collar us."

The man thinned his lips and studied Damian intently before nodding. "As you wish." He took one step back into the house before he paused. "Be sure about this, Damian. There's no going back once you've entered."

The warning was ominous and landed between them like a rock.

Amber started to inch backwards off the porch, but was halted by Damian's firm grip. Fire followed his touch up her arm and across her chest, pulling tight and hard.

"I'm sure," Damian stated crisply.

"I'm not," she whispered.

The man eased back farther and held the door open. "You may enter."

Damian exhaled and stepped forward, dragging Amber along with him.

What was she supposed to do now? Her feet dragged, and she pulled back, resisting Damian's hold. But they both knew she had no hope of getting away. It would be pointless to scream or struggle further since it was obvious the other man wouldn't help her and there was no one else around for miles.

Behind her, the door clicked closed, the sound echoing through the sudden quiet within the house. It resonated in her ears and transformed in her mind to the last nail being pounded into her coffin.

Standing there in the entryway of an empty house, sandwiched between two hard men, two strangers, the reality of her situation slammed into her.

She was trapped.

All possibilities of escape, of returning home, of the entire situation being a big, colossal mistake were wiped out when she crossed the threshold of the house. The chance to go back was gone. She felt that truth in every fiber of her body. The bird mark flamed to life on her hand and the stone hung heavy, hard and hot between her breasts.

Damian turned to face her, his grip still in place around her arm. His lips were pressed into a firm, thin line, but his eyes were on fire. They pulsed with the energy she felt. They had deepened to an almost black-blue and swirled with something undefined.

The energy burned and raced up her arm from where he held her, pushed at her senses and spoke of honor, truth and desire. A desire that coiled through her until her sex tightened and clenched in unknown arousal. She sucked in her breath at the sudden new sensation.

No man had ever affected her like that.

The virgin in her whimpered to know the secrets that whispered at the edge of the desire. The forbidden knowledge that she longed to understand and experience but never had.

In that moment, Amber was more afraid of the desire he stirred, of the longing that slammed through her heart than of whatever lay beyond the walls of the house.

# Chapter Eight

The air hung heavy, still and silent around the trio. No one said a word as the seconds ticked by. The oppressive air seemed out of place in the stark emptiness of their surroundings. It pressed upon Damian, the weight almost physical.

He couldn't remember when he'd felt so on edge. It had been a very, *very* long time since something had stirred him this much. Long ago he had learned that the only way to survive was to extinguish his emotions. To become as hard on the inside as he was forced to be on the outside.

And it had worked for a thousand years.

Now, this one speck of a female had his blood racing, demanding attention and creating a need for something he could not have. She was the Marked One. She had the prophesied sign of evil and destruction scored onto her delicate flesh.

How could he possibly be feeling anything desirable or protective for her? Unless he too was evil. Unless everything his people had been proclaiming about him was true.

*Never.*

But, there was nothing about Amber that even hinted at evil at this point. If anything, she was the exact opposite of evil. Innocent to an extreme that was hard to believe in today's world.

"Where are we going?" Amber pulled against his hold on her arm.

With more effort than he expected, Damian released Amber's arm and let his hand fall to his side. The loss of connection echoed through him and made him ache for more. Until all he wanted to do was whisk her away from there and anything that could harm her.

To where he could keep her safe.

Foolish.

He had to turn her in. She was his opportunity for redemption—his chance to finally return to the enclave and redeem himself to his father, his family and the entire community.

Steeling himself against the unrelenting pull he felt toward her, Damian looked to Xander and found himself fighting another battle. Xan, his one-time best friend, looked at him with zero emotion. Not a hint of the past. Of the closeness they had once shared. There was a time when Xan, Ladon and Damian had been inseparable. The Triple Terrors, a name pegged on them for the trouble they caused both in and out of battle.

Now, it was as if none of that had ever existed. Amber was his ticket to getting back everything that had been stripped so ruthlessly from him.

"Let's do it," Damian said to Xan, careful to keep all emotion from his voice. There was not a chance in hell he would let any weakness show. Not now. Not ever.

Xan studied him for a moment before he pulled two black collars from the hook next to the front door. To most, they would look like simple dog collars.

To Damian, they looked like death.

He concentrated on holding himself perfectly still as Xan approached. All one thousand years of calm fortitude were forced into use.

"What are those?" Amber demanded. "What's going on?"

Xan stopped next to him and stared, his coal black eyes peering into Damian's.

"You're sure?" Xan questioned again. Something Damian knew he wouldn't usually do. As head of the Energen Guard the force that protected and defended the Energen race—Xan never doubted his actions or offered second chances. The safety of the entire enclave fell under Xan's responsibility. A responsibility he owned.

"Positive," Damian responded even though he was anything but. For the first time in years he truly doubted his next move. It was not something he was used to, and he found it unsettling.

Giving a brief, crisp nod, Xan reached up and clipped the object around Damian's neck. Damian flinched, unable to restrain the reaction.

The collars were set as two half circles connected with a back hinge that enabled them to open and close easily around a neck. The hard, black metal felt cold against his skin and had the instant effect they were designed for.

"Like all circles created by my people, they will contain our energy," he told Amber around the tightness in his jaw. Every ounce of power he held was now contained. "As long as we wear the collars, we cannot wield the powers or use the energy as we were born to do."

He was a prisoner. He had willingly turned himself over to the very people who wanted to see him dead. He clenched his teeth and resisted the urge to pull at the restraint. He swallowed and cringed as his Adam's apple rubbed against the hard metal.

"Handcuffs for the mystical?" Amber quipped. "Well, then, you can put that other one away since I don't have any powers."

The rattling of a door handle forced Damian's attention from himself. Amber had eased her way back to the front door and was desperately twisting the doorknob in an attempt to escape. He felt a foreign sense of pride at her self-preservation instinct.

The two men watched her in silence until she finally gave up. She turned to look at them once she realized the door wouldn't open. Her lips were clamped between her teeth. His black trench coat swallowed her and made her appear small despite her height. Her gaze darted back and forth between the men, but she straightened her back and lifted her chin in a graceful move of defiance. She stood tall and assessed them with cool reservation. She wasn't cowering in fear or blatant denial of the events.

Damian held back the smile that threatened to break. Why in the world did her continual boldness, her unwillingness to give up, make him proud? It made zero sense and had no place in his emotions.

Emotions. There they were again. Yet another thing that made no sense. Why was he suddenly feeling when he had successfully shut out everything for years? Now was not the time to open that door.

"What are you doing?" Amber looked at Xan with hesitant eyes as he approached her.

"He needs to place the collar around your neck," Damian informed her, hoping to calm her some. "Let him. It won't hurt, and it's the only way we can leave this house."

She looked around Xan and met Damian's eyes. "I told you I don't need one. I have no powers. Trust me, after almost twenty-four years of life, I'd know if I did."

"It will be safer for you if you wear one."

Question and doubt were evident in her eyes, but eventually she gave a slight nod of acceptance.

Before Xan could move, Damian was next to him, taking the black ring from his hand. "I'll do it." The thought of another man touching Amber had his skin crawling with a possessiveness that startled him with its intensity.

Amber was *his* to protect.

Even as he rejected the thought, he was pushing Xan back so he could stand in front of her. She looked at him, her golden eyes showing everything she was trying so desperately to hide— fear, doubt, confusion, courage...and trust. That one nailed him like a knee to his groin.

He swallowed back self-loathing as he moved the collar around her neck. He deliberately let his fingers brush her soft nape, ensuring that none of her hair got caught in the hinge. The tiny click of the lock closing rang in his ears. He leaned forward under the pretense of fixing his scarf, which was still looped around her neck.

"Keep the necklace hidden," he whispered into her ear. The light smell of cinnamon invaded his nose and nearly brought him to his knees. How? More importantly, why did he just tell her that?

He'd acted on impulse.

She stilled, then nodded almost imperceptibly. He didn't doubt she would listen.

"It's time to go," Xan said. "I have been instructed to bring you directly to the Council Hall. I assume the full council will be present."

Damian turned to Xan and nodded his appreciation for the extra bit of information. They would be presented before the full group of council members, not just the five Heads of Houses. Not unexpected, but infinitely more challenging.

He guided Amber forward with a hand to her back. The lack of connection left him cold. The collars were blocking the flow of energy between them, something he hadn't anticipated. He had come to expect and welcome the heat.

His muscles tensed at that acknowledgement. She swiveled her head to look at him. She noticed it too.

Once again, he doubted his actions. His instincts were flashing bright red warning signals. But what were they trying to tell him? Whatever it was, he would need to figure it out fast. In a short time, he would be facing a community of people he hadn't seen in a millennium.

Since the day he was exiled from the enclave.

Amber paced around the small, empty room they were locked in. She itched with a suppressed craving that left her feeling both agitated and oddly empty. Her fingers rubbed absently over the smooth, hard surface of the collar around her throat.

"What's going on?" She paused and faced Damian.

Xan had led them out the back of the farmhouse into the warmth of a sunny spring day. Amber couldn't even process how that was possible. Understanding the events of the day had become an exercise in futility. So she simply stopped trying. Instead, she focused on taking in the details in the hopes she could use them to get away. The urgency to run had only increased with each mile they rode in the little golf cart closer to the large, circular building they were now locked in.

In the short ride, Damian had become her anchor and only constant in the perplexing world that surrounded her. Should she trust him? Probably not. But her options were slim.

He looked around the small room then rubbed his hand over the back of his neck. His arm froze when he touched the strange black collar. His jaw tightened and he dropped his hand.

"We will be presented before the full council, who will pass judgment on my claim," he finally answered.

"The claim that I'm the Marked One?"

"Yes."

"And then what?" She shoved her hands deep in the pockets of his coat to still her anxious movements, one hand brushing against the carved box from the stone. "What will happen to me?"

He looked at the ground. "I don't know. It will depend on if they believe me." He looked up, his face impassive. "If they believe that you are truly the prophesied one."

"I'm not," she insisted again. She looked at him and tried to convey the truth of her words. "There's no way I'm that person. I cannot manipulate energy or wield power over the elements of the earth. I'm just a simple antique dealer. Nothing more."

He stepped forward until he stood before her. "You are much more than that. I know this for certain." He reached up and tucked her hair behind her ear before he dragged his fingers through the long strands. "I can feel it. So can you if you stop denying it. There's a reason for the mark on your hand. A reason I was called to you."

Her heart raced not at his words, but at his closeness, his tender touch. She inhaled his unique scent, that hint of pine, a tinge of salt and grass...all the various aromas that were carried by the wind. The combination raced through her, tightened her nipples and made her ache.

"How?"

"I don't know." He stepped away, jammed his hands in his pockets and paced to the other side of the room. "I don't understand it all myself."

"But you still insist on turning me over to these people?"

A small tick flickered at the edge of his jaw. "I have to."

"Why? Why do you have to?"

It was his turn to pace. Brisk, quick movements back and forth along the far wall. Amber waited, unwilling to give him an out. Finally he stopped and faced her.

"It's my way back into the enclave. I was exiled a millennium ago. You're my ticket back."

"You're what?" She stared at him in shock, betrayal gripping her. "So my life is expendable and means nothing to you? This whole kidnapping me and claiming I'm some prophesied power of disaster is nothing more than an excuse for you to save face? So you can return to some community that kicked you out a thousand years ago?" She turned around, unable to look at him anymore. She didn't even trying to process the thousand-year time span he'd stated.

On second thought, she spun back and strode over to him. Before she could think about the consequences, Amber brought her hand up and slapped him across the cheek. The sharp smack of skin against skin echoed through the tiny room. Her own hand stung from the impact with his flesh.

His eyes widened and flashed. His nostrils flared and the tic went wild on his clenched jaw. But he didn't move. The silence hung between them, her haggard breaths the only sound in the room.

"I deserved that," he finally bit out. "But don't ever do that again. You will not get away with it next time."

The red mark was still bright and fresh on his cheek, and Amber had a need to make it redder. To make sure he understood just how much he'd hurt her. What did it matter at this point? He could harm her or she could wait for some assembling crowd to stone her death. She might as well get in some hits before she went down.

"You are a selfish ass," she said with a calm restraint she didn't feel. "For some stupid reason I'd started to trust you. I felt the energy between us." His eyes flashed imperceptibly. "Yes, that strange current of heat that passes between us at every touch, I felt it too. I listened to it and believed we were tied somehow. That you wouldn't hurt me. What a lie."

She reached back to hit him again, despite his warning. The force of her anger was put into the forward motion of her hand. She needed to hear that sound again and feel the pain against her hand. A physical communication of just how badly his betrayal felt.

Her hand was stopped just inches from his face, his grip firm around her wrist. They stared at each other, the anger stirring in his dark eyes only raising her own. She was tired of being walked over. Of being perceived as weak. And damn it, she wasn't going to let this man take her down. Not without a fight.

"I told you not to hit me again." The low warning was given in even, measured tones.

Her chest heaved with each gust of air she inhaled. "And I told you to take me home. You didn't listen to me so why should I listen to you?"

"Because I never threatened you with violence."

"No, you just plan on turning me over to those who will do it for you."

"That is not true."

"Then what is true?" she challenged, tugging on the hand still clamped in his wrist. "Do you plan to let me go? To take me home?" His eyes flinched almost imperceptibly, but she saw it. "No, I didn't think so."

She dropped her gaze to the floor as the resignation set in. Her hair fell forward to form a dark cloak around her face. The veil provided an almost tunnel vision down to the toes of his impeccable, black leather dress boots. The need to strike at him was still strong.

"You present an image of sophisticated righteousness, but beneath that cool exterior lies a heartless, selfish man. One who will use someone else for gain, even if it means hurting that person."

"That is not true," he venomously denied. His grip tightened on her wrist, but not enough to hurt her. He jerked her closer until her chest was inches from his, her eyes level with his neck. "You know nothing of me. I have sacrificed the last thousand years of my life because I believed in the truth. In good. In doing what is right."

"Then listen to me. Believe what I'm telling you."

"How do I know you're not manipulating me?"

"If your body responds to our energy the way mine does, then you'd know that I have no control over what is happening," she insisted. "The heat, the burning, the flash of sensation that eats at my core is not something I want. Something I'm manipulating."

The sound of his deep inhale broke the silence and caused her to look up in question. The second she saw the heated intent, the hunger that deepened the blue of his eyes until they were bright pools of desire, she realized her mistake.

She stood transfixed, unable to move as his head descended in a quick, conquering move. Fear stiffened her muscles as flashes of Nate invaded her mind.

Despite the quick, fierce approach, Damian's touch was gentle. His lips firm but yielding, not plundering. The light brush held such promise, such hints of passion that she found herself stretching up, reaching for more. Wanting more.

Anticipation flared, heating her from the inside out, blending with the sudden flash of energy to send hot licks of longing through her body. Some part of her brain realized she should be scared, that this was something she shouldn't want. The insanity of it was beyond reason. To desire the very man who had abducted her, put her life in danger, was crazy.

But she did want it. Desperately.

Her fingers clenched into fists as his free hand moved to cup her cheek, holding her still to meet his lips in another pass of sultry longing. His lips were soft, smooth silk that brushed over hers in question, doubt and desire. Each pass a bit harder, longer, more commanding.

Her pulse accelerated as the kiss deepened and the energy surged from the stone, whipping out coils of heat, overriding the collars and burning her with a desire that stole her breath. Every nerve ending was alive and vibrating with the sudden need for this man who held such questions and mystery. Who offered her a world of unknown passion and danger.

A low moan escaped when his heated tongue stroked over her lips—hot, tempting and inviting. Not taking. He let go of her wrist, and she tentatively rested her palms on his chest when the loud clearing of a throat rumbled behind them.

She stiffened. He froze.

A mumbled curse left his lips. His hold on her loosened as he lifted his head, his eyes guarded under hooded lids.

What was she doing? Abruptly, she pulled out of his grasp and stepped away from the inviting heat of his body. The energy sparked at the separation then slowly dissolved, leaving her empty.

"It's time to go," Xan said, his deep voice sounding like a freight train as it shattered through the tension in the room. "The council is waiting for you."

She looked at Damian, hope building that he would change his mind. That after that kiss he would realize she was innocent and wasn't the Marked One. That he would want to help and protect her.

Disappointment settled deep and hard when he nodded and moved around her toward the door. Between the two of them, he was clearly a bigger bastard than the circumstances of her birth had ever made her.

And she was a gigantic fool.

# Chapter Nine

"So you return." The voice boomed through the circular stone chamber, rocketing off the walls to bounce against Damian's eardrums. The room was filled with people, all sitting in raised, stadium-style seating ascending ten levels high. Every seat was filled, but the sound echoed as if the room were empty.

Amber and Damian were the sole focus. Every angle scrutinized and judged.

Sweat trickled down Damian's stiffly held back. He lifted his chin, refusing to be intimidated. He could feel the eyes on him. Hear the snickers at his return. Sense the condemnations that were still held against him.

"I have," Damian answered.

He stood next to Amber in the center of the chamber. Two lambs trapped, the wolves circling and hungry. He'd set the trap himself and now he needed to ensure that they both made it out safely.

"I hope whatever made you return was worth your freedom."

Was it? Doubt plagued him more than ever. The kiss had been a rash impulse, a lapse in control that he was now paying for. His attention had to be on the man before him. On what he had come here to do.

But the pull to protect her was raging so strong, it was hard to focus. The flash of pure energy that had fired through him when she'd kissed him back had spoken of desire and belonging that set his senses ablaze. The pure innocence that came from her made his chest tighten with the intuition that this was wrong. Bringing her here was wrong.

Turning her over to them, walking away from her was wrong.

Damian sniffed, and his lips thinned, but he schooled his features to show nothing. He reminded himself of his primary objective and forced the words out. "I have brought the Marked One."

A collective gasp echoed through the chamber, followed by a low murmur as the occupants leaned toward each other to debate his claim.

Damian didn't look at Amber. He couldn't. The flash of betrayal that had crossed her face after the kiss was seared into his memory. Instead, he trained his eyes on the man who stood on a raised pedestal about halfway up the row of seats.

Cronus, the council Elder, was cloaked in the formal, long white robe of the chamber room. Behind Cronus to the North sat the Head of the House of Earth robed in brown, and Damian knew without looking that each direction would find the remaining Houses—Air to the East, Fire to the South, and Water to the West. The chamber room was laid out like the compound itself with each elemental power aligned to the navigational direction it represented.

"The Marked One?" Cronus's voice rang out over the sudden din, hushing the crowd.

"Yes."

"Show us." A simple demand filled with challenge and doubt.

Damian stared at the elder, unable to react. This was the moment he'd wished for for centuries. It was his chance at redemption. So why was he stalling? *Damn it!*

Clenching his jaw and squelching the doubt, Damian turned to Amber and grabbed her arm. To her credit, she didn't pull away or even flinch. Worse, she just looked at him with blank, empty eyes. Her face was a stone façade of indifference.

A sharp pain jabbed at his chest, but he couldn't let it sway him. He lifted her arm and pulled back the sleeve of his long coat that she still wore until her hand was fully exposed. Gripping her wrist, he turned her hand over to show the mark to the council.

Once again, a collective gasp rippled through the room. There was a sudden shifting of bodies as people pushed and shoved to get a better view of the mark.

Cronus, however, didn't react at all. "A white bird rising. A simple tattoo that could be put on by anyone. That alone does not make her the Marked One."

Damian dropped Amber's hand and turned to face the challenge. "Correct. But this is not a fake tattoo. The energy she holds is more powerful and pure than any I have ever encountered."

"How did you find her?"

"The energy called to me. I followed it and found her."

Cronus lifted an eyebrow. "Why you?"

Damian clenched his fist and forced himself not to bristle at the question. "Why not me? I have done nothing but proven myself loyal since I was exiled. When will my penance end?"

"You killed my son!" The sudden roar interrupted Cronus and burst through the room, echoing off every wall and bounding back to slam against Damian from all sides. This time he did flinch. He couldn't stop the involuntary reaction.

"Kadmos!" Cronus admonished.

Slowly, Damian turned to face his accuser, the Head of the House of Air. He called upon the icy calm he had perfected years ago to maintain his composure and hide every bit of emotion that stirred within him.

"Father," he stated coldly. "I see a millennium has done nothing to alter your opinion." The bitterness in the words covered his disappointment.

His father stood, his face contorted in anger. The yellow robe of his house billowed around him as he stared down at Damian. "How could it change? You betrayed me. Your brothers. All of us. Do you expect us to forget that?"

Damian looked for Phelix and Loukionos, his younger brothers. They stood stoic but unified beside his father. Where he should be. Damian couldn't let the pain in. He had let go of that long ago, and there was no room for it now.

"Accusations that were never proven. Yet I have suffered the punishment all the same." Damian dismissed his father and turned back to Cronus. "And to further prove my loyalty, I have brought in the prophesied Marked One before she could be used by Gog and his followers to sway the balance of evil."

Cronus remained impassive. After a moment, he moved around the podium and descended the stairs. He moved with the smooth, sliding grace of a teenager that belied the three thousand plus years that he really was.

He stopped before Amber and looked her over. Again, she held strong and met Cronus's gaze without showing a single hint of what she was feeling. Without being prompted, she lifted her arm and pulled up the sleeve until the mark was displayed for Cronus to examine. The elder arched an eyebrow at her offering then cupped her hand in his large palm. He turned her hand from side to side in his thorough analysis of the mark.

The silence in the chamber was deafening. Everybody was focused and waiting for Cronus's proclamation. Damian's breath stuck in his chest as he waited for the words that would determine his future.

Amber winced when Cronus ran his fingertips over the mark. Damian inhaled and clenched his fist to keep from knocking Cronus away. The thought of Amber in pain caused him real, physical pain deep in his chest. Exactly where his doubt festered and burned and the energy waited to bloom and fire.

Cronus paused in his caress and shot a covert glance at Damian.

"In two days you will turn twenty-four, yes?" Cronus spoke his question softly to Amber, a lazy murmur that was imperceptible to all but her and Damian. Her brow furrowed before she gave a slight nod.

The elder gently replaced Amber's hand next to her side then shifted and turned until he stood before Damian.

"Well," boomed Damian's father. "What is the verdict? Is she really the Marked One? The one who was prophesied to hold the power of evil in her hand? The one who could destroy us all?"

Amber's breath hitched in surprise, but Damian still couldn't look at her. He didn't want to see the fear in her eyes or the pain that shouldn't be there. That he put there.

Cronus kept his gaze on Damian, but raised a hand to silence Kadmos. The elder was a few inches shorter than Damian, but he had the regal standing owed him by age. He was the oldest member of the North American enclave, an Ancient. That designation alone garnered him respect. But the elder earned his respect through his actions and unwavering guidance to the community.

*You have a large challenge before you, Damian.*

The words whispered in Damian's mind and startled him, but he withheld his reaction. Cronus was the Head of the House of Spirit and had the power to control the elements of the body. He could read minds and communicate via thoughts, but they were powers he used sparingly.

"The mark appears fake," Cronus stated to the room.

Amber gasped as the crowd murmured and his father growled. Damian just stared, too stunned to react.

*The time has come for you to rise.*

Quick as lightning, Cronus grabbed Damian's wrist and yanked on the fake skin that was skillfully attached to the back of his hand. The roar in his ears increased with each gasp, each exclamation of shock. But it was the slight intake of breath beside him that echoed through his mind.

Finally he turned. Amber stared at the mark now exposed on the back of his hand, a look of stunned fear on her face and in her eyes.

*Your suffering was not for nothing. Become who you were born to be.* Damian's gaze flicked to Cronus in question.

"The white dragon," Cronus bellowed over the rising din of the room, holding Damian's hand high. His grip was surprisingly strong and unrelenting. "The sign of Gog. A sign of evil. Clearly a sign of false words. Of false intent."

"No!" Damian insisted as his world crumbled around him. Again. "It is not true. I am not evil. I have never been evil."

"Words," the elder admonished. "Words of the Slander. Lies to hide the truth." He turned to Amber, grabbed her arm and raised it high until it was next to Damian's. "Two signs of evil. The bird and the dragon. Here to trick us. Here to destroy us."

"It's not true."

"Guards, take them to the cellars," Cronus ordered, dropping their hands now that his verdict was rendered.

The chamber broke out in chaos as people shoved and pushed to watch. The wolves darted and nipped as the circle tightened around the sacrificial lambs.

"Damian?" Amber stared at him in question. Her fear was no longer hidden, but instead slapped him in the face as strongly as her palm had. "What's going on?"

*Listen to the energy. Trust the truth it speaks.*

Damian was torn between Amber and the words Cronus whispered in his mind. The elder projected thoughts that made no sense, thoughts that contradicted his harsh judgment. Amber begged for answers he didn't have. The confusion clogged his throat and stalled his mind.

He had taken a risk with his life and Amber's. And it had failed. Now, she would suffer for his mistakes and blindness.

For his selfishness, just as she had stated.

"*Damian!*" Amber shouted over the rising noise. The strong show of indifference she had tried to hold crumbled under the sudden proclamation and revelations. She tried to lunge for him, to get his attention, but strong hands grabbed her and held her back.

"*Damian*," she yelled again. Maybe it was the desperation in her voice or the rising panic, but his gaze suddenly snapped to hers, pulled from whatever deep recess of thought he'd been trapped in. His eyes widened, then narrowed as he looked at her. His face hardened, anger quickly dominating his features.

Was he mad at her? What had she done? He was the one who had betrayed *her*. Who brought her here to be judged and probably executed.

She struggled against the arms that were pulling her away. Whatever their intent, it couldn't be good. The words slanderer, lies, evil, cellars, circled in her mind. These people clearly thought the mark was bad. That she was evil.

"Amber!" Damian's roar echoed over the crowd, stunning everyone into brief silence and stillness. Damian took the opportunity and lunged for her.

Even though the man had lied to her, abducted her and brought her here in the first place, Amber reached for him. She stretched her arms as far as she could and pulled against her captors.

She had to reach Damian. Just touch him.

The energy rolled within her like fire and ice, counter forces slamming against each other. The stone raged against her chest, adding its own energy to the mix of churning powers.

Power.

She felt full of unleashed power. Yet she couldn't get away from the hands that held her. Her struggles were weak attempts compared to the strength that continued to pull her farther away from Damian.

"Damn it!" Damian yelled as two guards grabbed his arms and stopped his advance. "Leave her alone. She's done nothing wrong. She's innocent."

No one heeded his words, but her heart soared foolishly.

"If she is truly the Marked One, then she is not innocent," the man who had judged them countered. Their persecutor stood calmly in the midst of the scene that had broken out around them. He was cloaked in a long white robe that, when paired with the straight white hair and beard, presented a classic image of a mystical ruler and only made the entire day's events seem even more preposterous.

"But I am," Amber insisted, refusing to give up. "I'm not evil. I have no idea what any of you are talking about. You have to believe me."

"We don't have to believe anything," the mystical man said. "The white bird tells us everything we need to know."

Damian was on his knees, forced down by the men who held him. But he still fought for release, his focus never leaving her. "It's fake. I put it on her hand. Judge me, not her."

His lie only made Amber struggle more. "I am innocent of evil, but the mark is real." The truth came out before she could second-guess the wisdom of it. She wouldn't let Damian be crucified for something that wasn't true.

The hold on her arms tightened, and she could not hold back the slight whimper that escaped as the pain raced into her shoulder.

Damian surged to his feet. "Let her go."

His eyes flashed with a menace of pure hate. His arms whipped out, thrusting off the hold of the two men who held him down. He executed a spin kick and punch that rivaled the best karate master and halted the advance of two more guards. His fluid movements were an odd contrast to the stiff executive attire he still wore.

She was almost at the entrance of the chamber when Damian broke free of the onslaught of attackers and raced toward her. Her hopes rose, and she fought harder against her own restraints. The energy pooled and centered deep in her chest behind the stone. She felt the power radiate outward, extending to every fiber of her body.

She called on that power and reached her hand out toward Damian. The hand with the bird. The damned cursed mark that had started everything.

Right before Damian reached her, more guards tackled him from behind. He slammed to the hard marble floor in a resounding thud of flesh and bodies. His eyes screamed of pain that matched the denial that left his lips. His need to reach her seemed as desperate as her own.

Her vision darkened as her world slowly narrowed to the man struggling before her. He was wild, primitive and desperate in his attempt to reach her. Why? The question itself didn't require an answer. Not if she listened to the energy that pounded within her.

A fist cracked against the tender flesh of Damian's cheek, his head rocketing sideways from the force of the blow. The pain echoed across Amber's cheek. Hard. Instant. Brutal.

She gasped at the sudden bolt of pain. A physical touch when none had occurred. It was yet another in a never-ending series of stranger-than-life events.

Without thought or conscious effort, Amber called on all the pent-up power that now pounded through her. Her only thought was to get to Damian. She had to help him and stop his pain.

With a strength that exceeded anything of her own, Amber kicked back while pulling on her arms. Her foot connected with flesh, the corresponding grunt a sign that her aim was true, and her arms were suddenly free.

"*Damian*," she called as she sprang forward, one hand clasping instinctively around the stone beneath her shirt, the other outstretched. The white bird was reaching for him.

He rolled, lunged and extended his hand. His firm, hard grasp closed around her hand just as her feet were kicked from beneath her. The energy was instantaneous. It shot up her arm, raced across her chest and connected with her own center of energy. It ignited with a burning flame of power that sucked the breath from her even before she crashed to the cold, marble floor.

Damian's grip was solid. Warm. Everything.

She looked up and his eyes locked with hers. A clear, piercing blue that screamed of promise. His lips curled up, an out-of-place grin dancing across his features.

Confusion pummeled her right before the world turned black and she was consumed by a thousand pinpricks dancing across her flesh. She knew that feeling. This time she welcomed it.

And she accepted the fact that her life was now in Damian's hands.

# Chapter Ten

The sensation of plunging down the steepest hill of a rollercoaster turned Amber's stomach each time they solidified then quickly faded back out in a flash of light. At some point in the riotous journey, Damian had gathered her tight to his chest, and she clung to him with a desperate grip.

Finally, the motion stopped along with the pinpricks on her skin. She held on and took deep, calming breaths, forcefully willing her stomach to settle.

"Are you okay?" His hold on her loosened, the deep timbre of his voice loaded with honest concern.

"What just happened?"

He exhaled and his breath ruffled against her temple. "Somehow, you did the impossible."

She blinked, pulled back and looked into his eyes to see if he was serious. "What? I didn't do anything. You're the one who zapped us out of there." His arms tightened around her, just a hint of resistance as she attempted to put space between them. She couldn't think with him this close, his body touching hers so intimately, the energy burning within her. "But then, it was your own selfishness that put us there in the first place."

The defensive, verbal barb hit its mark. He looked away, but not before she saw the guilt flash in his eyes. His face tightened as he dropped his arms and stepped back. The instantaneous loss of his energy hit her deep, almost as if she'd lost a valuable piece of herself.

How? Why? Logically, she should despise this man after what just happened.

Unable, or more honestly, unwilling, to process the conflicting thoughts, Amber changed her focus to their surroundings. They were standing in the middle of a rustic, yet cozy living room. A large leather couch was flanked by two matching chairs and situated in front of a large brick fireplace. The room itself was clean, neat and very masculine, decorated in deep browns, greens and blues.

The architecture of the room was unique in that the room was one large circle. The curved walls were void of pictures or decorations, but the accessories weren't missed because all the focus was on the large bank of curved windows that composed one-third of the room. The floor-to-ceiling glass offered a stunning view of the snow-covered hillside and valley below. The open landscape provided a feeling of isolation, of floating alone on top of a cloud.

The beauty was breathtaking and called to her in a strangely familiar way.

"It was your power that overrode the energy cuffs," Damian said, yanking her back to their conversation. "I don't know how you did it, but you shouldn't have been able to. These collars are forged with the strongest energy and, as far as I know, have never failed. But our combined energy provided a power strong enough for me to port us out of there."

Amber's hand went to the collar that circled her neck. She twisted the hard metal against her skin, the anxiousness returning to make her skin crawl with the need to move. She remembered the feeling of power that had surged through her when he'd touched and kissed her. How, even now, she craved his touch.

"I don't understand."

"Energy is what powers the world. It is never created or destroyed, only redistributed and transformed," Damian explained, stretching his neck as if to escape his own collar. "Circles are the only way to contain the energy, and whoever casts the circle defines the dynamics of the circle. Basically, what energy can enter and exit. The Energy races use circles as a form of protection. Since people are nothing but energy, a cast circle can prevent people from entering and exiting. With the collars, the circle contains the energy within our bodies, preventing our internal energy from exiting, and also keeps us from being able to use any of the external energy that is always around us."

He stepped forward and unclicked the lock on the collar circling her neck. Her breath expelled in relief as the tight hold that had been clamping down on her was removed. The restlessness that had plagued her eased as the energy surged through her limbs, reigniting the slumbering cells and revitalizing her as it linked with the stone, then reached out to connect with the energy around her. She was quickly becoming attuned to the feel of the energy. It was unnerving yet powerful.

And the fact she recognized that made her muscles tense in pure shock.

He cast the collar dismissively onto the sofa next to them. "And the collars worked, right up until we kissed." His eyes darkened and dropped to focus on her lips. Her mouth parted to let a small, inhaled hiss escaping as desire ripped through her.

His nostrils flared, and he tilted toward her before he straightened and turned away. He shoved his fists into his pockets as he paced to the windows and stared out at the peaceful scene. His profile was hard, sleek and professional. He was the executive preparing for business negotiations.

Almost absently, he pulled his hands from his pockets and rubbed his fingers over the dragon mark on the back of his hand. Amber's fist clenched as she felt his touch whisper over the bird mark on her hand. How?

She backed away, her hand closing over the suddenly pulsing stone that was still hidden against her chest. It was a protective move to put more space between her and the man sporting the dragon mark.

The very symbol she had been warned to stay away from.

Internally, she warred with the conflicting information that assaulted her. Her instincts said Damian was safe and good. He had saved her, pulled her from the awful crowd of people who had declared her evil, a harbinger of destruction. But they had also said he was bad. That the marks on *both* of their hands were the sign of evil. And he had taken her to those people in the first place.

She hugged the thick warmth of Damian's coat closer to her body despite the rivers of sweat that raced down her back. It offered a meek layer of protection. One she desperately needed at the moment. She forced a swallow, determined not to cower or freak out over everything that had happened, even if she would be justified in doing so. She locked her knees and forced her shoulders back.

She knew she wasn't evil. But was he?

"How come you hid your mark from me?" She waited until he turned his head toward her then lifted her chin to indicate the dragon on his hand.

His gaze dropped as he moved his hand to stare at the mark. The white dragon was as intricately sketched as her bird. It stretched over the back of his hand, wings spread wide. The mouth of the dragon was open, baring its teeth and looking as if a breath of fire was eminent.

His eyes closed, and a brief hint of vulnerability softened his features before the hardness returned. He opened his eyes and shot her a look of indifference. "It wasn't something you needed to know."

She met his challenge head on. "And it had nothing to do with the fact that, twice now, I've been told the dragon was a sign of evil? That you have the exact symbol I was told to stay away from?"

Damian's eyes narrowed. "Who told you to stay away from it?"

She licked her lips. "Just a man."

He stepped toward her. "The same man who gave you the stone?"

Damn, he was quick. Her hands fidgeted deep within the pockets of his coat. "No."

His eyebrow rose in speculation before a smile curved his lips, the simple act lifting the darkness that had plagued his face just moments ago. "You're a bad liar, beauty. The blush gives you away every time."

She turned away, hating the fact that he was right. She could never pull off a true lie without feeling immediate guilt which then blossomed into a telltale flush. Tucking her hair behind her ear, she changed the subject.

"Where are we?"

"My safe house."

She turned her head to follow his movements as he strode across the room. "What do you mean, safe house?"

He stripped off the sleek suit jacket, revealing the tight, hard muscles that bunched and flexed across his shoulders as he tossed the expensive jacket over the back of a chair. His tie came off next and joined the discarded jacket before he unbuttoned the top buttons of his shirt.

Amber licked her lips, her bottom lip staying between her teeth as her gaze dropped to the tight contours of the delectable bottom that was on display beneath the expertly tailored slacks. She attempted to swallow, the sudden dryness in her throat stoked by the flame of heat that coursed straight to her gut, then lower. The feeling was foreign and startled her with its intensity. She inhaled sharply and stiffened all over again.

Why did she respond to him like that? He was everything she shouldn't want. Was it the bad boy syndrome, her overt desire to break away from the strict harping of her aunt and try something dangerous? Not that he presented a dangerous façade with his executive front. However, the control that contained the anger simmering just beneath the polished surface screamed of the danger and power he could unleash.

She closed her eyes to block out his image, and the move inadvertently brought the feel of the energy into focus. Oddly, it was becoming an almost viable, living thing. And if she opened her mind and senses just a little, she could hear what it was saying.

Her eyes flew open. *No.* God, what was she thinking?

"The circular shape of the house was built and cast by me," Damian said, opening a door on the far side of the room and entering. "No one can enter unless I give them permission. We are safe from the Guard or anyone else who happens to find this place." His voice became distant as he moved away from her.

Amber latched on to the distraction and took another look around the room that consisted of a kitchen to her right with a long bar to separate it from a small dining area and the cozy living area she stood in.

With more questions in her mind, she hurried after him, her curiosity increasing with each new bit of information. Her progress came to an immediate halt when she slammed into a wall of apparently nothing.

"What the hell?" She rubbed her forehead. "What was that?"

She stared into the open doorway at what she could clearly see was Damian's bedroom. Tentatively, she reached out her hand and tried to push it across the threshold. It came to a hard stop at the plane of the doorway even though there was nothing there to block it. A faint hum buzzed over her palm as she held it against the invisible barrier.

"Ahh, Damian?" Amber called out. "Can you help me here?"

He appeared, bare-chested, from another doorway at the side of the room. His dress shirt hung open and untucked from his slacks. The wide expanse of exposed muscle and hard, sculpted abs fuddled her brain and caused her to flush with heat once again. She licked her lips and willed away the telltale flush.

"Sorry," Damian said when he saw her standing at the entrance to his bedroom. He stepped through the doorway to stand next her and took her hand, the energy flaring instantly. "You may enter, Amber."

The vibration disappeared, and her other hand went past the doorway with ease. She tilted her head and cocked an eyebrow at Damian, the question obvious.

He smiled almost sheepishly, an act so out of character for him that it gave Amber more pause than the doorway. "It's another level of protection. My bedroom is another circle with more shields. I forgot to grant you permission to enter."

"But there was nothing there." She looked up and around the doorframe as he let go of her hand. She was still confused, but somehow she was able to walk uninhibited through the doorway into his room.

"Energy doesn't need physical walls to hold its form, only a guideline. And," he continued as he followed her in and went back into what she guessed was the bathroom, "after a thousand years, I'm good at what I do. But I needed your energy to remove the restriction. This damn collar is preventing me from doing even simple things like that."

She sank into the black leather chair that sat to the side of the door. "Are you really that old? I mean, you don't look that old." Hell, he looked closer to thirty. The thought that he had actually been alive for a millennium was another tidbit of information that got clogged in her brain.

He reentered the room wearing nothing but jeans and the black collar that still circled his neck. He definitely wasn't a soft-gut, flabby CEO. No, the clearly defined six-pack, narrow waist and hard, toned chest and arms were the exact opposite of that. She tried not to stare at the blatantly sexual display, but her eyes wouldn't follow the commands of her brain. Sure, she'd seen naked chests before, but never in the intimacy of a man's own bedroom. The air in the room was suddenly stifling, and his coat became more of a sweltering shroud than a comforting cocoon.

"Yes," he said as he pulled open a drawer and extracted a pair of socks, the movements showing off the muscle definition that bunched and flexed across his back. "Because our species absorbs and uses the energy around us, we can sustain the health of our bodies for much longer than others."

As much as Amber's anal-retentive side would have liked to dig into the details of that latest piece of information, there was simply too much stuff to process. She exhaled and let it go. The how and why of everything was irrelevant compared to the what.

"What do we do now? It seems unlikely that I can just go back home and pretend nothing happened." As much as she wished that could be true, the logical side of her knew it wasn't.

Damian opened another drawer and removed a black T-shirt. "We run." He turned back and looked her over.

"What?" His blatant perusal and the fact he'd caught her staring made her cheeks heat. "Why do we need to run?" Damn, she was beginning to sound like an insatiable two-year-old, peppering questions to the point of irritation. But she needed to know. Her mind refused to settle and just go along with whatever he had planned.

"We run because by now half the Energen Guard will be assembling to track us down. They can follow the energy trail that porting leaves behind, which is why I had to do all of that popping in and out to get here." He pulled on his shirt, the dark cotton clinging to his chest. He rubbed a hand over his hair, setting the short, blond stands into a spiky disarray before he sat on the edge of the bed and slipped on his socks. "And it won't be long before the others catch wind of what you are and begin to hunt us as well."

Her attention yanked from his body and focused in on one word. "Others? What do you mean, others?"

"The ones who are truly evil. Who work for the Slanderer, Gog. The ones who will want to use you and the powers you hold to execute their plans. Which, trust me, aren't very pleasant for the human race."

"Oh, great." It just kept getting better and better. "So we just keep running indefinitely? That doesn't work for me. I have a life that I would like to return to at some point."

Finished with his socks, he stood and rested his hands on his hips. "That's probably not going to happen."

Her chest constricted as the blank reality of that set in. "What does that mean?"

He walked over until he stood before her, forcing her to look up to meet his gaze. "It means that it is now my responsibility to keep you alive. To protect you until we understand what that mark on your hand means and your life is no longer in danger."

His eyes darkened, and his lips thinned as a look of determination settled across his features. "But the chances of you ever returning to your old life are slim to none."

She swallowed, pushed down the panic that once again threatened to overtake her. She pushed herself up from the chair, keeping her focus firmly on his eyes. A person's eyes always spoke the truth. Her new position put her within inches of his body, but he didn't back away. Didn't move at all. Except for the tic on his jaw which now jerked in hard, sharp twitches.

"I don't want this," she whispered.

"If it's any consolation, neither do I."

"Why do you care?" She had to know. "Why did you lie back there and say you put the mark on my hand? What made you change your mind?"

The tic jumped with the tightening of his jaw. His eyes darkened, his brow drew together and his muscles stiffened. But he didn't look away. Amber held her breath and waited. His answer was suddenly more important than she had originally intended.

"You," he finally admitted, his tone low, intimate. "Despite what the prophecies say and the mark is fabled to mean, I don't believe you're evil. That you would *choose* evil. There is too much innocence in you."

"How do I know I can trust you? After all, you are the one who abducted me and turned me over to them in the first place."

He brought his hand up and cupped her cheek. "As you told me before, if you listen to the energy, you will know I am telling the truth."

His touch brought heat, hot and liquid through her system. The energy sang, whispering its soft melody of truths. This time, she opened herself to them and listened. They spoke of pain and betrayal—his own, not hers—of truth and commitment. And of that slow, building desire that tempted and pulled with its own tune of enchantment.

She felt the heat rise up her neck and over her face. She pulled her gaze away and found herself staring at the black, metal collar.

"How does the energy do that?"

His hand fell away from her cheek. "The energy doesn't lie. It's connecting us, speaking to us. Telling us things our conscious mind might ignore or miss. The energy communicates on a deeper, subconscious level that evades the defenses our minds erect. It's all about feeling and sensing. Not logic."

"Well, that just sucks," she mumbled. For a woman who preferred logic, that bit of info was damn disturbing.

His deep, sudden chuckle had her snapping her head up in surprise. "Yes. Sometimes it does," he agreed.

"So if the energy doesn't lie, why do your people think you're evil?"

"Good question," Damian grumbled, the brief hint of lightness morphing to a hard scowl. He turned away and stalked backed to the bathroom.

She followed him, not ready to let the subject go. She moved through the door and saw that there was a large walk-in closet to the right before the room opened into a large marble bath. Amber stopped dead as she watched Damian pull a black metal knife from a drawer in the closet. He slid it out of its sheath, flipped it side to side and tested the sharpness of the edges against his fingertips. She swallowed and retreated a step.

"They're to protect you, not hurt you," Damian said keeping his eyes on the collection of weapons displayed in the large, cloth-lined drawer before him. His movements were efficient and knowledgeable. He handled the knives with practiced ease, a comfort that displayed a completely different side from the staunch CEO.

He lifted a harness from a hook, slid it over his shoulders and settled the straps until the broad cross was centered on his back between his shoulder blades. He reached behind him and snapped two knives into the empty sheaths on the straps so they were inverted and easily accessible. With quick competence, he snapped and clipped more knives around his frame until Amber lost count of exactly how many weapons were on his body.

The change in him was masculine and deadly. When he turned to face her, her breath caught at the lethal image he presented. The black attire, the harness straps that pulled his shoulders back and broadened his chest, the multitude of knives on his belt and strapped to his forearms all combined to transform him into the bad boy she'd thought of earlier. His eyes were dark, his jaw set, as if the addition of the weapons opened a door to another side of him. One he kept tightly hidden behind the fancy clothes and reserved demeanor.

She licked her dry lips and released her trapped breath. Her body flushed in heat, as she tried to push back the elusive need that was building deep in her womb.

A need she sensed only he could end.

Damian watched, enchanted by the little pink tongue that darted out to lick over Amber's soft lips, the movement both innocent and sexual. His cock tightened and responded almost instantly when her slightly larger bottom lip was sucked between her teeth to be tenderly nibbled. Hot flashes of the kiss they'd shared scorched his mind. The kiss had been relatively tame by most standards, but it had affected him more than any before.

What was she doing to him? It was if he were waking from a long slumber and finding his entire world had changed. It had been a very long time since he'd responded so instantaneously, so fiercely to another. No, he wasn't celibate, but after a few hundred years, the whole sex thing became more about basic release than true need.

Desire.

Another emotion he'd effectively blocked until Amber walked into his life.

"Unless you're ready to be kissed again, beauty, I'd stop that sexy little lip nibble you've got going on," Damian bit out, his voice hoarse from the frustration tightening his vocal cords. The dragon twitched and stirred in agitation on the back of his hand, sending ripples of sensation over his skin.

Her face turned an instant shade of deep red that fanned over her cheeks and down her neck. She slowly released her lip and dropped her gaze to the ground.

Sucking in a breath, he brushed by her and reentered the bedroom, the confined space of the closet too tempting for his over-zealous libido. He was seconds away from shoving her against the wall and claiming a real kiss from her. Something he was sure she wasn't ready for.

"Why did you kiss me before?"

The softly spoken words rang with doubt and had him wanting to murder the person who had put it there.

He turned back to face her. She stood in the entrance to the bathroom, her hands shoved deep into the pockets of his oversized coat. Her cheeks were still flushed, but her gaze met his boldly as she waited for his answer.

Damn. She was such an enticing mix of innocence and smoldering fire it was near impossible to resist. Fuck it. Three long strides and his arms were around her, her body clasped tightly to his chest.

"I kissed you because I find myself so fucking drawn to you I can't stop myself." Shocked at his own harsh words, at the side of him that was slowly stretching and breaking free of the tight hold he'd clamped on it, Damian stiffened and waited.

Amber gasped in surprise, but her golden eyes turned a dark, molten brown as she stared at his lips. That was the only invitation he needed.

His mouth claimed hers with a demand tempered by caution. He sensed her desire mixed with curiosity and a touch of fear. His lips brushed over hers, tempting, sucking, enticing until she slowly relaxed and she shifted her hands up to rest on his shoulders.

Damian's erection rubbed stiff and hard against her lower stomach, and he was thankful for the padding offered by the coat she wore. He called upon every ounce of restraint he had to hold himself back and wait for her. Her lips were soft as silk and slowly becoming more confident with each brush. His hands crept up her back over the sleek strands of her hair to cup the back of her head. She moaned lightly in her throat and sank into him even more, pushing her soft breasts into his chest.

Stifling his own groan, Damian brushed his tongue over the soft, wet crease of her lips. Her mouth opened, and the tentative touch of her tongue against his was enough to set his world on fire. The energy burned and flashed through him, igniting a longing for more. A possessive need fired, calling out to the primitive animal within. It was a need that set his skin aflame and shut down all thoughts but her.

Every fiber of his being yearned to possess and claim her as the energy pushed and called for her.

He skimmed over her tongue, enticing it to explore and dance with his own tongue. The feel of her confidence rising, of her strokes getting stronger, more assured and aggressive only heightened his own burning passion.

She snaked her fingers into his hair, rubbed his scalp then pulled, driving his mouth down tighter onto hers. This time he didn't try to hide the deep groan that rose in his throat. Damn, she was going to kill him. He had to stop. Now. Or he wouldn't be able to. She was rising into her need, feeling the passion and opening to him, but she wasn't ready for everything.

Not yet. Not now. And neither was he.

Gently, he pulled back and she whimpered in protest. Her eyelashes fluttered open to reveal eyes full of wonder and questions.

All his life he'd been taught, been told, to listen to the energy, to trust the truth that it tells. But it was the energy that had betrayed him. Spoke falseness about him that had resulted in centuries of pain. A pain that still festered and stung.

Could he trust this? Now? When so much was at stake?

It was that doubt that had him dropping his arms and stepping away. The risk was too high. The energy flashed then dropped like a bomb, hard in his gut. She watched him, cautious in her appraisal. Slowly, she tucked her hair behind her ear and brushed it over her shoulder.

He wasn't ready to contemplate what his attraction meant or if it had anything to do with how his mark had changed again. The dragon that had cursed him for a millennium and was the root of his pain and torment had somehow changed from a wingless to a winged dragon between that morning and when Cronus had revealed his secret. And now, it almost seemed to purr with contentment whenever Amber touched him.

Irritated at himself and the entire situation, Damian rubbed a hand over the back of his neck. He flinched and cursed under his breath when his palm hit the hard, metal collar.

"Would you like me to remove that?"

"Yeah, but it's not possible." He gave it a hard tug as proof.

"Why?"

He sighed and dropped his hand. "Because it can only be removed by the person who put it on."

She cocked her head and furred her brow in thought. "Then why did that man allow you to put on mine?"

He smiled and rested his hands on his hips. He liked that about her. The fact that her brain never seemed to stop. "Another good question. My guess would be that it was a small concession based on our past." It would seem their one-time friendship did count for something.

"Can I try?" She looked so hopeful, he couldn't say no. Hell, what would it hurt?

He nodded and she stepped up to him. She tilted her head back and forth a few times, apparently trying to figure out the lock before she lifted her hands and grasped the collar. Her fingers were warm against his skin, and he inhaled at the flash of heat that raced through him. She fiddled and pulled at the lock, her brow creased in concentration. Her lip was once again clamped tight between her teeth.

"It won't work," he told her.

Her eyes brightened and she smiled right before a spark of sensation sizzled against his neck, then a soft click echoed through the room. Well, fuck, she'd done it. Impossible. How?

She opened the collar and pulled it away. He stretched his neck and dropped his arms to his sides as the dampened energy fired back to life. It raced through his system, singeing the nerve endings and igniting the power. He stretched his fingers and reached out to the energy around him.

"You shouldn't have been able to do that," Damian repeated, giving her a tight smile. "But thank you."

She shrugged her shoulders and grinned. "It must be my soft touch."

Yeah, right. That was it.

Unable to resist, he lifted his hand and focused on the leather jacket that hung from a hook next to the door. As if an invisible string connected his hand to the jacket, it sped through the air and landed in his grasp. The power vibrated through him as he remembered the thrill, the overwhelming sense of strength and rightness that came with using his gifted powers.

"How'd you do that?" There was no fear in her words, only wonder and curiosity. That strange feeling of pride bolted through him once again.

The woman who had slammed into his life only a few short hours ago and had so quickly changed everything he believed was one a man could truly come to appreciate. One a smart man would run from before he became lost in her. But then, something told him being lost in her would be the closest thing to nirvana he would ever experience.

# Chapter Eleven

Amber swallowed at the sudden flash of desire that sparked in Damian's hard gaze. How did he make her flush with heat with just a look? He shrugged on the worn leather jacket and rolled his shoulders to settle it on his frame.

"Every Energen is born with an affiliation to one element," he said in answer to her question. "We use the energy to control that element. I can control the element of air."

Her mind spiraled around that piece of information. He sat on the edge of the bed and pulled on a pair of scuffed, black leather boots. Finished, he stood. His transformation from stoic CEO to rebel fighter completed.

Her thoughts blanked and her lip took another beating from her teeth as she took in the hard-edged image of pure masculinity Damian presented. Her heart accelerated and her nipples tightened. It was as if the relatively useless and unnoticed peaks were suddenly demanding attention after years of being ignored. Not to mention the speed-dial link they seemed to have directly to the other ignored area between her thighs.

His kiss had turned her muscles to mush and seemed to have killed off some brain cells too. She should have resisted his touch, pulled away before his lips lured her back to trap her in this spell of lust. But it was virtually impossible to resist him. Her body responded to him, the energy, the pull he seemed to have on her despite the logic against it.

"We need to get out of here," he said, stepping closer to her. Her lip throbbed in protest when she bit down harder to keep from retreating. "We've stayed too long, and I'm certain the Guard will be tracking our trail by now."

"I need to go back to the shop," she managed to insist through her parched throat.

His face turned hard, the lightness that had previously lifted it gone. "I told you, you can't. Not anymore."

The need for something normal made her push. "I need to check on my aunt. She'll be worried when she returns to the shop and sees the destruction. She's older, and I have to let her know I'm okay."

"You can call her."

She shook her head. "No. I need to see her. Please." Amber was surprised at the quake in her voice. At how important this was to her. "After all that's happened today, I need to see her to make sure she's not hurt. Before I can go forward with whatever is happening to me, I need to know she isn't harmed. I don't want her to worry."

He looked over her shoulder, his lips compressed in silent debate. "You understand that by going to her, you could be bringing the danger to her?"

It was risk she had to take. Something was pushing her to go back. It was the same something that had pushed her to New York City and to the stone. She nodded and added one final argument. "I think she knows something about what's going on. About why I'm involved."

He exhaled through his nose and his fingers flexed on his hips. "Fine. I probably owe you this." He looked back at her. "But we can't stay long."

"Thank you," she whispered, feeling more vulnerable than she had since he'd kidnapped her from the shop.

"You better hang on," he said, stepping closer. His strong arms circled her and pulled her snug against his chest. The energy pulsed and burned between them with a strength that nearly buckled her knees. The absence of the collars allowed the flow to move unrestricted and the energy seemed to be growing stronger with every second they were together.

Damian cleared his throat, his fingers tightening on her back. "We'll need to energy hop again, just in case we have followers."

105

"Was that the strange rollercoaster ride of flashing in and out that we did before?"

"Yes."

Great. Hopefully, her stomach would handle it better this time.

She slipped the metal collar that she was still holding into her coat pocket. It clunked lightly against the wooden box, and she smiled at the small collection of oddities that was collecting in the pocket.

Amber circled her arms around his waist and hid her face against the curve of his neck. His scent washed over her, and she tried to dispel the sense of rightness that settled within her. The energy sang a sweet, high tune that trembled down her back and wrapped her in its warm embrace.

She acknowledged the stupidity of what she felt right before the prickling sensation started again. Just in time to block the acceptance that whispered at the back of her mind.

They solidified in the alley behind the antique shop, the tilting, acidic burn in her gut a little less than the last time. Amber stayed within the tight, warm circle of Damian's arms until her stomach settled.

"There is something disturbing about that whole mode of travel that goes far beyond what it does to my stomach," Amber said between breaths.

His deep chuckle rumbled in his chest. "You get used to it after a while."

"I'll take your word on that."

She finally loosened her hold and stepped away from him. The air actually snapped and popped at the separation with little sparks of static electricity.

Ignoring the oddity, she turned and quickly opened the back door, the urgency to see her aunt pummeling through her now that she was there.

"Aunt Bev," Amber called. "Are you here?"

"Amber?" Her aunt's voice had a high-pitched, hopeful note to it and came from the recesses of the showroom. Amber hurried down the hallway and almost collided with her aunt as they met in the doorway between the hall and the showroom.

"Oh, Amber." Aunt Bev sighed, relief washing over her face in a waterfall of emotion. "I was so worried about you."

Amber hid her surprise when her aunt enveloped her in a warm, hard embrace. The rare show of outward emotion startled her and made Amber worry even more about her own predicament. Her aunt pulled back and rubbed her hands down the front of her sweater and over her wool skirt in a pretense of smoothing out the wrinkles.

"Well, I'm glad you're okay. I was worried sick when I returned to find the back door unlocked, the shop destroyed and you missing with your purse and phone still in the office." Her aunt turned away and walked stiffly back into the destroyed remains of the showroom. "Thank goodness Joseph decided to escort me home from the island. If it wasn't for his calm assurance that you were all right, I would've been a frazzled mess and the place would be swarming with police looking for you."

The tribal shaman stood calmly in the center of the room. His long hair had turned white many years before and was pulled back into a neat, single braid down his back. His face was creased with age and worn tough by the elements, but his straight back and almost regal carriage kept him from appearing old. The faded jeans and flannel shirt he wore were his uniform of choice during the winter months and added to his image of stability.

"Why didn't you call the cops?" Amber questioned

"We will," Joseph answered. "We were waiting for you to return first. The one who did this destruction is long gone and won't be caught anyway. There was no rush."

"Who's that?" Aunt Bev demanded, her face pinching in a look of disapproval.

Amber felt Damian's presence behind her, the energy moving to life even without his touch. It was comforting to have him at her back. Especially when faced with the rising ire of her aunt.

"It's all right, Beverly," Joseph intervened before Amber could respond. "He is the one we've been waiting for."

Amber's attention whipped to the shaman. "What did you say?"

Joseph smiled. "The gentleman behind you. We've been awaiting his arrival for many, many years. I am relieved to see that he has found you."

Just when she thought her world couldn't get any crazier, it did. She could feel Damian's anger rising behind her, the energy pooling deep and frustrated at the shaman's mysterious words.

His hand on her back had her moving into the room, Damian intimately behind her. The stone flared to life at his touch and reminded her of what had started all the craziness that had invaded her life since that damn night in New York City.

The reminder sparked her own frustration at the secrets and lies. The cryptic caginess from people she trusted.

"What are you talking about?" she questioned, struggling to hold on to her calm, to maintain that last link with sanity. "I'm tired of being manipulated and used. Of being treated like a child when I'm not one."

"You will find the answers when you are ready," the shaman replied.

She inhaled sharply. "No! You know what's going on, and I deserve some answers. Now."

"Amber," her aunt admonished. "Watch your tone. Joseph is your elder and will be treated with respect." The older woman moved to stand next to the shaman, a guard in grandmother clothing. "He's done nothing but protect you since your mother failed so miserably in that job."

"*Stop it*," Amber bit out, heat flaring across her cheeks. "Just stop it. I am done with everyone measuring me against my mother. Of constantly having her failures rubbed in my face. Despite her flaws, she was still my mother." She released a shaky breath. "And she paid a very high price for her crimes. So please, just let her rest in peace."

The silence hung in the room like the deafening quiet between a lightning strike and the burst of thunder. Her aunt's face had paled, her hands clasped tightly at her waist, taken aback by Amber's sudden attack. Never, in the over fifteen years of living with her aunt, had Amber ever spoken to her like that.

A sense of power surged through her. Not at taking her aunt down, but at finally, *finally*, standing up for herself. For saying the words she'd wanted to say for years.

Joseph rested a hand on Aunt Bev's shoulder, a silent show of support. Likewise, Damian's strong hand settled on Amber's shoulder, his strength pouring into her. His claim staked. The sudden face-off would've been almost comical if not for the seriousness of the situation. The room crackled with the tension.

The shaman cleared his throat, a failed attempt to clear the air. "There is much the two of you must learn," Joseph started, raising a hand to silence her protest when she opened her mouth to interject. "I know it's frustrating, and I'm not trying to be mysterious and confusing. But many things are best understood when you learn them yourself. And, truthfully, I don't have all the answers."

"Tell us what you know," Damian demanded, his voice pounding into the room with its force.

The shaman observed them as if he was debating what to say. When he finally spoke, his eyelids drooped and his face slackened, a distant appearance cloaking him. His words came out in an almost trance-like cadence.

"A thousand years of exile, a thousand years of rebirth. Taken down in shame to rise in glory. At his side a virgin bride, the hidden bird to bind his soul. To this end the world will flow. Without the rise, the world will fall. One of light, one of dark. Two to wield all five. Circles will rise and must hold strong. Together the two will lead us all."

The chill returned to invade and spread to every appendage even as beads of sweat broke out on Amber's forehead and her arm hairs stood on end. She swallowed past her arid throat and tried to quell the rising anxiety. Damian's hand tightened on her shoulder, his unease radiating into her with each deep breath he sucked into his chest.

The pending threat of doom hung like a black cloud in the room and was as suffocating as a wool blanket in July.

"What foolishness do you speak, old man?" Damian's crisp words cut through the tension. "Where did you get those words?"

Joseph eased back with a simple blink of his eyes. "They are words that have been passed down through my family for generations. We are the protectors of the innocent. The keeper of the words. The seers of my people and the holders of the one truth."

"The words are nothing but garbage," Damian snapped.

"Are they?" Joseph challenged, apparently not at all intimidated by the man that towered over him. "It is my job, the job of my family, to protect the line of the innocent. To keep the last lineage of the great Moshup alive and pure. The end of that line is Amber. She is the last living descendant of the great giant who led and helped to build the Native American communities along the eastern coastline when we were but a fledging race of beings struggling to survive."

Amber gasped, disbelief consuming her. How could that be true? What did it mean?

Joseph narrowed his eyes at Damian. "Do my words touch too close to the truth? Ring of a rightness that is too frightening to accept?"

"Watch yourself, old man."

"You do not scare me, old one," Joseph replied. "I only fear for what will happen if you do not accept what is before you."

The bird on Amber's hand fluttered its feathers, stretching its wings in preparation for flight. To defend. The sensation itched over her hand and warmed her skin. It was as if the mark was becoming a living, breathing entity that moved and communicated with her through the energy. Although it remained flat and unmoving on her skin, within her she felt every movement, every emotion it projected. Intuitively, she knew to listen to it, despite how illogical that was.

"Joseph," her aunt's quiet voice quivered between them. "What is going on?"

The shaman stepped toward Amber. Damian immediately moved in front of her, blocking Joseph's path. The man stilled his advance, his eyes showing approval.

"I will not harm her. I have protected her for twenty-three years. Kept her safe"—Joseph paused and looked down at the dragon mark on Damian's hand before he lifted his gaze to stare into Damian's eyes—"for you."

Amber's stomach dropped clear to her toes, and she gaped at Joseph in disbelief. *No.* Absolutely not. She stepped around Damian to face Joseph. Any fear or residual panic was pushed back by her overriding need to take back control of her life. "I don't know what you're talking about, Joseph, but I am not some piece of property to hand off like a cheap whore." The indignation fueled her words and flushed her cheeks. "I do know that I wasn't kept or prepped or protected for anyone. I am my own person. I make my own choices, my own decisions."

"Of course, child," Joseph replied almost patronizingly. "And every choice you make, every decision you make has the potential to change the outcome of the Great War to come. I am not your enemy, and I wanted your man to understand that."

Her cheeks flamed at his words, and her lips compressed in a mix of irritation and embarrassment. "He is not *my* man."

"Whatever you say," Joseph responded.

"Forget it." Amber turned away. The feeling of being boxed in—of the walls closing in around her until she was trapped with no way out—made her skin crawl in rejection. "I'm done with this. I only came here to check on Aunt Bev and to let her know I was okay and to find out if *she* had any answers for me. Instead, I find yet another man spinning prophecies and warnings about my life. About who *I am*." She spun back around to face down Joseph. "It's time I made the decisions about my life. And I will *not* be forced into a role based on the words of some ancient prophecy or made-up lineage."

God, that felt good. The power from standing up for herself sailed through her and warmed her blood with hot licks of fulfillment. On a roll and unable to stop the cleansing purge that seemed to be rising uninhibited from within her, Amber glared at the three people who were each staring at her with varying looks of shock, amusement and approval.

"Do any of you realize the day I've had? This morning I was a normal woman, being so bold as to attend a protest against this guy and his wind turbines." She pointed accusingly at Damian, who didn't even have the courtesy to flinch. "Next thing I know, he's magically appearing out of nowhere, spitting accusations that I'm some predefined emissary of destruction. Then I'm whisked through thin air, judged by a race of beings I didn't even know existed, and accused of *pretending* to be this Marked One, declared evil, and ordered to the cellars."

Her aunt's face had turned a pasty white during her recap. Maybe Aunt Bev didn't know everything that was going on, but it was past time she found out. Undeterred, Amber glared at her betrayers and continued. "Now I return to find that the two people I trusted most in this world have been lying to me my entire life. In fact, they've actually been waiting to turn me over to what? My death? The sacrificial lamb offered up for the greater good?" Her aunt's hand fluttered uneasily at her throat. Joseph stood stone faced at her side.

"Well, no thank you. I don't want the job. And I refuse be used or manipulated. I don't care what each of you *thinks* I am." She gave each occupant of the room a hard, piercing glare. "Because I know what I'm not. And I know that none of you have control over me. And that I definitely don't need any of you to manage *my* life."

Wanting to keep the feeling of triumph that coursed through her, Amber stalked out of the room, down the hall and out the back making sure to slam the door behind her. The loud bang echoed through the silence and off the brick walls of the buildings. She exhaled a shaky breath and watched the white puffs of vapor form in front of her face. She took off at a brisk walk, exiting the alley and heading down the street. She had no focus, her only intent to get away.

From the words. The feelings. The confusion.

How could all of this be happening? If it weren't for the brisk air brushing her cheeks and nipping at her ears, she'd be tempted to believe it was all a very bad dream. But it wasn't a dream, just a demented reality that threatened to pull her under and drown her within the depths of its complexity.

Her boots moved briskly over the sidewalk, causing Damian's coat to flap against her legs. Once again, she was thankful for its warmth. She'd been wearing the damn coat for most of the day, and his scent was twining its way around her, tingling her nose with hints of pine. Damn it. She couldn't get away from him even now.

What had Joseph meant with his strange words and even stranger assumptions? Kept her safe for Damian? What the hell? This wasn't the dark ages where women were property owned by men to sell and barter as they saw fit. She didn't belong to anyone, and she definitely wasn't going to be meekly handed over to some overbearing, overconfident, over-assuming man. In trade for what? Saving the world? Ha! There was nothing to save and she wasn't anyone's hero. Period.

A light from an overhead street lamp flickered above her before going out. The dark descended around her and pulled her quickly out of her musings. A sudden, unnatural chill descended in the air.

She jerked her head around, taking quick looks over her shoulders, peering into the darkness that surrounded her. Goose bumps riddled her flesh, and the hairs on the back of her neck rose in warning. Increasing her pace, Amber hurried down the deserted sidewalk toward the next globe of light. It flickered and went out just before she stepped into the safety its pale, yellow light cast.

Fear skittered through her as she froze in understanding. The stone burned in warning. She swallowed thickly and blinked back the tears that formed at the edge of her eyes. In all her ranting, all her adamant declarations that she didn't need anyone, she'd forgotten the fact that she was being tracked. For whatever reason, whether she wanted to believe it or not. Whether she understood it or not.

And she knew beyond all doubt that those very beings that wanted her, hunted her, were now surrounding her. And she was alone, just like she'd wanted.

# Chapter Twelve

The door crashed behind Amber as she exited the shop and the sound echoed through the room like a bullet—hard, sharp and deadly.

Damian took in the pale face of Amber's aunt and the emotionless mask of the old man who had just turned his world on end. The blistering bursts of Amber's fury and indignation still lingered in the tight confines of the room and rubbed against him. He wanted to run after her, to keep her close, where she belonged. But he needed answers, and he could still feel her through the energy.

"I need your knowledge, old man," he demanded. "I don't have time to dance around words and guess at meanings. I need to get to Amber, so tell me what I need to know. Now."

Joseph stepped closer to Damian, but showed no fear. Only respect. "As a descendant of Moshup, Amber is like you, only she doesn't know it. She has no knowledge or understanding of what she's been groomed for or of the challenges that await her."

"What challenges?"

"The world is unsettled. The elements in turmoil. The environment failing. War is coming, as you know. You finding Amber is the catalyst to the rest."

Damian cursed, frustration mounting with every cryptic drop of information that was leaked to him. "And what is that supposed to mean?"

"All I was ever told is that when the Chosen One finds the innocent, together they will rise and unite in glory for the rest to follow." The old man pointed at Damian's hand, clenched at his side. "The white, winged dragon is the mark I was told to watch for. You are the Chosen One. Amber is yours."

What in the hell was this man talking about? "Chosen One? What crap do you speak? According to *our* prophecies, Amber is the Marked One. The one who has the potential to destroy the world."

"Or save it," Joseph interceded quietly, completely unruffled by Damian's verbal attack. "I don't know the prophecy you speak of. Obviously, there are more pieces to this puzzle than we have been given. It's up to you to put them together."

The old shaman stepped directly into Damian's personal space, tilting his head back to maintain eye contact. "The Chosen One will rise, a virgin bride at his side. Don't let the fear of the past keep you from accepting your fate. Like Amber, you have a role to play that is much bigger than just you. The red dragon stirs, even now. You know this, if you listen."

The truth of what the old man said rang like a gong in Damian's head. In his heart and soul. The energy within him hummed in fired acceptance even as he resisted everything he'd just heard. It couldn't be right.

He—the one who'd been exiled for a thousand years—was supposed to save the world? With a virgin bride to boot? Right. The thought was comical, but the old man's face held no amusement. In fact, the strength of his beliefs burned bright and strong in his dark eyes. He was as firm in his beliefs about Damian as Damian was in his own about Amber.

*Shit.*

Before he could question the shaman further, the energy shifted, turned and rounded on him in dark cascading waves of blackness. The weight pressed on his shoulders, warning and telling him of the darkness that was closing in. Circling, taunting, and playing with them.

With Amber.

*Fuck!*

The dragon writhed on his skin, his wings stretched, his claws extending. The fire burned deep in Damian's gut in preparation for battle. It was time to fight and protect what was his.

Amber's breath hitched, icy and cold in her chest. The darkness settled around her, heavy and daunting. She backed up cautiously, her gaze darting into the black depths of the night.

She'd stormed off in a fit of anger that had taken her out of the busier waterfront area into the quieter residential streets. Now, it was completely dark, not a single light showing to offer aid, and she was alone.

A low chuckle vibrated through the night, an evil laugh laced with anticipation that stopped Amber's heart. She was so dead.

The bird flickered back and forth over her hand in caged irritation. It wanted to fight and defeat the enemy.

Amber wanted to run.

The stone pulsed with deep bursts of hot energy that flushed through her in a steady rhythm of warning. The fear tasted salty on her tongue, or maybe that was blood from biting her cheek too hard.

God, where was Damian? Why did she leave him?

In a warm wave of soothing energy, Damian appeared at her side. A savior at her beck and call. Amber was so relieved to see him, she immediately launched herself into his arms. "*Damian.*"

Instantly, the light prickles covered her skin, and she waited for the rolling pitch of her stomach to start. But it didn't. With a hard thump, they reappeared back on the street only feet from where she had been.

"What happened?" Her panic flared bright and hot at the realization they were still in danger.

Damian hauled her back quickly, shoving her behind him and using his own body as a shield before her. "We're trapped."

"What? How?"

"We're in a circle," he answered gruffly, his attention focused on the darkness around them. "And they used it create their own."

Amber did a quick scan of their surroundings to see that, in her efforts to get away from the shadows, she'd come to a stop in the middle of a grass island. The road circled their spot providing a nice turnaround or a hidden trap for the unsuspecting. "Well take it down."

"I can't. Only the caster can take it down."

On a whim, she raised her hand and tried to do it anyway. She'd removed the collar when he'd said she couldn't—maybe this was the same. The energy buzzed at her challenge, sending ripples of cold barbs through her. She thought of breaking down the invisible barrier, but the current struck out with a force that knocked her back and left her dazed. Yeah, that option was closed.

Shaking the lingering numbness from her arm, she scrambled for another solution. "So cast a smaller one around us."

"The energy won't allow it." Damian reached back and extracted a knife from a sheath on his belt. Keeping his back to her, he thrust the handle toward her. "Here. Take this. Use it if you need to."

"What?" she sputtered, her fear temporarily pushed to the back as she tried to process his latest move. "I can't take that." Like she would even know how to use it.

He pushed it at her again. "Take it," he said, his voice leaving no room for argument. "Our only way out is to defeat them."

Exhaling a shaky breath, Amber accepted the offered weapon. The knife felt heavy, deadly, in her palm. It was about five inches long and reminded her more of a dagger than a knife. She clenched the weapon in her fist and lowered her hand by her side.

Her mind scrambled for another way out but came up with none. "So we're screwed?"

"No, we fight."

Out of the shadows, a fireball sailed across the space directly at them. Amber froze in shock before she ducked behind Damian's back. The fireball deflected around them and smacked into the unseen energy circle about three feet behind her. The heat flared outward and brushed against her cheeks before fading.

"What the hell was that?" She was not prepared for shooting balls of fire.

"He controls the element of fire," Damian huffed as he lifted his hand at another fireball that was blasted at them. Somehow, the shooting ball of flame bounced off an apparent invisible shield about two feet from Damian's outstretched hand and sunk to the grass.

Once again, questions bombarded her brain, but there was no time for inane thoughts. Now was about reflexes, wit and survival. She stiffened her back, swallowed and let the energy flow through her. She would fight and defend. Damn it, she wouldn't cower and run.

The bird stretched and rolled in approval.

"And don't let them grab you," Damian added. "One firm grip, and they'll port you faster than you can blink."

Great. Another thing to worry about.

"Isn't this nice?" A deep, guttural voice spoke out of the darkness. "Two lost souls, alone and trapped. You make my job so easy."

Amber leaned around Damian's girth to see a man step out of the shadows on the other side of the deserted street. The man was all muscle and the image of black death. Hair, long leather duster, T-shirt, leather pants, boots—all black. The evil energy emanated from him and reached with icy tentacles across the distance.

Damian clenched and unclenched his hands at his sides, his only answer to the man's taunts.

"You could hand her over and make this easier," the man suggested, a sarcastic snarl curling his thin lips. "No? Then have it your way."

With a flick of his wrist, another fireball sailed across the open space. The flames hissed and stroked the air with harsh rasps of fury as it soared through the night, a bright, flaming ball of pain and death.

Amber stood behind Damian, trapped in a shocked state of awe, the moment surreal. The dancing ball of flame streaked through the night, a blatant symbol of the drastic curve her life had taken.

The fireball whizzed over Damian's head and slammed into the energy wall behind her. She hunched her shoulders and ducked as it disintegrated in short sparks of heat and light that rained down on her like snippets from a sparkler.

Damian swung his hand high, commanding. Amazingly, a lightning bolt shot down from the sky to hit were the attacker had been standing a half-second before. Sparks flew up where the lightning hit the earth. The man dodged, rolled and stood in one fluid motion. A fireball appeared in his hand and was immediately launched at them.

Amber gasped, the air sucked from her lungs, as she was clamped to Damian's side by his vise-grip hold before she could even begin to process the incredible events. In the next instant, she was lifted into the air and held, suspended off the ground, the fireball soaring beneath their dangling feet. They were literally floating above the ground.

"*Oh, God.*" Her arms locked around Damian's torso as they remained in the air, dodging left and right to avoid a bombardment of fireballs. "You have got to be kidding me!" Amber was willing to believe, but lightning, fireballs and levitation were seriously testing her mental stability. She fought the reflex to shut her eyes and hide her face in his chest.

No, this was something she needed to see to believe.

Damian was a study of complete focus. A small bead of sweat coursed down the side of his stern face, and his eyes narrowed, brow furrowed and lips thinned in concentration. His arm was steel around her, every muscle in his body pulled tight and hard as he weaved them back and forth through the air.

Amidst the air dance and fireballs, a dense cloud of fog rolled in out of nowhere and surrounded them in a cool blanket of invisibility. Amber's already racing heart went into overdrive, hammering so hard against her ribs she was surprised they didn't break. She couldn't see anything, but at least the fireballs had stopped. She felt her feet touch the ground and exhaled in relief.

"Stay behind me," Damian demanded as he pushed her back to where he wanted. "And duck if you see a fireball coming."

"Not funny."

"Not trying," he rumbled back.

Before she could curse him out, flames sprung up from the grass and cut through the fog. The heat evaporated the mist and once again exposed them to the enemy. Damian quickly swung his arm up to command another lightning bolt at the man.

The action volleyed back and forth, no one getting the upper hand. Amber followed Damian's orders to a tee. She might be stubborn, but she wasn't stupid. Obviously, this fight was beyond her measly self-defense skills.

She inched back, keeping her focus on the battle before her. The power, skill and amazing abilities of the men were both frightening and breathtaking. It was beyond anything she'd ever imagined.

Amber cringed as a fireball hit Damian in the thigh, the flames lighting up his pants before he executed a duck and roll to put them out. Both men were breathing heavily, their chests heaving in and out as they sucked in deep breaths of air.

"Are you done playing yet?" the low, gritty voice called out.

Damian remained silent as he edged his way toward her. His back was to her, his face hidden from her scrutiny. Was he okay? His hands were held up and ready as blood oozed down his leg from the fireball wound.

A fine sheen of perspiration had formed on her skin, making her feel chilled and clammy. She hated the feeling of helplessness, of there being nothing she could do to defend herself or to help Damian.

"Come on, Damian. You might as well give up," the other man taunted. "You know fire always trumps air. Just ask you brother." An evil chuckle rolled across the space. "That's right, you can't. He's dead." The man whipped out another fireball.

Damian flicked up a hand, forcing the fireball to bounce off the unseen shield of defense.

Now that was a nice trick to have.

Catching a movement out of the corner of her eye, Amber jerked her head around to see another man appear out of a black cloud of smoke. His focus instantly went to her, his eyes narrowing with sinister intent.

Amber jumped as the stone started to vibrate between her breasts. Seriously? Heat was not enough?

Suddenly, fireballs started flying at them like big, flaming snowballs. Damian held the force field, deflecting what he could, but many of them still went whizzing by her, leaving hot trails of vapor to brush against her skin.

With Damian distracted, the newest member of the party began to inch his way toward her. Six foot five inches of pure menace stalked her with deadly intent. He was dressed completely in black like his comrade, and his long, blond hair gleamed in the darkness. His face was void of expression, and set rock hard to match the rest of him.

The stone was a hot, bursting flare between her breasts. Large amounts of energy pulsated into her body, filling her, preparing her. Her bird circled and screeched in warning.

Damian was occupied deflecting fireballs. This new guy was all Amber's. She needed to act. Not think, just do.

She inhaled, exhaled, then once again followed her instincts and reached between the folds of her coat to clutch the stone under her shirt. The energy calmed her.

She was strong. She was a fighter.

Releasing the stone, she crouched and waited as the blond man moved closer. Sweat beaded on her forehead as she met and held the deadly stare of her stalker.

"You can't run." His low voice shredded her nerves.

Damian turned and quickly forced a lightning bolt at the man, but was dragged back to the other fight when a fireball whizzed by his head.

Self-preservation had her backing away as the stalker advanced. He moved her backward until the invisible wall of energy made her stop. Her back quickly felt scorched as the energy vibrated and hummed against her. There was nowhere to go.

The stalker, just feet away, raised his arm to strike her or grab her. It didn't matter which one—neither was acceptable.

In the distant fog of her brain she heard Damian roar her name, but her focus was on the man before her. His lip was curled in victory, his eyes hooded, black and evil. She dodged his strike, made a jab with the dagger still clutched in her hand and did a quick spin. Automatically, her left hand shot out to defend against another strike, the lessons from the self-defense classes rising to help her once again.

Out of nowhere, Amber felt a surge of energy shoot through her. It felt like an inferno burned from her chest, through her body and out her extended hand. She watched in stunned amazement as a blaze of fire blasted from her hand to hit her attacker in the chest. The man roared in pain before he flailed back then tumbled to land prone and unmoving on the ground. A dark, singed circle was imprinted on the center of his chest, smoke swirling in lazy circles out of it.

*Holy shit.* Amber twisted her palm to stare dumbfound at the completely normal surface. She just saw fire shoot out of her hand, but there was absolutely no mark. Her palm was a healthy, normal, unmarred pink. What. The. Hell?

The energy still hummed within her, forcing her to act. To think. She quickly scanned the area. Her heart jump-started again when she saw two sets of eyes staring at her apparently as stunned by her actions as she was.

Damian met her gaze and grinned. Something akin to respect shone in his eyes, illuminated by the residual fire that still burned in the grass. He nodded, and the warmth of his approval had her straightening her back and tilting her chin up in acknowledgement.

The brief moment, the sense of closeness, ended quickly. The other man whipped another fireball and hit an unprepared Damian in the shoulder. Shock and anger lit his face as the force of the strike sent him spinning and stumbling to the ground with a strangled curse.

"Damian!" Amber could not hold back the cry. Foolishly, she had distracted him. She sprinted to his side. He was still on the ground, but had managed to prop himself up on an elbow and was making an effort to get to his feet.

Amber dropped the knife and knelt, reaching to touch him. Her hands stalled in mid-air when she saw the black and bloody wound of scorched flesh that covered his upper chest and right shoulder.

"Are you okay?" Dumb question. Of course he was not okay.

"What are you doing? I told you to stay back," he growled.

The sternness in his voice reminded her of the danger. Before she could answer, Damian swore and yanked her arm so hard she tumbled forward to slam against his chest. He let out a groan of pain then his hand was lifting to command another lightning bolt at the enemy.

"*Look out.*" Damian roared in her ear. She found herself propelled in a violent circle as he twisted them out of the way of an oncoming fireball. Somehow, she landed back on her knees facing Damian, her back to the enemy, her hand in his.

Risking a quick glance over her shoulder, she saw the enemy advancing on them. His arm swung up, and she knew something bad was going to happen. All these men had to do was raise a finger and all kinds of bad crap happened.

Instinct had her free hand rising to repel whatever he shot at them. The energy surged and the incoming fireball was deflected away to land a good ten feet away from them.

"Oh my God." She froze, her breath catching in her chest. That was not possible. She couldn't do that. What was going on?

Damian's stunned voice broke her stupor. He shook her slightly when she did not respond. "Amber. Focus." He gripped her elbow and forced her stand with him.

"Well, well. Isn't this sweet?" The snide voice had her whipping her head up to glare at the enemy. "Too bad it's all going to end so soon. It's been so fun playing with you, Damian. Battles are no fun if they end too quickly." He paused to run a slow, taunting perusal over Amber. "But I really do need the girl now."

"Fuck off, Tubal," Damian snarled, his hand tightening possessively on Amber's elbow as he tried to push her behind him again. She wouldn't budge. She was done hiding.

Tubal extracted a long, knife-like sword from under his jacket and advanced on them. His steps were slow and predatory. "She just displayed some impressive power. I can't wait to play with her. To turn her, and then use her."

The man's voice oozed menace. If he was waiting for a reaction, she gave him none. The dark energy stroked against her, the cold edges circling and enticing her with their lure of seduction. Of the power the dark energy could give her.

Damian pulled on her elbow, inching them backwards in a subtle evasion tactic. "Don't let him bait you. Don't give him what he wants."

Tubal's deep, sinister laugh rolled through the air. "I always get what I want. You should know that better than anyone, Damian."

Amber shook off the cold and let her rage simmer and boil, the energy steaming and brewing within her. The culmination of the day of pain, upheaval and shock festered just below the surface of her tightly contained emotions. Now this evil asshole thought he could just poof in and take her too. Take her, use her, then kill her.

Not a chance.

Damian's hand flexed around hers, pulled her attention and pulsed with power. Words whispered over the energy, binding with her subconscious to speak their intent. And she got it. Somehow, she understood what he wanted. The energy flowed powerful and strong between them, entwining with the stone and caressing her bird.

Damian halted their retreat and lifted his free hand over his head. The air quickly started to turn, twist and swirl into a vicious tornado focused completely around the enemy. It sounded like a freight train had entered the circle as the wind tore ferociously at their attacker, but left them completely untouched. Damian looked at her expectantly, a trickle of sweat running off his forehead and down the side of his face.

*Now.* The words whispered across her mind, and slammed into her consciousness. The energy spiked hot and hard behind the stone.

Amber lifted her hand and focused all her thoughts on the tornado. She felt the anger boil higher as she thought of all that had happened. Of all she had lost in the span of twelve simple hours. In less than one day, the life she had once known was gone forever.

She let the pain and frustration flow through her. Let it simmer and fester until it meshed with the energy to unite in a potent mix of power and wrath.

*Enough.* The thought roared through her mind and with it came the power. The hot, burning flames shot from her hand, burst through the tornado and blasted into her target. Their evil nemesis went flying, so focused on the tornado he had no inkling the fire was coming. The brief look of surprise that lit his face was priceless, the shock and anger satisfying, then his body slammed into the earth with a deadened thump.

The man lay motionless on the ground, a small smoke trail rose from his chest, the lingering evidence of what she'd done. Amber dropped her hand as relief flooded through her. Her knees weakened and trembled with the suppressed fear that finally surfaced at the elimination of the threat.

Damian dropped his arm and the tornado drifted away. The wind stopped, the air stilled. The energy that had been circling them—trapping them—quietly drifted down and evaporated along with the flames that had been continually burning in the small patch of grass.

Darkness and quiet settled over the street with unnerving calm. With the energy field gone, the common night sounds returned. The bark of a dog, the rustle of the wind through the trees, the purr of a car motor on a neighboring street. It was as if the energy field had blocked the sounds from entering and existing as well.

The energy slowly dissipated and settled within her. The stone cooled and her bird fluttered, turned, then rested.

A bone-deep exhaustion swamped her as she acknowledged the adrenaline drain that made her hands shake. Amber released the breath she had been holding and gulped in much-needed air. Lingering scents of smoke, burnt grass and something else she refused to think about assaulted her nose and made her gag.

Damian toppled to his knees and fell forward to brace himself on his hands. His back heaved up and down as he pushed great gusts of air through his chest.

"Damian." Amber bent down, frantic to help. "What's wrong? What can I do?" She tentatively placed a hand on his good shoulder, leaning forward to peer at his face. "Damian, please. Tell me what I can do."

He lifted his head just enough to enable his pain-filled eyes to meet hers. His lids drifted closed as he breathlessly spoke on an exhale, "Kill him...I must finish him." Damian struggled to get to his feet, pushing up before he toppled back to the ground with a low groan.

"Finish him?" Amber shook her head in confusion. What did he want? Every fiber of her body was screaming to get the hell out of there.

"I need to kill him." His raspy voice was barely audible as he once again tried to push to his feet only to fall back to his hands and knees. His struggle was filled with pain and gut-wrenching determination despite his body's refusal to cooperate.

Before she could argue with him, a black cloud formed next to the enemy's fallen form. Amber jumped to her feet and quickly found the knife she had dropped earlier. She gripped it tightly in her fist, her previous exhaustion dismissed in preparation for another attack.

Her breath caught and held when the cloud dissipated to reveal the outline of a woman. The darkness hid her features, but Amber could see the wispy flow of long black hair as it curled down her back and surrounded her face.

The air dipped cooler as an undeniable wave of worry and suppressed fear hit Amber. The woman crouched and laid a gentle hand on the man's forehead. The stranger turned her head and pierced Amber with a hate-filled glare. A quick flash of violet sparked from her eyes before the two disappeared into the night.

"Noooo!" Damian roared as he lunged to where the man had been. He stumbled forward until he stood heaving over the now empty space. His head fell back, and Amber cringed as a howl of pure torture tore from Damian's battered body.

Unsure of what had just happened, of what was causing Damian's pain, Amber slowly moved to his side. The look of utter defeat on his face was a deep contrast to the victory and relief she was feeling. They were alive. They survived.

But Damian looked as if he wanted to die.

She hesitantly reached out to touch his arm and held her ground when he winced and pulled away. She kept her grasp firm and refused to back off. The need to comfort, to help him, overpowered any fear or need to retreat.

"Damian." She kept her voice low, but strong. "We need to go." The misery that swept through the energy tore at her heart. But she wasn't going to broach the subject of his pain right now. She knew they weren't safe and getting out of there seemed obvious.

He nodded, then swayed. Amber shoved the knife into her coat pocket then tucked herself next to his side to hold him steady. Supporting two hundred and thirty odd pounds of man was no easy feat, but she pulled on the last of her strength and kept him standing. He groaned under his breath and grimaced, but stayed on his feet.

He had kept his word and risked his life to save her. She owed him.

"The tower," he mumbled low and husky against her ear.

"What?"

"Newport Tower," he said on an exhale. "Go there."

"Can't you port us out of here?"

His head shook. "Too weak..."

Great. "Why Newport Tower?" Even as she asked, she realized the question was irrelevant. Damian had done nothing but protect her since he'd pulled her out of the council chamber. He had to have a valid reason for going to the strange circular structure. Amber got her bearings and calculated where the city landmark was located. "This way."

Together they shuffled down the street, his weight pressing down on her shoulders. The night was silent, the shadows offering both protection and danger. This time she stayed out of the light, aware that Damian's barely conscious and beat-up state would draw too much attention if they were seen.

The energy pressed on her, blending with the wind and pushing at her back. Nudging her forward, shoving its will alongside her resolve and forcing her onward. Amber stumbled, and Damian followed, his weight throwing them forward and close to tumbling headlong into the cement sidewalk. Bending deep, she forced them upright, knowing she wouldn't be able to get him back up if they fell.

The sweat ran in steady streams down the side of her face and soaked through the back of her shirt. Her hair, a constant cause of annoyance, hung around her face in limp, sticky strands.

A movement in the darkness ahead of them had Amber slowing, then she stopped, her senses alert. Fear gripped her even as she gathered her courage. Her limbs quivered and strained under Damian's weight, and she wondered how she would make it to the tower.

A figure moved within the shadows, definitely a person.

The energy slipped through her, sluggish, drained, but desperately trying to vitalize and prepare her. Her bird circled, swooped and arched, claws extended.

She would fight. She would defend.

Or she would die.

# Chapter Thirteen

The wind gusted icy and cold down the deserted street causing a can to clatter against the pavement, pushed along by invisible fingers. The sound rankled Amber's already frayed nerves and only served to highlight just how alone they were. The empty tree branches swung and bobbed against the pressure of the wind, their shadows dancing over the ground, shifting and swaying in a rhythm set by another.

Amber brushed her hair back from her face, tightened her jaw and waited.

She tensed as the silhouette moved. Coming closer, the sound of boots clumped on the sidewalk. She had no idea how she would defend them, but she'd already done so much that day that she'd never thought herself capable of. This was just one more hurdle she would manage.

Joseph stepped out of the shadows into the dim light of the overhead streetlight, a deep crease of concern pressed into his furrowed brow. Amber's breath expelled in a deep gush of relief, causing her knees to sag under Damian's weight.

"Will you let me help?" Joseph's seemingly odd question caught her off guard and gave her pause.

"Do you mean us harm?" She didn't feel that he did, but then she'd learned so brutally today that impressions didn't mean anything. Her bird—the intrusive mark that had come to life so vividly that day, the one she had intuitively begun to listen to—tucked its wings in rest.

"No, child. I would never harm you." He cast his gaze over the slumping form of Damian and took a step closer. "I will help, if you allow it."

Her limbs shook under the strain of holding Damian upright, and the shaman's offer of help seemed like a gift from the universe. She nodded.

Joseph stepped up and tucked himself under Damian's other arm, mindful of the gaping wound on his shoulder and upper chest. Damian groaned in protest and tried to pull away.

"It's okay, Damian," Amber soothed. "Joseph's going to help. I don't think I can get you to the tower by myself." Her words must have registered because he stopped his struggles. She knew Damian was still semiconscious because she wouldn't have been able to hold him up if he had been completely passed out. As it was, her legs and back sighed in relief when Joseph took some of Damian's weight.

Together, they moved slowly through the city blocks, Joseph silent the entire way. He never even asked where they were heading. Amber had a hundred questions for the shaman, but it took all her effort and concentration to keep Damian upright, to keep her feet moving. Each step felt like a giant leap with cement blocks tied to her feet as they hiked up the hill toward the tower. The physical strain kept her mind blessedly blank.

Finally, they made it to the park where Newport Tower was located. The circular, stone structure was ancient and had been the topic of speculation and research for many years. Amber had never given it much thought, but now the anomaly of a building pulled at her. It seemed to welcome her with a warm rush of belonging.

The tower itself was about two stories tall and made entirely of stone. The intricate masonry work was stunning and amazing given the time period when it had been built. The best guess was sometime predating the 1400s, thus the questions of who had built it and how.

It had eight cylindrical columns that formed symmetrical stone arches around the base with smaller windows along the upper portion above the arches. The top, if there ever was one, had long ago toppled, leaving the building open to the environment.

Amber paused at the edge of the park to catch her breath and process her next steps. The tower was completely enclosed by a high, black, metal fence. It was also lit up like a flaming Christmas tree. Big floodlights were situated around the perimeter of the structure in an effort to keep vandals out. Which was all good and nice, but didn't help her at all.

"Come, child," Joseph prompted as he started moving toward the tower. Amber had no choice but to trudge along with him. She didn't even question how the shaman seemed to know that was her destination.

The stone on her chest warmed and began to pulse in time with each step she took closer to the tower. And with each step, Amber felt the energy thicken around her. It brushed against her cheeks in soothing caresses and hovered around her mind in acknowledgement.

All around them the darkness stretched into the silence. The unusual quiet was unsettling given that it was still early evening. The wind blew strong and hard into her, blowing her hair off her face and out of her eyes in a helpful stroke of assistance.

Joseph led them to a gate in the metal fence that was sealed with a large, bolted lock.

"Great," Amber sighed, the strains of defeat settling through her. "There's no way in."

"Do you believe?" Joseph looked at her around the stretch of Damian's chest. His eyes were shadowed. But the expectation was there in his voice.

She let her head sag in resignation, heavy under the physical and mental weight. "Believe in what, Joseph?"

"In what you are. In what you are meant to do. Meant to be."

Did she? It was a question she simply didn't have an answer for. "I'm not meant for anything. I'm just me."

"And just you is everything," the shaman insisted. *"That's what you need to understand.* You, in all your innocence and simplicity, are exactly what you need to be."

Damian groaned. Amber's gaze lifted to his face, and she was shocked to see him looking at her. His lids hung heavy over his midnight eyes, pain etched into his furrowed brow, exhaustion evident in the effort it took to keep his eyelids up. He didn't speak, but the impact of his gaze slammed into her, snapping hard and fast against her chest.

"What do I do?" The question escaped her lips without thought.

"Use what is around you to get to the circle." She felt the approval in Damian's voice as his instructions whispered hoarsely through the night.

The slamming of a car door echoed through the silence followed by the *bleep, bleep* of the doors locking. A tree creaked in resistance as the wind blew across the park and pulled at her hair. But Damian wasn't talking about those things.

The energy, the force that she was just starting to accept, swept over her skin, bypassing her doubt and denial to wrap itself around the tiny ember of belief. And once it found the kernel, it fueled the acceptance until it burned through her.

Amber reached out and wrapped her fingers around a cold, metal bar in the gate. The vibration caught her by surprise and she inhaled against the feeling. She closed her eyes and listened. Ancient lyrics of power and struggle flowed through her. So much information, but none of it understandable. Confusion riddled her, and she closed her eyes harder in her effort to block out the jumble and focus on the immediate need.

It was Damian who cleared her thoughts. She felt his energy as it joined with hers. His was weak, faded, but pushed forward to aid her anyway. Amber opened herself further, to the possibilities, to the unbelievable.

Her bird screeched in joy and turned its face into the wind in delight.

The power surged and burned from the stone. Once again, it wound around the mingling energy and strengthened the bond. She focused on the bar within her grip and thought of her need for the lock to open and the lights to go off. She pushed the thought along on the energy, used the invisible power to obtain her wish.

The soft click and slide of the lock opening on the gate pounded against her eardrums and barely preceded the plunge of darkness behind her eyelids.

Amber gasped and opened her eyes to total blackness. She jerked her head around to see that every light surrounding the tower was extinguished along with every streetlight lining the perimeter of the park. The metal gate squeaked on its hinges, her movements forcing the door inward to open slightly.

"I did that?" Her voice shook, her disbelief coming out in the wobble of words.

She looked up at Damian, but his eyes were closed once again. His head hung down and bobbed slightly as she gave him a small shake. Her own doubts were forgotten when pressed against the need to help Damian.

"Damian," she said sharply, hoping to keep him awake. "Stay with me. We're almost there."

She gave a shove to push the gate open farther then stepped forward to enter the enclosure. Only Joseph wasn't moving with her. She shot the shaman a questioning look.

"This is where my journey ends," he answered. "I cannot enter. The rest is up to you."

Doubt reared its ugly head once again. "But I can't do this by myself."

"And you are not alone," the shaman said. "Reach out to what is around you like you did just now. Trust what is within you. Trust the one you are with."

"Do you ever give a straight answer?" Her annoyance at the man, at the entire situation, vented itself in the angry tint of her words. At the same time, she knew it was useless to sputter at the shaman. It wasn't going to change what she needed to do.

She released an exaggerated sigh and pushed her shoulder into the gate as she braced her legs and back for Damian's weight. "Let's go, Damian. Just a few more steps."

Joseph stepped away, and she looked back for one last indication of support. The shaman took another step back, smiled slightly and inclined his head, returning the silent plea with the grace of his age.

She bit her lip and looked forward. She stumbled through the gate with Damian, over the small grassy area and through one of the tower arches. The second she entered the building, the power struck her hard and strong. Her steps faltered, but she regained her balance and pressed forward to the center of the circular structure.

Slowly, she lowered herself and Damian to the ground. His arm slid off her shoulders as he executed a controlled tumble to lie on his back on the cold, stiff grass. His head tipped sideways and his lips parted, letting a small groan escape before he appeared to pass out completely.

She blinked back the hated tears and bit down on her lip when the overwhelming feeling of defeat sunk hard and fierce within her. What was she doing? Who was she kidding? There was no way she could do any of the things everyone seemed to believe she could do. All the wild and crazy assumptions that so many had made about her weren't true. It was too much.

But there before her lay a man who needed her right now. Who for some reason, did seem to believe in her. He'd risked his life for *her*.

And as much as she wanted to shut her eyes and deny it, she had watched fire shoot from her hand. Flames that had exited her palm with a force strong enough to take down two powerful men.

She inhaled hard, held the air deep in her chest then exhaled, blowing away the self-pity in a gust of carbon dioxide. She watched the fog form before her face, the vapor cloud billowing up before disintegrating. Damian's big coat gapped open as it pooled around her knees in a puddle of fabric. She shivered, the coldness of the night creeping in to chill her heated skin.

She looked toward the gate for Joseph, hoping he could tell her what to do, but the gate was closed, the shaman gone. There was no one left to lean on. Her fist clenched in her lap, and she reined in the thoughts that threatened to crumble her last wall of internal strength.

With a quick shake, Amber raised her head and looked around the interior of the building. It was about the size of a small dining area with the arches providing an open feeling of exposure even though the two of them were bathed in complete darkness. As she looked at the tall, thick columns that supported the structure, she knew instinctively that they aligned with the cardinal points of a compass. The configuration was comforting in a strange way. One she didn't understand.

The power in the small space was strong and old. It pushed against her exposed skin and she let it in. Let the external energy enter and mingle with her own. And it whispered to her once again. Built her up and strengthened her from within. She reached out and grasped Damian's cold hand between her two warmer ones. His eyes fluttered open at her touch and she leaned over to look into his eyes. The visual connection pulsed through her with the power of the energy.

There, in the very center of the circle where the energy was a pinpoint of strength, she connected with Damian in an unspoken thread of understanding. His energy flowed into her from the callused palm of his hand. A hand that was strong and capable. One that had defended her without hesitation.

The pull was impossible to resist or deny.

It made no sense. Blood still oozed from both his shoulder and leg wounds, and he was clearly weak and in need of medical attention. Why didn't she take him to a hospital? Why did she bring him here to this lonely, mysterious circle based on his one command?

Because she trusted him.

The realization dawned bright and clear in her heart and mind. On both levels, she trusted this man who, with his mere action of appearing in the shop that morning, had forever changed the course of her life.

For good or bad, she was connected to this man in a way she didn't fully understand.

Her bird tumbled and preened, swiping its feathers in a dance of joy. The satisfaction filtered through Amber, confusing her even more. It was obvious the strange mark approved.

Damian still held her gaze, his eyes dark pools that blended into the night. He tugged lightly on her grasp, pulling her closer. She leaned in, expecting him to tell her what to do next. Why they were there in the ancient circle.

He whispered something that she missed.

"What?" She leaned in closer. "I can't hear you."

Her hair fell forward, casting them in a veil of further darkness and creating an illusion of total isolation. He lifted his head with apparent effort and caught her lips in a deep, aggressive kiss. The power assaulted her, and she opened her mouth to let him in. To feel his tongue as it caressed hers, claimed her and demanded more. His hand came up to palm the back of her head even though she had no desire to pull away. She wasn't afraid.

No. She wanted more.

The ancient power surrounded them and flashed with bright pops of light. The world spun and tilted as she sank into the kiss and the longing that stirred within her. To everything she had dreamed of, but never reached for. The rightness plunged through her, gripped her hard and sent her reeling.

The energy built and crashed around them, pulsing with each brush of his tongue against hers, with every breath that drew them together, that bound them tighter, until it shifted, split, then slammed together in a shattering clash of power.

The ground rolled, and the wind gusted and howled around the circle. Amber broke the kiss and braced herself over Damian, providing as much protection over his weakened body as she could. The energy pressed hot and heavy on her back. Her muscles strained in the effort to keep her weight off Damian, to hold herself above him and away from his injuries.

The eerie creaking of metal, the distant roar of an angry beast pummeled her mind and froze her blood. A shiver wracked her from the inside out and sent rivers of fear racing through her.

The weight lifted from her back at the same moment that the wind died and the ground stilled. Her eyes flew open in the sudden stillness; she'd been unaware of their clenched-tight state. A quick check showed Damian still and unconscious once again. The dark red tinge of his lips stuck out sharply against his pale skin, emphasizing his vulnerability.

"Damian," she breathed, bringing her hands to his cheeks. His skin was cold, but his energy flowed stronger, more consistently under her palms.

"Touching," a voice purred through the stillness, throaty, soft and unmistakably sinister. "If it weren't so pathetic."

Amber whipped her head up, swallowing the gasp that formed in her throat. Her gaze zeroed in on the tall, dark-haired woman who leaned against the metal rails on the far side of the fence. The woman pulled her own gaze up from the leisurely perusal she was giving her blood-red nails to peg Amber with a glare that tightened the mass of knots in Amber's stomach into an intertwined jumble of dread.

Amber straightened and pushed to her feet. The woman mirrored her movements, shoving away from the fence to face Amber. The hip-length, black leather jacket the woman wore hung open over a black T-shirt that pulled tightly across her breasts and emphasized the slim lines of her waist. Her long legs were encased in black jeans and thigh-high leather boots, the three-inch spiked heels adding more height to her already imposing six-foot frame.

In contrast to the hard lines of the woman's body, her features were full, lush and strikingly beautiful. Recognition hit Amber even as the energy churned with sickly unease. This was the woman who had appeared back at the fight to take the injured enemy away.

Her bird screeched and lifted its sharp, deadly talons, ready to fight.

"Who are you?" Amber demanded, putting strength in her words to cover the weakness in her locked knees.

The woman tossed the mass of long, dark curls over her shoulder as a cold smile slid over her lips. The emptiness that filled her dark eyes was far more chilling than the quickly cooling elements.

The pause vibrated through the air, the woman drawing out the tension. Amber held her silence and met the unspoken challenge, refusing to cower.

The women let out a sharp, tilting laugh before she finally answered the question. "I am Kassandra, the first wife of the Shifter leader, Tubal. And *I* am your death."

# Chapter Fourteen

*Like hell she is.* The denial flared instantly and furiously within Amber, awakening every lagging, fatigued nerve and stoking the flame deep within.

"Really?" Amber countered. "I can't tell you how many times I've heard that today. And look, here I stand."

The woman, Kassandra, started a slow, stalking pace around the perimeter of the fence. She pursed her lips and cast a sidelong look at Amber. "Luck, I'm sure. But all luck must end."

Amber turned, keeping her body aligned with the enemy. Her boots nudged Damian, reminding her of the precariousness of her position. But she would not fail him. The resolve settled deep in her bones and filled her with a blinding call to protect.

"You're looking a little trapped, my dear," Kassandra taunted as she continued her stroll, trailing her fingers over the bars and letting the tips of her long nails click against the metal. "Where's your luck now?"

Amber let the bait fall untouched. Instead she focused on the energy, pulling it into her, absorbing its strength.

"What? No reply?" The evil woman stopped, rested a hand on her hip and tilted her head in casual contemplation. Amber wasn't fooled.

"Well then," Kassandra purred.

With a flick of her wrist, a fireball appeared and sailed through the slats of the fence, bullseyeing on Amber. Just as quickly, it smacked into the invisible barrier of the energy that protected the circle within the building. The heat flared and washed over Amber as the fireball disintegrated in a burst of snapping sparks.

"You bitch! You need to die," Kassandra shrieked, all pretense of casualness dropped.

Amber released the air trapped in her lungs, careful to keep her relief hidden. She said a thousand mental thank yous to whoever had created the circle she was now safely encased within. Damian had seen to her protection before his injuries had taken him under.

She smiled, years of taunting and torment honing her verbal battle skills. "I really feel like living today." Just in case, she eased her hand into the coat pocket and clasped the hilt of the dagger. "But thank you for the visit."

Sarcastic kindness was always more effective than brute words.

"You won't be so cocky when I'm done with you." Kassandra sneered, a dark veil of evil cloaking her. The coldness slithered toward Amber, snaking through the energy barrier to pull at her once again.

"Nor you," Amber managed to respond. Her voice had gone husky, her body suddenly liquid as the bitter cold energy circled around her. The crisp currents felt so refreshing, enticing after the heat. A part of her wanted to go to it. Wanted to accept all the darkness offered.

"Yes, that's it," cooed Kassandra. "Doesn't it feel nice? Welcoming? We can help you, lost one. Teach you. Show you the way."

Her words were an enticement, pulling Amber in along with the cold and dark. It was the wish for everything to be clear.

Amber felt her feet shuffle forward almost against her will before her boots thumped into Damian. He was still unconscious on the ground, a barrier between Amber and the Shifter enemy.

Amber lurched back, yanking her mind and body away from the dark pull of evil. *"No."*

The Shifter snarled, a threatening sound that matched the malevolence that emanated from her. A series of fireballs left her hands and flew through the air in rapid succession, every one bursting against the unseen wall in hollow echoes of failure as they broke apart and vanished into nothingness.

The warmth returned to Amber, blanketing her in its protective security. It took every ounce of fortitude Amber had to stiffly stand there without flinching or ducking. To watch the fireballs burst, flash and die just six feet before her.

Trust.

In the span of a day, she'd learned to trust the energy. And she believed it would keep her and Damian safe. Still, it was a bit like not flinching when a rock flew at the windshield of your car.

Ducking was not an option.

Amber forced her smile to shine full-force, brittle as it might be behind the façade of confidence. Just as long as the enemy didn't know that.

"You think this is funny?" Kassandra fumed once she'd given up on the fireball bombardment. "You won't for long."

From the corner of her eye, Amber saw the black cloud forming, which she now knew meant reinforcements had arrived. How many? She wasn't taking her focus off Kassandra to find out.

"You can't break the barrier," Amber said, hoping to hell that was true.

"But we can wait." Kassandra pivoted around and threw her arm out, gesturing toward the residential area they were in. "At some point, the cops will come, the day will dawn and you will be forced out by simple human means. Then you won't be so safe." The smile that lit her face was anything but friendly.

Damn. Sweat threaded down Amber's spine, but she kept the smile plastered on and gave a casual shrug. "Who said I plan on being here that long?"

"You have no way out." Kassandra pointed to two spots behind Amber. "As you can see, you're surrounded."

Ding. There were two others behind her. "Thanks for letting me know. I'll bank that for future reference."

"Bitch." Kassandra sneered. "I can't wait to wipe that fucking smile off your face. You can't beat us. You're a pathetic, powerless, sitting duck. Why Tubal wants such a weak excuse of a Shifter is beyond me. If it was up to me, you would've been killed at birth like all runts should be."

Shifter? What the hell was she talking about? Amber squashed her curiosity, once again ignoring the bait. "Well if that's true, then you can't *really* kill me. Can you?" Amber said as she ran a hand through her hair to let the long strands weave through her fingers. "If your husband wants me, maybe he's just tired of you."

The haze of fury that covered Kassandra's face was underscored by the flush that turned her flawless skin to a molten red.

Pulling courage from the depths of her verbal sparring repertoire, Amber flicked her eyebrow up and cocked a mocking smile. "Jealousy does not look good on you." Confidence was so easy to project when safely encased behind bulletproof glass. Or a fireball-proof energy shield, as the case may be.

Her words hit their mark with larger results than Amber could've ever imagined. And given all that she had experienced that day, her expectations were pretty wide open.

A gale force gust of air rushed at the round little building that was currently protecting her. The wind rattled through the metal fence bars, cutting harshly between the rails as it slammed into the invisible barrier and was redirected around the perimeter of the structure. The trees swayed and creaked in violent protest against the unnatural power.

Then, in a quick, smooth movement of interlinked motion, Kassandra changed forms. Her beautiful, womanly shape changed before Amber's dumfounded eyes.

To a dragon.

A big, green and gold, reptilian, scaled dragon.

Amber blinked, licked her lips and resisted the proverbial shake of the head to clear her sight. She swallowed and clutched the dagger even tighter in her fist as if a little knife would protect her against a big flipping dragon.

A wall of flames fired out of the dragon's mouth and shot toward her. The heat seared her face and engulfed her body, but the flames were held at bay by the energy barrier. *Thank God.*

The dragon before her reminded her of the ones she'd seen at the Chinese New Year celebration. It was about ten feet in length, wingless, with a body reminiscent of a snake. Of course, the New York dragons were men in costumes.

This dragon was very, very real.

And very, very angry.

Behind her, Amber heard two more angry growls right before the heat hit her on both sides. This time, she couldn't stop herself from looking. Pivoting to her side, she saw exactly what she'd anticipated.

Two more dragons.

How? Maybe she should have gotten a clue by their very name, Shifters, but she had barely wrapped her mind around the fact that there were beings in the world that could control the elements and energy of the earth. Shape-shifting dragons were in a completely different realm of belief. One that defied all logic and suspended rational thought.

Yet there were three dragons definitely prowling outside the fence.

Where were the cops when you needed them?

For that matter, where was anyone? There was obviously some kind of power being used that she didn't understand. One that prevented others from hearing and seeing what she saw. She would gladly relinquish her privileged status to anyone who wanted it.

The dragons released simultaneous breaths of fire that scorched her from three sides and raised the heat in the circle to oven-ready. The heated air singed her lungs when she gasped, trying to breathe through the terror. Her face felt flushed, burned, as the interior space of the circle increased with each flash of dragon fire. She needed to do something. Correction—she needed to get them out of there before they became dragon dinner.

With considerable effort, Amber blanked her mind to all that threatened to crumble her. She mentally pulled the shutters down on all of the impossible. On dragons and fireballs. On teleporting and energy manipulation. On prophecies and destiny. Instead, she focused on survival. That was all she could do at the moment. The only thing that was truly important.

Keeping her focus on the dragon Kassandra, Amber stepped over Damian so her feet straddled his hips. The dragon tossed its head and bared its teeth in a threatening sneer. Hot puffs of smoke lifted from its nostrils in snorting grunts. The long tail swooped back and forth in a display of agitation, the spiked end swinging with deadly practice, ready to pummel its mark.

Amber looked down and inched her feet in until her boots tucked snugly against Damian's lower ribs. The connection was essential. On her chest, the stone came to life. The mystical pendant that now held her as solidly as a pair of handcuffs. The slow heat pooled in her chest and raised her already boiling temperature higher. But it was comforting in a way that calmed her soul and opened her mind to listen.

To feel.

Outside the circle, the dragons paced and growled. Periodically, heat would flush over her as one of them released another breath of flames that kept the interior space near boiling. But Amber pushed that aside.

She slid her hand from her pocket and lifted her arms until they extended perpendicular from her body, her wrists tilted back leaving her palms parallel to the two columns at her sides that aligned to the east and west navigational points. How she knew this, she stopped questioning. The answers simply hummed within her.

The energy guided her.

There was power in the directions. In the alignment of the points that pulled from the earth's energy field. The forces that held the earth in place and kept it rotating in a defined rhythm.

This was the power she was seeking.

The energy slammed into her chest and shattered against the stone. Her head flew back at the force, but she kept her feet planted, her back straight. It felt like a lightning bolt to her chest. The excess power sizzled over her skin and rang in her ears.

The stone became the apex of the power, pulling it in from each direction until it centered within her chest. The energy was the drug she'd always craved, but hadn't known it. It connected with her nerves and raced through her blood, lifting her higher in a rush of adrenaline. It coursed down her legs and funneled into Damian. His hands clenched around her ankles, the pressure of each finger pushing against the leather boots to imprint on her skin. Amber forced her head to tip forward so she could look into Damian's eyes. They were opened and staring at her in undisguised awe.

"You are stunning."

Amber sensed the words more than heard them as they lifted from Damian's lips. Her chest tightened at his unexpected praise. She *felt* stunning. Powerful. Something she'd never expected to feel.

Her heart cracked a little more at his simple acceptance of *her*.

Another punishing blast of heat upped the urgency and forced Amber to focus. The power had built to a combustible force within her chest, pushing against the walls, demanding release.

She tilted her head back to look at the open sky above. The roofless building provided a clear view of the suddenly cloudless sky. Amber clasped her hands directly above her head. The vertical point drove a spike down the heart of the tower like the centering point on a compass.

The power surged, thrust and rammed down through her with a force that shook the foundation of the stone tower and almost dropped her to her knees. But she held strong, the energy funneling through her from the very crux that made the earth rotate in space.

In the next instant the prickling started on her skin, the pinpoints of sensation followed by the turning of her stomach. In the distance, she registered the thunder of angry roars.

Holding, she let the power build. Let the strength pour from her as she focused on escaping. On leaving the tower. On safety.

At the last second, right before the power peaked, Amber dropped to her knees and hugged Damian to her chest. Space and time melded together as they ascended into nothingness.

# Chapter Fifteen

The landing was gentle, smooth in its execution. Amber wasn't fooled. She sprang to her feet and crouched in defense over Damian the second her senses registered that her body was once again solid. She closed her hand around the hilt of the dagger, yanking it from the depths of the coat pocket to extend it before her. A minimal shield against an unknown enemy.

Damian stirred and pushed himself to a sitting position before he slowly rose to his feet. She quickly gave him a once-over before her focus turned back to the room. At least he was standing on his own.

"Where are we?" Her words echoed in the sparse room even though she had taken care to speak them softly. She turned in a circle to verify that they were alone before she straightened to her full height and let the knife drop back into the coat pocket.

"I don't know," Damian answered, his voice deep and throaty as he surveyed their surroundings. "I've never seen this place before."

Amber took in the dark red carpeting and the deep rose wood that covered the walls, leaving a vague sense of being trapped inside a wine barrel. The circular formation of the room picked off her newfound respect for the seemingly unobtrusive geometric shape.

"Can you port us out of here?"

Damian closed his eyes, and she waited a beat before he gave a quick shake of his head. "No. The casted circle won't allow it." He opened his eyes and looked at her. "But it doesn't give off a malevolent vibe."

Amber arched her brow in question.

"As you become more attuned to the energy, you can pick up its vibrations," he explained. "All energy has a feel based on how it is used with every connotation having its own rhythm."

"Like the energy has feelings?"

"Kind of. It picks up and retains the intent of the user. Just like an engine retains the heat after it's been turned off, the energy holds the signature of purpose."

"And the energy of the circle we're in is good?" She let the hope show in her voice.

He stroked a hand over his jaw in thought. "It's more like ambivalent."

"Well, that's better than evil," Amber said before exhaling a deep breath. She moved away from Damian and took a closer look at the room, every instinct still on high alert.

The circular room was void of windows, but large enough to keep it from feeling like a cell. The space was broken only by a single bed that sat low to the ground on a black, wooden frame and a small side table that sat next to it. The low light in the room was coming from the lamp on the table and the crack beneath one of the two doors in the room. The deep purple duvet was pulled neat and crisp over the bed and accented with an arrangement of black and cream pillows decorated with variations of Chinese themes.

She turned her focus back to Damian. The wound on his shoulder was still bloody, crisp and painful looking. He was a little pale, but considering he had been basically passed out and unconscious just a few minutes ago, he looked remarkably good. The relief that flooded her was more than just the basic thankfulness that he'd be okay. She was smart enough to recognize just how attached she was becoming to him. The thought of losing him went far deeper than the simple fear of losing the man who offered her protection.

"How are you feeling?"

His features tightened before he paused in his own surveillance of the room to look down at his shoulder. He shifted the injured shoulder around, wincing slightly before he stopped the movement.

"Better," he finally answered. He lifted his gaze to hers. "Thanks to you."

"Yeah," she scoffed. "Thanks to me, you were injured in the first place."

"No. Thanks to you I'm up and walking already." The firm timbre of his voice negated her instant surge of denial. "It was your power, the energy you pulled in at the tower that infused me and accelerated the healing."

She shook her head, clenched her lips and looked away. "I don't understand." She blinked back the stinging that sparked and burned in her eyes. "I'm sick of not understanding."

Damn it. She would not cry now. Not in front of him. Inhaling through her nose, she forced her muscles to relax with the slow exhale. With effort, she returned her gaze to meet his. The concern she saw there almost undid her. Almost. Because it couldn't be real.

"You've been through a lot today." He lifted his hand to brush her hair off her shoulder so it rested down her back. "You've faced every obstacle thrown at you, every wild truth despite their impossibilities, and you didn't crumble or cower from them. That takes strength. Courage. So give yourself a break. Understanding will come."

The sudden warmth that flooded her had nothing to do with the stone or energy. He looked so honest, sincere in what he said. Like he believed his words.

"Why do you care? Only hours ago you were offering me up as a sacrifice to your people. A pawn in your game of redemption."

He sighed, clenched his hands on his waist and dropped his head to let it sag in a brief pose of guilt. Her heart seized, betraying just how important his answer was to her.

Straightening his back, he met her gaze. His lips thinned, but his eyes pierced her with their intensity. "I will always regret that. If I had listened to the instinct that burned within me, I would have *never* turned you over." He stepped closer, a move that put him firmly in her space, but it wasn't an attempt at intimidation. Instead, it was comforting. "If I listen to the energy, trust it as I've told you to do, I'd believe that you *are* the one for me."

Her lips parted slightly, the air slowly leaving her constricted chest. He brushed his fingers over her cheek until he cupped the side of her face in his palm. His energy whipped through her from the simple touch, pouring out of his palm to burn her insides. The hunger weakened her knees and scorched her throat to the dryness of a barren desert.

"If I ignore the prophecies, the absent words of faceless spirits, I know that you are all that is good. The white bird is as evil as my white dragon. I don't care what everyone else thinks. What they say. If I trust the energy—" He cursed softly, then swallowed. "If I trust the energy, then I care about nothing *but* you."

His eyes burned with the conviction of his words. She wanted to believe him. The urge to lean into him, to simply shift forward and let him catch her, was almost too powerful to resist. But there was more. More to him and to everything that was happening. If she trusted the energy like he was urging her to, then she needed to know what that more was before she could surrender.

"Why is it so hard for you to trust the energy?" she probed, treading as gently as the reedy currents warned her to. "What happened that has led you to doubt exactly what you tell me to believe?" He flinched ever so slightly, but she caught the movement and pushed anyway. "How can I trust the energy when you don't?"

"An excellent question, young one." The voice shot through the silence, breaking the moment with the sharp force of a pickaxe.

Damian turned, his hand reaching for the knife strapped to his back and letting it fly in one smooth motion. The weapon shot through the air toward the wiry Asian man who had appeared behind him.

In a blink, the man disappeared. In his absence, the knife speared the wood wall with a dull thud and stuck. *Fuck.* How had he let someone sneak in behind him? A juvenile mistake.

"I am not your enemy," the voice said from behind him again.

Damian spun, reaching for another knife as he moved.

"*You*," Amber exclaimed as she pointed at the man. Her other hand slammed over her chest as she shuffled away from the intruder. "*No.* You can't have it back."

Amber's face was etched with panic, her hand clutched possessively around the stone that hung under the jacket. Damian recognized the man as the Spirit Ancient from the alley in New York City. The one who'd rattled off the prophecy and disappeared.

Protect. Defend. Save. The words slammed into Damian as he shoved Amber behind him.

"I do not want the stone back," the man calmly stated. "It belongs to you. If that were not true, then I never would have given it to you."

Damian kept the knife raised and ready. "Who are you? What do you want with us?"

"I want nothing from you," the man said, stepping forward until he stood within the shaft of light that sliced out from the cracked doorway. "I brought you here to give you a moment of safety. To rest and heal before your journey continues."

Amber pushed her head around Damian's side, his tight grip on her arm preventing her from moving completely out from behind him.

"Why?" she demanded, her voice strong despite the anxiety he felt coursing through her. "Why do you keep coming to me?"

The thin Asian man tilted his head, and the two strips of white hair that hung like long ropes from the ends of his Fu Manchu mustache swayed in time with the movement. "Why?" he repeated, a note of curiosity in his voice. "Because you need help and I can provide it."

The white silk of his loose, traditional Chinese jacket rustled softly as his hands rose from their position behind his back until he held them toward Damian and Amber in a show of trust. "You called for safety, Amber. The energy answered and, with my help, brought you here. Trust the energy to heed your call and keep you safe."

"How do you know my name?" Amber demanded before Damian could. What game was the Ancient playing?

The man smiled mysteriously, letting his hands fall back to his sides. "Because you are the Marked One. Because I am old and know more than you. I trust the energy. It talks to me. I listen."

Damian inhaled and reached out across the energy, letting the vibrations flow around him. The power assaulted him in a gust of brute force, but it was not malevolent.

"Again, Ancient. Why are we here?" Damian demanded.

"Because the Chosen One has found the Marked One," the man calmly replied.

Damian's jaw tightened against the implication, an instant rejection of the statement. But this was the second time in a day he'd been told that. By two men he did not know, both telling him to believe. Was it true? Damian told Amber to believe, should he?

"There's no way I can be this Chosen One, a title I'd never heard of before today," Damian deflected, the cynicism dripping from his voice. He speared the Ancient with a cold stare, daring him to contradict his word. "Chosen inspires the connotation of someone special. Someone picked from the crowd to do something or be something special. We both know I am not that."

A sacrifice—now that, he could believe.

"What do you mean, Chosen One?" Amber said as she pushed her way from behind Damian. She swiveled her head, shooting questioning looks between the two men. "What haven't you told me, Damian?"

"It's nothing," he denied. "Just words from foolish old men."

Her eyes narrowed. "Is it as nothing as me being the Marked One?" The iciness of her words sunk into Damian.

"I don't know," he found himself answering honestly. "Lately, it seems I know nothing."

A light chuckle drifted through the claustrophobic room. "The first step in understanding everything." The Ancient smiled at his own caginess as if all the events were suddenly clear. "I found you both when you were lost. But it is up to the two of you to find the path and lead the way."

"Found us both?" Amber questioned, her sharp mind catching the hidden points when Damian's had missed it.

"In New York City," the man replied. "The Year of the Dragon celebration. A year that will change everything. A year that has been a millennium in waiting. You needed the stone and he needed to prepare. That was all I could do then."

"So it was you who gave Amber the stone?" Damian said. "Where did it come from?"

The Ancient waved his hand in dismissal. "Details that do not matter at the moment."

"Why me?" Amber whispered, the soft words barely audible in the silent room. She lifted her head and looked at the Ancient. A man she recognized, but didn't seem to trust.

Damian was learning the calm, collected face Amber presented hid her true feelings. It was her way of deflecting and hiding her emotions from others. A tactic he understood.

He reached out and grabbed her hand. There it was, the niggling of fear, the thread of panic, the trace of desperation—all of them clearly discernable over the energy. He pulled her to his side and wrapped his arm around her shoulders. The urge to keep her safe—to keep her—took over every thought within him. She resisted him at first, but then she melted against his side, the fight leaving her.

The Ancient walked toward them. Damian stiffened and pulled Amber tighter to his body. Although he detected no threat from the man, he wasn't prepared to trust him either. Too many years of doubt stood between him and blind faith.

No matter what the energy said.

"You will understand the why when you are ready," the Ancient told Amber as he stopped a few feet from them. "Now, you need sleep. Food. A shower. I will provide those. Tomorrow, we will talk. But for now, you will rest. This room is safe—no one can enter without my permission." The man walked to the open door, his white slippers silent against the plush carpet. He pushed the door open, allowing more light into the room. "The bathroom is also safe and fully stocked. A luxury I think you could both use."

The man bowed slightly, then disappeared without a sound.

# Chapter Sixteen

Amber stepped out of the bathroom, a towel wrapped tightly around her head, confining her long hair. She had her dirty clothes back on, but her skin was clean. Her mind soothed. Or, at least, tired enough to stop thinking. The long, hot shower had done its magic, releasing the knotted muscle aches and replacing them with a bone-weary exhaustion.

The smell of teriyaki hit her nose, and her stomach growled in response. Damian looked up from his perch on the edge of the low bed. He'd removed his ruined jacket and shirt, making the burn wound—which he had adamantly refused to let her treat—look even worse when highlighted against the bronze expanse of his chest. He looked her over from head to toe before he cleared his throat and stood.

"Feeling better?" he said softly, the husky notes stroking her skin in a warm glow.

She nodded. "Yes. Much." She clutched her hands, forced her gaze away from his naked torso and stepped away from the door. "Your turn."

Being alone with a male, sharing a bathroom, completing mundane tasks were all out of her scope of experience. The intimacy of the situation unnerved her more than the threat of dragons or fireballs.

"Here," he said, stepping behind her. "Let me help."

Before she could refuse, he gently unwrapped the towel from around her head, letting her wet hair fall free, but catching it with the towel before the strands soaked her shirt. With the softest of touches, he rubbed the thick towel over her hair, periodically squeezing and rubbing until most of the water was absorbed into the cloth.

Amber closed her eyes and let the tender touches relax her further. His kindness, the juxtaposition of the stoic warrior quietly drying her hair was more poignant than any words he could have said. Her bare toes curled into the soft carpet, the fibers scrunching under the pressure.

"Stay here," he said, the warmth of his breath caressing her neck. In a second he'd returned from the bathroom with a brush.

"I can do it." She cleared her throat to remove the scratchiness that had assaulted her voice and extended her hand.

"So can I."

The brush massaged her scalp and tugged lightly as he patiently pulled it through the long mass. She lost track of time, forgot about all the stresses that pushed at her and simply let him take care of her. The steam from the bath heated the room and brought with it a damp moisture that cloaked the air in weighted heaviness.

The nerves that held her stomach tight loosened with each touch. With each soft pass of the brush, the feeling of belonging grew within her. The stone hummed a warm, consistent murmur between her breasts and the energy flowed languidly through her in rhythm to Damian's patient brushing.

"Your hair is beautiful," he said close to her ear, the heat of him warming her back even though he didn't touch her. "It amazes me that it's as silky and smooth as it looks." He ran his fingers through it. "So soft."

"Thank you," she whispered, not knowing what else to say.

"Has it always been this long?"

She turned her head to look at him over her shoulder. His face was sincere, questioning. "Yes. As annoying as it sometimes is, it's a part of me. A part of who I am." She looked down, the force of his gaze too powerful. "I think I would be lost without it."

The brush stilled, and she felt the flush creep over her face. Why had she told him that?

His hands held her shoulders when she tried to step away. She heard the quiet thud of the brush hitting the carpet before he rubbed the tight muscles at the juncture of her neck.

"You are not your hair," he said, his voice both firm and gentle. "You would be beautiful with or without it. Strong if it was long or short. Courageous even if you were bald. The outer trimmings do not change the core of who you are."

Unbidden, she leaned back into the steady pressure of his hands. Her head tilted forward and she sighed. "It would seem that you have a very different perception of my core than I do."

"Isn't that true of most people? It's very rare that we see ourselves as others see us."

A short puff of air left her nostrils in a sound of agreement; a small smile curved her lips. "Very true." His fingers continued their gentle rubbing of her neck up to the base of her skull. Amber bit her lip to keep the moan from escaping. After a moment she asked, "So how do you see yourself?"

He chuckled, the low tones scurrying over her spine. "The important question is how do *you* see me?"

His hands didn't stop their work, but she felt his body tense behind her. The expectation hung in the air, her answer far more significant than the simple question posed. Her tongue bathed her dry lips with moisture, and she closed her eyes to shutter her thoughts even though he couldn't see her face from where he stood.

She pulled strength from the darkness, inhaled deeply, exhaled it all. Her voice was low, but steady when she finally spoke.

"I see the strength of a man who bears the weight of many without complaint. One filled with loyalty and honor despite the injustices that have been committed against him. A man courageous enough to stand up to his people even though it meant abandoning all that he wanted."

His hands stilled. She heard him swallow. "And you see this in spite of all that I've done to you?"

She turned to face him. His grip tightened on her shoulders when she met his probing gaze. She may have had her doubts about all that had happened to her, about everything that had been said about her. But she had no doubts about the man before her.

"And what exactly have you done to me?" she challenged him. She reached up with a shaky hand and circled the burn wound on his shoulder with her fingertips. "You've protected me when you didn't need to. You've saved me when you could have turned your back. You were, *are*, willing to sacrifice your life for mine. So tell me why I would see anything different?"

The pain that slipped across his face surprised her. She'd said too much. Again. Damn it. She had no experience with these types of situations. Of expressing her emotions, especially to a man. Instead of comforting him, she'd caused him pain.

She looked away, dropped her hand and tried to step back. Again, he stopped her. Why? His hands slid up the sides of her neck until they cradled her face. A slight pressure forced her head up until she met his gaze. The pain she'd seen was gone. In its place was a tenderness she'd never seen in him. His features had softened, his eyes a deep blue that held her in a paralyzed trance.

"Because I started all this," he said, his voice low, insistent. "It's because of me that you are here. That people are after you. It's my fault that you are hunted." He shook his head and looked down. "My selfishness has caused all this."

She chuckled, a brief rumble of disagreement. "I don't believe any of that." His head lifted, his eyes narrowed in doubt. "This was all set in motion before you showed up. From the second that Asian man gave me the stone, my life was changed. I might not understand everything, but I know that without question. You are not at fault for where my life is." She tentatively pressed a hand to his bare chest. The heat warmed her palm, the energy tunneling down her arm to burrow into her chest.

"No," she whispered, the trepidation making her voice soft. "You are only a part of where my life is going."

"Amber," he breathed, his thumb caressing her cheek. "You offer too much. There is so much you don't know about me. About my past."

"Then tell me. Trust me to understand. Trust that the energy is right."

That fast, he shut down. Abruptly, he stepped away. His hands dropped to grip his hips. He looked away, his focus on the open doorway to the bathroom. The hard lines of his profile were void of all tenderness, chiseled now out of stone.

The silence spread between them, the gap widening to form a plunging cavern of unsaid words. Amber crossed her arms tightly across her chest, her hands gripping her arms in an attempt to hold the pain inside. To keep it locked away where no one would see it.

Damian moved toward the bathroom without a word or glance in her direction. The door clicked quietly closed and the innocent sound broke her heart open.

She squeezed her eyes shut, but surprisingly there were no tears to hold back. The rejection—his rejection—stabbed at her, a thousand knife wounds aimed at her heart. How could it hurt so badly?

Her bird curled inward, tucking its wings tightly around its body. A lone tear rolled from its eye, the single drop shed for her.

Amber shivered; the cold invaded her system and plagued her with self-accusations. All the blistering taunts, blatant hatred and disgusted glares she had lived with her whole life came racing back to beat at her mind. Tortured memories that held her in their icy grip.

Damian didn't believe in the energy. He didn't trust it or her. Apparently, she wasn't good enough for him. He'd said she was brave, strong, courageous—all noble words, but none of them expressed his feelings toward her.

Again, she was the fool. She'd been willing to trust, to believe, so easily. Longing for love so desperately that she jumped—no, vaulted—at the first sign of interest from a man.

Pathetic.

But no more.

Straightening, Amber loosened the death-clamp on her arms and slowly exhaled. The soothing breath blew away the self-deprecating tirade she battled. She picked up the forgotten brush from the floor and pulled on the strength Damian spoke of. She dug up the courage he professed she held and turned her back to the bathroom door. She moved away from him, steady steps toward the bed where the food waited on a tray, the dishes encased under metal lids.

Calmly, she set the brush on the bedside table and crawled onto the bed. The pain securely trapped back inside. The thoughts banished.

Her heart beating but locked tight against further invasion.

The water rushed over Damian's head, sending hot pellets of damnation into his shoulders, across his back, into his heart. He'd hurt her. *Fuck.*

Of course he'd hurt her. She'd opened herself to him, showed him her shining light of innocence, trusted him with her hope. And what had he done? Kicked her in the gut and stole her candy all in the same asshole stroke.

He *was* evil.

Had to be to do that to her.

Damian groaned, rubbing his palm over the pain in his chest. Not the battle wound, but the soreness that radiated from deep in his torso.

He tipped his head back and let the water sluice over his forehead and stream down the sides of his face. The steam rose around him, the water heated to a scorching punishment. He deserved more. Shame rammed against the brick wall encasing his emotions. The wall toppled with barely a protest. But then it had been slowly crumbling since he'd first touched Amber.

Cursing—violent, harsh words—Damian shook the water from his face and yanked the soap from the holder. A millennium. A thousand years of fucking isolation. Years of loneliness that had stoked the simmering anger, the burning resentment that ate at him over the injustices piled on him. Of the false accusations and betrayal until he'd finally closed off the emotions. Buried them all before they buried him.

Until Amber.

*Damn it.*

He scrubbed the soap furiously over his skin, scouring harshly as if the simple bar could cleanse the dirt from his soul. His shoulder protested, the stiffness and pain a reminder of what was at stake. Of exactly how deadly this battle was and how threatened Amber truly was.

The subtle cinnamon scent of the soap reached his nose. His nostrils flared, opening wide to inhale the aroma. His dick throbbed as her scent surrounded him. He'd been hard since she'd stepped out of the bathroom all fresh and soft. The slight hesitancy in her movements, the uncertainty that radiated from her. It called to him. She called to him.

Images of Amber assaulted his mind. Of her standing up to him, challenging his assertions of who she was. Of her fighting to get to him, to save him from his people. Of Amber standing over him, hair lifting with the energy as she reached for the power and used it. Each image showed who she truly was. Why she was the Marked One.

There was serious power within her. Still fresh, untapped. Innocent like her.

So was he to believe that he, Damian, was the Chosen One?

So much had happened so fast that he hadn't even had time to process all that *he* had learned today. The shaman had said that Amber was his. Saved for him. *Fuck.*

Damian scrubbed a hand over his face, trying desperately to make sense of it. The logic didn't match what he was feeling. What everyone was trying to tell him. Amber wasn't the only one whose world had turned upside down in a day.

Slamming the soap back on the shelf, Damian cut the water and stepped from the shower. It was time to face the mess he'd created. Hiding in the bathroom wasn't his M.O. They needed to talk—about the facts—and keep the emotional stuff out of it. It didn't matter what she thought of him.

His dragon spread its wings wide and hissed in denial.

What did it know anyway? Hell, the damn mark had sprouted wings today. It was yet another thing that eluded explanation. After a thousand years of torment because of the white fucking dragon on his hand, the damn thing decided to grow wings. On the day he found Amber. Coincidence? Not hardly.

But what the fuck did it mean?

Yanking his jeans back on, Damian rubbed the towel over his hair then gave the locks a quick finger comb. Leaning forward, he checked his shoulder injury in the mirror. The wound from the fireball was already partially healed and would probably be gone by morning. The burn mark on his thigh was smaller and shrinking at a steady pace. Amber's little boost of energy seriously accelerated his healing time.

His shirt was toast, and he didn't see a convenient change of clothing lying around, so shirtless he would have to stay. The hole in his jeans only added to the *GQ* cover look. He scoffed at his appearance. It was a far cry from the CEO image he'd begun the day with.

Twisting his head to the side until his neck bones cracked and his spine groaned, Damian stretched the muscles and prepared for the upcoming clash. Amber should be pissed at him. He deserved it.

He jerked the door open, a quick pull that released the captured steam in a silent swoosh of air. His bare feet hit the soft padding of the carpet without a sound.

Amber sat cross-legged on the bed, the food tray to the side of her, her hands clasped in her lap. Her back was straight and she didn't look at him. He scooped up his jacket and the pile of weapons he'd left on the floor then moved to the other side of the bed, setting the items down but ensuring they were still close.

He resisted a sigh, his lips thinning. He'd caused this rift between him. Now how did he cross it?

"You didn't have to wait for me," he finally said. She looked up at him, a blank, emotionless stare, before she turned away and removed the lids covering the plates of food.

"I didn't mind." She set the covers to the side before she picked up a set of chopsticks and held them out to him. "I hope you can use these. He didn't give us forks."

Her voice was flat. Pleasant, but lacking all the warmth of earlier. *Shit.* He wanted that back. Wanted to see the light in her eyes, the flush of her cheeks and hear that warm, silky voice as it challenged him. Pushed him to confront what was holding him back.

The mere fact that he wanted to do that, wanted to do whatever it took to get that warm, fighting Amber back startled him to his bare toes. It also told him more than any shaman or Ancient ever could.

Damian placed a knee on the bed and accepted the offered chopsticks from Amber. The mattress tipped slightly as he sat down on the soft surface and faced her. The silence stretched between them as she sorted out the meal and handed him a plate. Despite the fact that his stomach cramped in hunger, the enticing aroma sparking the instant craving to eat, he had lost the desire to eat.

His dragon paced impatiently as they mechanically consumed their meal. Damian resisted the urge to bounce his knee or fidget under the stretching tension that bridged between them. The light click of the chopsticks, the soft clink of the ice cubes, the slight rustling of material as Amber shifted her legs; inconsequential sounds that echoed in the deafening quiet.

"Sorry."

Damian set his empty plate on the tray and waited for Amber's response. He knew his coarse apology wasn't even close to what was required.

"No problem," she said placidly, her eyes on her plate, her motions flowing without a pause. "You owe me nothing, so there is nothing to apologize for."

The cold words pierced his chest. She used her chopsticks to smoothly scoop up the rice and lift it to her lips, her movements as unemotional as her words. He could be a bug or lump of coal sitting across from her for all the attention she gave him.

His focus was one hundred percent on her. On her soft lips as they opened to accept the rice and then move ever so slightly to chew the food. His body responded to the non-sensual actions. His blood heated, his pulse accelerated and, unwanted, his dick hardened.

Looking away, he inhaled a quiet breath and forced his hands to relax their fisted hold against his desire.

"You're wrong," he finally admitted, his voice still grating with his barely suppressed need. "I owe you an explanation at a minimum."

She lifted her gaze to assess him with guarded eyes. Her face remained impassive, but she set her plate aside and gave him her attention. Finally.

"All right, I'll listen." She clasped her hands in her lap and waited, giving nothing.

Where did he start? Why was he willing to tell her things he'd kept silent about forever? The answer hummed over the energy and pulsed in his chest: because she meant more than anything he'd encountered in his too-long life.

She *was* everything to him, if he was willing to take the risk.

# Chapter Seventeen

"The energy betrayed me," Damian said, the low gravel of his voice scratching through the heavy silence to crunch under the weight of the emptiness that separated them. He had shifted to rest against the headboard, his fist clenching the opposing wrist as they rested on his bent knees. "I find it hard to trust in something that has caused me so much pain. To trust something that lied to me, about me, is nearly impossible for me to do."

The admission was pretty much what Amber had expected. That much had been obvious—what she hoped for was the reason behind the distrust. But she refused to ask, to beg further. Anything he gave her had to be given freely or it would mean nothing.

So, instead of responding, Amber removed the tray, now littered with empty plates, to the floor next to the door she assumed was an exit. With her back to him, she took a steadying breath, then straightened and returned to sit on the corner of the bed. The corner farthest from Damian.

He watched her with hooded eyes, the emotions hidden behind a shield so thick it was impossible to tell what he was thinking, let alone feeling. Amber clasped her hands in her lap to hide the telling shake, tightened the lock around her heart and presented the same stoic face that he displayed to her.

One that she was well-versed in. He wasn't the only one who'd lived a life of betrayal.

Damian closed his eyes before he let his head sag against the dark wood headboard. "I haven't told this story since it happened a thousand years ago." His lips moved, but the rest of his body remained still. "I haven't trusted anything or anyone since the night I lost everything."

With his dark, penetrating eyes hidden behind his closed lids, Amber's lower lip was immediately attacked by her teeth. She allowed the nervous habit to fester while he wasn't looking. It also kept her from breaking the silence that once again circled them in strained intimacy.

She would listen. *She* owed him that much.

Anything more, he would have to earn.

Damian struggled to block the images that threatened to break him. After holding back the reel for so long, refusing to let the movie play or even let the highlights be displayed, the sudden release of the show was enough to crush him if he let it all go at once.

He would start with the basics. Maybe easing into it would be easier.

"Energy—the most powerful element on Earth," he began. "It is what we, the Energy races, have fought over since life began and the power of the energy was defined. A fight that still rages. Different locations, different players. But still, it plays on. Energen versus Shifter."

He paused and waited behind the safety of his closed eyelids. She said nothing. He heard her nearly imperceptible inhale. But he felt her almost like she was curled beside him, holding him tight against the memories that threatened to choke him.

She hadn't spoken a word, but she was listening. Waiting.

His need to tell his tale was suddenly as strong as his need to hold her tight to his side where she belonged.

The resounding truth of that image pushed him forward into the darkness of the past. The present evaporated as he returned to the dark events that had occurred a thousand years ago. When his brother was still alive. When he still believed in the energy, in the truth it told.

He felt the words leave his mouth, but his consciousness wasn't in the present. With the release of the show, he let the past roll in and take him under.

*The field was dark, the sun long gone. The night hung heavy and waiting around the figures contained within the large ring of fire.*

*The circle cast, the battle prepared.*

*Khristos, Damian's older brother—the eldest of three—and heir to the House of Air, stood strong, tall and courageous in the center. His blond hair fanned around his head with the stroke of the wind, his muscular frame tense and ready. The firelight danced across his bare chest and gleamed off the sharp edge of the sword clutched in his fist.*

*Behind him huddled a small, thin female. She crouched in fear, almost lost in the deerskin cloak that hugged her body. She hid her face in her hands, her shoulders shaking in uncontained fright.*

*The Shifter, dressed in black, dark hair long and uncontained, stood across from his brother. A cruel smile lifted his mouth, a long, black blade held at his side.*

*Damian stood outside the flames, outside the circle. Looking in, but unable to enter. Arriving too late to join the fight. Too late to help his brother.*

*Heat radiated from the fire, scorched his flesh and blistered his hands as he fought to enter the battle. To break down the shield that barred him. The Shifter had cast the circle, and the energy forbade Damian entry. Held him out while it trapped his brother and the woman he protected. Inside the circle, the war raged between the two combatants: Air versus Fire. Energen versus Shifter.*

*The metal clang of clashing swords rang hollow and high across the open expanse of the field. The energy peaked and flowed as the fight crested and volleyed.*

*Disbelief pummeled Damian when Khristos lost his footing, stumbled, then fell. Damian punched at the wall of flames, desperation pounding in his chest, blanking his mind to everything but the need to help. To save.*

*A need denied.*

Damian's dark tunic burst into flames, his driving desire taking him too close to the inferno that blocked him. Absently, he stripped and discarded the clothing. The flesh burns ignored.

The Shifter launched a fireball, the tumbling ball of flame nailing his downed brother in the chest. Denial roared from Damian, the sound echoing across the night on empty waves of pain. Sweat rolled down his spine and dripped from his forehead. His hands were raw, blistered and burnt from the blaze before him.

The agony of the burns was nothing compared to the torture of his own inability. Of helplessness.

Surprise, pain and anger flashed across Khristos's face before he slammed into the ground, the force of the fireball grinding his back into the cold, hard earth. A piercing scream wrenched through the still air, the female a mass of frozen terror as the Shifter advanced on them.

His brother made a desperate attempt to defend the woman. He scrambled backwards on his elbows, dragging the terrified female with him. Khristos used the last of his waning energy to blow the Shifter back in a failed attempt to hold off his aggressor.

A faint wisp of hope stirred within Damian when his brother struggled up to regain his footing. Khristos could not be defeated. He was the strongest brother. A brave warrior. A proven, trained fighter. He had taught Damian everything, was one of the most respected members of their enclave.

Khristos could not die.

The Shifter flung another fireball into Khristos's chest; the force of the impact lifted his feet off the ground, suspending his body in the air before he slammed down to the hard ground.

Harsh, violent rejection curled in Damian's gut. Blatant refusal to accept what he watched. What his eyes saw, but his mind could not process. Wet trails of liquid streamed down his face unchecked.

His brother rolled to his side, defeat etched into the lines of pain that sprang from his eyes and circled his clenched lips.

The Shifter's deep laugh echoed through the thick air—evil, victorious, merciless. The female's whimpering scream followed. The two sounds at complete odds yet synchronous.

Khristos struggled to lift his torso and brace himself on his elbow. His bleak eyes met Damian's through the flames before he blinked and turned away. Resignation settled across his battered features.

Without warning or giving away any intent, Khristos lifted the sword he still clenched and plunged it through the back and into the heart of the hunched-over female.

She jerked in surprise, her head lifting in reflex to reveal eyes filled with acceptance. Her red lips opened in a silent scream, her strained features growing lax as death closed in. She slumped forward, her long hair falling down to cover her face, the dark veil hiding her last breath as it exited her lungs.

The raging roar from the Shifter overpowered Damian's howl of denial. Disbelief washed through him as he launched himself once again at the fiery wall before him. He threw himself at the flames again and again, each attempt to penetrate the barrier blocked. He kicked at the blaze until his leather boots smoked and hissed.

There was nothing, nothing he could do to stop the inevitable.

The all-consuming madness that engulfed him prevented him from noticing the stench of burning flesh and hair as the fire scorched and smoldered up his back, down his arms and over his now bloody and black hands. The peeling and bloodied skin was invisible to him as every ounce of his attention was focused on his brother.

Khristos slumped back to the ground, his chest heaving in labored breaths. His head was turned away, preventing Damian from seeing his face.

The Shifter stormed to Khristos's side, the rage vibrating off every movement he made. "You will pay for that!"

His low, growling threat was given right before he raised his sword and drove it down to slice through Khristos's limp wrist.

*The fierce movement severed the hand in one swing and removed his brother's last defense.*

*The piercing cry of pain that left Khristos's mouth was only the first, as the Shifter continued around his body, slicing and cutting at will.*

*The fight fizzled out of Damian. All he could do was watch in mute numbness as his brother's life torturously ended.*

*Khristos's pain-filled cries eventually stopped, and the silence that followed felt unnatural. The harsh whispers of the flames as they danced and weaved around the circle mingled with low grunts and throaty laughter of the Shifter as he finished his kill.*

*The enemy stalked around the bloodied, mutilated carcass of his brother. The man's gaze sought and found Damian's outside the circle. His lip curled in vindictive hatred, his eyes hollow and cold.* "Are you ready for this one?"

*Damian's mouth opened in refute, his stomach heaved, his arms reached out to stop the sword, to protect his brother. But it did not matter.*

*There was nothing he could do. And the Shifter knew it.*

*The Shifter gripped his sword with both hands, raised it high and paused as he held Damian's attention.*

"Watch and remember." *His eyes glinted with pure evil.* "It was I, Tubal, leader of the Shifter force. In the vengeance of Gog, it was I who killed this Energen."

*The sharp, metal blade hissed through the air as it was leveled downward at Khristos's neck.*

"Noooo." *Damian's tormented screech of rage left his mouth as he watched his brother's head being severed from his once strong body. The evil rolls of laughter that bounded out of the Shifter's chest were background noise to the roar in Damian's mind.*

*Then there was nothing. The entire world went silent.*

*There was only the muffled sound of his pounding heart as his knees hit the ground. His lungs were raw as if they had been burned from the inside out. The pain was excruciating, almost debilitating.*

Pure and true hatred seeped into his skin, into every pore of his body and filled him like nothing else ever had. He stumbled to his feet, prepared to fight. For revenge. To kill the bastard who had taken his brother.

The Shifter smiled as he wiped the sweat from his brow. "Are you ready for your turn?"

The muted taunt barely penetrated Damian's senses as he watched the enemy remove Khristos's blood from his sword with slow, deliberate swipes on the grass.

Tubal. The name was forever engraved in Damian's mind.

The circling wall of flames that had barred him from helping his brother withered and smoldered out with a slight hiss.

Instantly, Damian charged. All rational thought was gone. The burning need for revenge blinding him to everything but the man standing passively before him. Kill him.

The Shifter held his ground as Damian stormed toward him. The cruel grin curved his lips, and his eyes sparked with anticipation.

Damian lifted his sword, a guttural, primal growl heaving up from the depths of his chest. Triumph sparked in the Shifter's eyes, then he disappeared. Dissipating before Damian's sword could cut through his chest.

The downward momentum of Damian's weapon carried onward, pulling him forward as the metal sliced into the ground right between Khristos's neck and severed head.

Damian froze. Shock paralyzed him before he recoiled, stumbling as he choked back the bile that rose in his throat. He felt more than saw the other bodies as they formed around him on the perimeter of the circle. The Guard had arrived.

Damian tried to dissipate and give chase to the enemy, but he was too weak. His body too burned, his energy too diminished to port and follow Tubal's energy trail. No! Not now, he needed to follow. Needed to avenge.

He cursed the flames, his own weaknesses.

He felt his muscles weaken and his bones collapse, then the hard grit of the dirt as it bit into the tender flesh of his burnt hands and cheek. Through the vacuum that consumed him, he heard Xander delivering orders, sensed the movement as the men jumped to his bidding.

The grass whispered slightly as the booted feet approached his downed form. Damian kept his eyes closed when he heard the soft stretching of leather as the owner of the boots crouched.

"I do not understand, Damian." Xander's leather gloved hand enclosed his upper arm. "Why would you kill your brother?"

"No!" Damian roared, suddenly finding strength. He wrestled his arm from the hold and scrambled backwards away from his friend. His gaze pivoted to his brother's mutilated form, to his sword lying between the severed head and body of his brother. "I did not kill Khristos. How could you think that?"

# Chapter Eighteen

Damian took a deep, steadying breath, the stench of burnt flesh gradually leaving his nostrils. He rubbed his eyes, pushing the memories back along with the acid that burned in his throat. Slowly, he lowered his hand and returned to the present.

Amber sat beside him, having moved from the end of the bed at some point during his story. One hand rested on his knee, the heat of her palm warming his skin through the material of his jeans. Her energy filled him, pooling into him from the one simple contact point.

Like always.

"They blamed you?" she said softly, her probing eyes searching his face.

"Yes."

"Why didn't they believe you?"

He looked down, away, anywhere but into her too-trusting eyes. "The first reason was the mark." He lifted his hand to show the white dragon on the back of it. "My mark changed to this that night. When I was born, I had the mark of the eagle."

Flipping his hand around, he stared absently at the innocuous mark. "Well, this mark minus the wings. Those didn't appear until this morning, after I met you."

His dragon stirred at the mention of the wings, fluttering them lightly as if to taunt him with the appendages.

Amber shifted, pulling her legs under her as she leaned forward and grasped his hand. She smoothed her fingers over the dragon mark, causing the dragon to arch and growl in contentment.

"How did the wings get there?"

He shrugged and rubbed his free hand through his hair. "Just another in the growing list of questions."

"What was the second reason?" She lifted her head to look at him. "You said the first reason was the mark, what was the second?"

Sheer force of will kept his leg from bouncing in agitation. His lips tightened as he fought back the bitterness. "The energy. The energy said I helped to kill Khristos. That I had a hand in his death."

"How?"

"I don't know," he bit out, the anger and frustration hurling their ugly venom at her. She flinched. He ripped his hand from her tender grasp and anchored his fists in his hair. "I don't know. Don't you see? The energy lied. Somehow it spoke untruths about me. It manipulated the entire enclave into believing something that was not—is not—true."

Her warm palm fluttered to his bare chest.

His breath froze as a thousand bolts of lightning fired into him. He dropped his hands and watched her, wary, uncertain. Vulnerable.

Exposed.

All fucking emotions he didn't want to contend with, but she blew him wide open. She forced him to confront them.

She tilted her head to the side, her hair falling in a waterfall down her shoulder. Her eyes narrowed in concentration as if she was listening to something.

"I don't hear it," she said quietly. "I hear only the truth in what you just told me. I hear your pain at the betrayal. At all you have lost. But I do not hear the lies."

"Then you are the only one." The defeat in his voice did not surprise him. After so many years, the thought of anyone believing him was a long-forgotten dream.

"Maybe you only need the right one."

"What do you mean?"

Ever so slightly, her palm smoothed back and forth over his chest. Thoughtful, exploratory. "What do you believe, Damian? Do you believe you are responsible for your brother's death?"

On reflex, he shook his head, but halted abruptly. Did he? Damn. "I could have done more," he finally said. "He shouldn't have died while I stood by and did nothing."

"What could you have done?" Her inquiry was probing, but not pushy. The impact of her question was eased by the softness in her voice.

"I don't know...anything but stand there and watch."

"Do you *really* believe that?" Her hand stilled on his chest. "That you did nothing? Or is the guilt keeping you from seeing the truth?"

This time he was the one who flinched. The immediate denial was poised at the end of his tongue. Maybe it was the lack of judgment that mingled with the simmer of dare in her penetrating eyes that halted his automatic response. There was no cruelty in her words, only a question he wanted to deflect. It would be easier to deny and dodge—the tactic he'd been employing with dismal results for way too long.

What was it with this woman? A day in her presence, and he was purging his soul. He needed to man up and pull away. Put the emotional wall back in place before the barricade was permanently destroyed.

But he couldn't stop. The energy pushed at him to trust her. Believe in her and what she offered. Did he dare trust it?

Did he dare believe again?

Forcing his jaw to relax, he finally admitted, "Of course I feel guilt. He was my brother. The cherished and honored heir." He thrust a finger at his chest. "I was supposed to protect him. Guard him. And I failed." Failed. Miserably.

"It sounds to me like he failed." She didn't falter despite the murderous glare he sent at her. "He lost the battle, not you. He took the life of the female, not you."

"What do you know?" He pushed her hand from his chest, her touch too intimate. His defenses too fragile to stand hard against her attack.

She clasped her hands in her lap and looked down. After a moment, she tilted her head up to look at him with shuttered eyes. "I know what it's like to bear the shame of someone else's actions. I know how hard it is to hold your head up against false accusations. I know the pain of being ostracized for something you had no control over."

And just like that, his defenses threw down their battle weapons in a surprising defeat. Her quiet admission stunned him. Humbled him with its blatant honesty. She did understand. Not just hypothetically, but from experience. And she waited for him, every muscle stiff from the exposure.

He cupped her face, his thumb caressing the soft skin of her cheek. She relaxed and pressed her head into his palm. Again, the vulnerability that hid just below her surface glimmered in the faint light of the room.

"There is much I don't know about you," he murmured.

She looked away, briefly, before her spine straightened and her gaze returned to his. "Who was she? The woman your brother was protecting, then killed?"

Accepting the topic volley back to him, he sighed and dropped his hand. "I don't know. No one ever told me."

"Do you know why he killed her?"

Another shrug. "I can only assume it was to keep her from the Shifter."

"Tubal?" Her brow furrowed in thought. He could practically see the wheels of her analytical mind turning. All the information turning and tumbling in her head as she tried to make sense of it all. "The same man who attacked us tonight?"

"Yes."

"The same man who wants me?"

His jaw tightened. "Yes."

Understanding dawned on her face. He stiffened, anticipating what was next. Pity was for losers. A worthless

177

emotion that would make him feel smaller than a weeping toddler.

But it wasn't pity that gleamed in her eyes. If anything, it was a deadly intent that almost mirrored what he felt.

She leaned in, her eyes narrowing. "The same man who claims I'm a Shifter?"

What? Where'd that come from? He sat up. "There is no way you're a Shifter, Amber. There is not an evil thread in you," he insisted adamantly. His own eyes narrowed. "When did he say you were a Shifter?"

"It was the woman, Kassandra," she said very calmly, as if none of it were disturbing to her. "The one who took Tubal away. While you were passed out in the tower, she came back. She claims Tubal wants me because I'm a Shifter."

"Not. A. Chance. In. Hell." The anger fired in him, immediate and all-consuming, hardening his voice. Sealing his resolve. There was no way Tubal would ever get his hands on her.

A conspiratorial half-smile curved over her lips. "Then next time, we'll need to ensure that he doesn't get away." Mischief sparked her features. "Of course, next time, I just might take him out for you. It seems my little flamethrowing trick packs a mighty punch." She wiggled her fingers in a taunting jibe.

The tension left him. His head sagged back against the headboard, a smile curling the edges of his mouth.

"Getting cocky already?" He lifted an eyebrow in question. "But there is the small detail that you must remove his head in order to truly kill him."

Her grin fell, her face blanched. She sat back and licked her lips. "Yeah. Okay. So maybe I'll just leave the actual killing part to you."

He laughed. A full chest roll that startled them both. Impulsively, he reached out and pulled her tight against his side. Her eyes opened wide. Surprised by the move or the contact?

"Deal," he said, his attention following the tip of her pink tongue as it slicked across her lips. "It's my job to slay the dragons for you."

"Ah, speaking of dragons." Her eyes narrowed again as she poked him in the chest. "You could have warned me about that."

He chuckled. "And you would have believed me? They're kind of one of those things most people need to see to believe."

Her eyes rolled up and she shook her head. "And levitation, fireballs and teleporting aren't? I think I'm pretty much past the whole seeing to believe standard."

"And could you have said that five hours ago?" His question brought home just how quickly everything had transpired. How much she had endured and absorbed in a day. He lifted a hand to her cheek before he let his fingers trail through the soft strands of her hair. He couldn't get enough of the silky mass. "You've endured much today. And yet you can still joke with me. How?"

She stretched out her legs and laid her head on the uninjured side of his chest. Her fingers traced a light path around the mostly healed wound on his shoulder, the soft strokes heating the desire that flamed to life at her contact.

"Because it's you," she finally said, the words releasing faint whispers of air against his skin. "I understand now why you don't trust the energy. What it's telling us. But for me, it hasn't lied. For whatever reason, in the course of a truly messed up day, I have come to believe in what it's telling me." She took a deep breath and released it. "And it's telling me to trust you. It's telling me to be with you."

She pushed away so she could look in his eyes. "Do you know why?"

Hell, no. He had no idea why the energy would give him such a gift. After all it had taken from him, it was now handing him her. A treasure he wanted to keep.

One he would be stupid to throw away.

His arm tightened around her. "No. I don't," he answered honestly. "I don't understand any of it. But how could I doubt a gift as perfect as you?"

She looked down, the quiet echoing around them. "I'm not perfect."

He tilted her chin back up. "Neither am I. No one is. But as a gift into my life—you are perfect." The doubt in her eyes shot a hole right through his heart.

"Who hurt you?" he probed gently.

"Who hasn't?" she replied so quickly he knew it was honesty, not sarcasm speaking. Just as quickly, she tried to push away from him.

He held tight. "I won't hurt you, Amber." She stilled, then slowly met his gaze, the hesitation another shot to his heart. "Not anymore. Never again." He brushed her hair over her shoulder. Her hand fisted on his chest.

Never again did he want to hurt her.

Against his better judgment, he leaned in and kissed her, his restraint holding him back as he waited for her. Thankfully, she didn't hesitate or pull away. She met his lips, opening to him. God, she was so innocent. So untainted.

But her lips were strong, sure. Not questioning or doubting. Her tongue licked over his bottom lip in a soft stroke of invitation.

All questions of right or wrong were crushed under the petal-soft touch. He pulled her tighter to his chest and entered her welcoming mouth. He almost groaned under the hot onslaught, the tentative brush of her tongue as it met his, the slight hint of cinnamon that filled his taste buds.

She moaned sweetly as her fingers laced around his neck to pull his lips tighter against her own. He could feel the passion unfolding within her, the blossoms spreading under the warm glow that fired between them. Through them. She invaded his mouth and he let her explore. He gloried in the swipe of her tongue, the little nips and licks over his lips, the hard crush when she plunged into the depths of his mouth to reach every hidden crevice.

She was hot, sweet. Beautiful.

His hands fisted in her hair to keep them from going to the soft breasts that brushed torturously against his chest. His cock throbbed in hard demand under the tight confines of his jeans. A demand that had never really receded, but was now screaming to be filled. By her.

But he held back. Afraid to push her, to scare her away. She vibrated with vulnerability when it came to sex, and he wouldn't rush her.

*Fuck.* The shaman's words blasted into mind. *His virgin bride.*

Was it possible? Was it not? He should stop.

Suddenly, with the stealth of a seasoned warrior, Amber shifted to straddle his hips. Her lips never left his as she ravaged his mouth. Her hands ran up his chest, stopping to brush over the taut peaks of his nipples, sending sharp nails of need through him. When the warm juncture between her thighs settled on his erection, he was lost. She moaned and rocked gently on his lap.

Blistering desire stunned him senseless. Her growing passion matched by her increasing confidence shattered all thought. All resistance.

He was lost to her.

He tasted so good. Better than anything that had ever crossed her lips. Like spice and desire. The sensations burst inside Amber as she came to life with a need, a want so strong she couldn't contain it. Hot flames, a pulsing burn, an undeniable ache between her legs right where his rigid cock met her body.

She rocked on it again. She was unable to stop the instinctive movement. God, it felt so good. He felt so good. His mouth was hot, welcoming. There was no demand. No pushing. It was all about her. What she wanted.

He knew. Somehow, he knew what she needed. Let her lead even though she had no idea where she was going.

And she didn't feel shy or insecure at all. Confidence reigned dominant within her. He groaned and thrust almost unwillingly upward into her aching core.

He pulled his mouth from hers, his hands fisting in her hair pushing her back so he could rest his forehead against hers. Heavy breaths panted thick in the quiet.

"Amber," he groaned, a deep, throaty sound. "If you don't stop now, I won't be able to."

She pushed in to lick his lips. He groaned again. "I don't want you to," she admitted. No, stopping was the last thing she wanted.

Finally, she wanted it all. Wanted to know what was at the end of all this feeling. At the end of the desire and passion that burned in her like a raging inferno.

He pushed her back until their eyes met. He stared into her, looking deeper than any man ever had before. "Are you sure? Do you know where this is going?"

Unwanted, the heat spread over her face. "I'm not a child, Damian, nor am I naïve. And I know exactly where this is going." She looked him over then threw out the challenge. "Do you?"

He inhaled sharply, his nostrils flaring. In anger? Desire?

In the next instant she was flat on her back, Damian looming over her, his body pressed hard between her legs. The challenged accepted.

"I would never think you naïve," he growled, the intensity in his eyes burning her soul. "It's your innocence that I question. I cannot give it back to you if I take it."

*Ping.* The lock around her heart broke apart into a thousand pieces.

This man was all hers.

"I don't want it back," she whispered, brushing her fingers over his chiseled cheek. "Ever. It's yours." How did he know she was a virgin? A small part of her wondered, but it didn't matter right then. Not then. She looped her legs around his thighs and pulled him tighter to her body.

"Fuck," he whispered, his eyes closing, his arms shaking. "You're going to kill me, Amber."

"Then kill me too," she said before she pulled his mouth back to hers. She wanted this. Needed this. Him.

There was no holding back this time. Damian took her mouth, plundering the hot depths like a man possessed. His tongue sought hers, stroking, guiding, stoking the flame that burned below.

His energy flooded her, pulsing out to her limbs in time with the rapid thumping of her heart. In time with his until they were unified. Synchronized to a single beat.

Incredible.

God. She was swimming in feeling. Sensation. Her hands brushed down the hard muscles of his back. So broad. Defined. Smooth.

His mouth left hers to trail a line of kisses down her jaw until his hot, wet tongue traced her ear. She sucked in a breath before a moan tore from her throat, a deep, guttural sound that pooled up from the depths of her chest. Her feelings bordered on desperate.

She wanted everything without knowing exactly what she wanted.

His hand smoothed up the sides of her ribs, under her shirt until it cupped her breast. She arched into his touch. "God, Damian." She tossed her head to the side as he nipped her earlobe, his hand skimming across her nipple. The sensation shot straight to the hot spot between her legs. "I need..." What? Something. "More..." It was all she could get out.

Growling, he pulled back to slide both hands under her shirt. The material bunched on his wrist as his callused palms moved up her sides. The roughened hands of a warrior, not an executive. How had she ever believed he was just a CEO? The fire that burned in his eyes was all fighter. Conqueror.

"Lift," he demanded. She did, arching her back and lifting her arms until her shirt was removed. The flame in his eyes scorched her, the hot desire smoothing over her naked flesh as his gaze slowly perused the new offering. "Beautiful," he murmured absently as he lightly grazed the lace edging of her bra. The soft touch sent chills through her and caused her breath to hitch.

She felt beautiful and she absolutely loved the feel of him looking at her. Him. The first man to ever see her so exposed. Yet there were no insecurities. No doubt within her at all.

Only need. Want.

Her bird cooed deep in its throat and arched its head, the satisfaction emanating out of the vibrations in its chest to resonate within her. The stone burned, heavy and welcomed between her breasts. The energy pulsed around it, around them and into her.

Damian's finger circled around the outer ring of the pendant, trailing sparks of liquid fire in its wake. His small homage to the entity that had united them. The stone glimmered in the dim light, the colors dancing and rolling with the waves of energy.

Finally, his finger moved aside to dip below the lacey material and ever so slowly brushed across the hard tip of her aching nipple. She gasped, arched, the lightening hot ping of need tightening in her core. The simple touch was amazing.

He smiled. "You like that."

Not a question. Not one she could answer anyway. Her voice was stuck. Frozen as he removed the material completely, discarding her bra and baring her breasts fully. Her nipples stiffened, puckering under the heat of his stare, under the brush of cool air.

She couldn't move. The anticipation locked her immobile.

Finally, he cupped her breasts, pressing lightly before his fingers reached up to pluck then squeeze the rigid peaks. Her back came off the mattress, a silent moan opening her mouth. Her body sang with feeling at the sharp pleasure-pain that shot through her.

This. This is what she'd wanted. What she'd waited for.

But more. Definitely more.

He watched her, passion etched over his hard features, his lips ripe from their kisses. He stilled and held her gaze.

"There is so much I want to do to you, Amber." His rough, gravel-edged voice flowed over her like an ancient mating call. "With you. Will you let me?"

He asked. Her heart broke wide open, the exposed feelings thumping in acceptance within her heart. He asked. It was a simple courtesy that meant so much to her. More than he could possibly know. Offered freely, not because of her past, but because that was the kind of man he was.

Her hands smoothed up the powerful arms that bracketed her body. Over the rounded muscles of his biceps, shoulders, then down the hard plain of his chest until they reached the rippled edging of his abs. Only then did she meet his eyes. Eyes that freely displayed the passion and desire that smoldered within him. Eyes that held so much more that she was afraid to define. Afraid to hope for.

"Yes," she whispered. "Show me."

His head dipped, his eyes closing in a brief silent acknowledgment before he dropped to seal his mouth over her nipple. *God.* Heaven. Pleasure. Her mind blanked. Feeling took over everything. Hot, moist. Unbelievable.

Her head tossed, her hands clenched in his hair. His teeth grazed the edge of the peak, then bit down. Her legs tightened, spasmed around his to pull his hard erection against her throbbing sex. Pleasure. Pain. Hot, aching need. Everywhere.

Damian bathed one nipple then the other with lavish attention. Stroking, nipping, sucking until she teetered on the edge of exploding. It was incredible. The fresh scent of the earthy shampoo, the dark edge of pine and thunder bathed her nostrils. She squirmed under him, unable to hold still. Wanting to absorb him.

Have him.

Finally, his head lifted and she pulled him to her mouth, needing the heat and the connection that bound him to her. His tongue fought with hers, the battle even, the sparring equally matched. His hard chest rubbed over her wet and begging nipples, the pressure shooting to her womb. God, she ached.

As if he read her thoughts, Damian's hand moved down her waist to run over her bare skin at the edge of her jeans.

"Damian," she breathed, arching her hips to meet his hand.

"Last chance, Amber."

She yanked his mouth back to hers, showing him how much she wanted him. She pushed him back and held his gaze. "Don't you dare stop." She would die if he stopped.

He reared back, kneeling between her legs. His hands brushed her stomach, circled her belly button then unfastened her jeans. "I wouldn't think of it."

She watched, entranced. Her chest heaved with each breath, the anticipation mounting. The light rasp of her zipper purred through the room. She moaned, her fingers stroking over the tender flesh of her stomach before they gripped the hard muscles on his forearms. The muscles flexed and tightened under her grasp.

Sweat gleamed on his skin in the pale glow of the bedside light. His chest expanded, contracted in a deep cadence that matched her own. Slowly, he pulled the material over her hips, down her legs, the brush of the fabric a gentle caress against her hyper-sensitive skin. Reverently, he looked at her, his gaze passing over the length of her body.

His fingers hooked under the edge of her panties, his eyes lifting to ask a final, unspoken question. She held his gaze and shifted her hips up in answer. He inhaled, then slid the final obstacle down her legs. The cool air brushed over her, clashing against the heat that burned within her. She shivered.

"Again, beautiful," he said, his searing look saying more than the words. Fully exposed to him, she had never felt more secure. His hands smoothed up her legs. A kiss dropped on her knee. Her inner thigh. *Oh God.* The top of her pubic bone. Her legs flinched closed slightly.

"Trust me, Amber," he breathed across her lower stomach. His hot breath shot straight to her womb, tightening the ache that burned below. She squirmed, her feet rubbing anxiously into the soft velvet of the duvet.

"I do," she panted. "I just want..." She tossed her head. "I don't know..."

His fingers pressed between her legs, one strong pad circling her vagina then running up to rub against her clitoris. Her back sprang off the mattress; white lights flashed behind her closed eyelids as the sensation bolted through her sex, over her womb and nailed her heart.

"That," she panted. "That..."

His finger pressed harder, circled, toyed with the ache. "Have you ever had an orgasm, Amber?"

*Oh God.* Did he really just ask her that? Her mind grasped for answers, battling against the sensations as his fingers continued to play with her most private area.

"Yes," she finally admitted, the honesty breathing out of her. No place to hide. "But never with..." She couldn't finish.

His finger plunged into her inner canal. Hard, demanding. A small scream left her mouth, her hips thrusting up to meet the invasion. The pleasure.

"But, never what?" he demanded, his voice harsh, yet soft. "Finish it, Amber. Say it."

She couldn't think. The pressure built with each thrust of his finger. Then his lips closed on her, his tongue stroked over her pulsing clit and she was lost.

"Say it," he growled against her, the vibrations echoing through her. She writhed uncontrollably under him.

"A man," she finally panted. "Never with...anyone." He nipped her inner thigh, the bite shooting a tantalizing mix of pain and pleasure into her core.

"You're killing me, beauty." Then he was gone, his heat removed, his fingers absent.

"No," she cried out, reaching for him. Needing him to continue. She bolted upright, ready to follow only to freeze. His jeans dropped, and he straightened, beautifully naked.

She swallowed.

Gorgeous. Hard, naked flesh. Head to toe solid man. Warrior.

The energy hummed around them. The anticipation pulling tight as he knelt on the bed then edged closer. Sweat broke and trickled enticingly down her chest, between her breasts. She licked her lips and reached. Unable to stop. Not wanting to stop.

To hell with not knowing what to do. Instinct controlled her now, every action primal. Her hand lifted, then hovered over his hard erection. His breath ceased, every muscled tightened.

"Touch it," he ordered.

She did. Her hand shook before it closed around the velvet skin. So hard underneath. She was in awe. Enthralled. She stroked it, slowly up, down. His breath hissed. His stomach clenched, his muscle rippling at the sudden movement. She stroked again, her motions dictated by nature. His cock was thick, long and unbelievably alluring to her. She wanted to lick it. Explore like he did her. She moved her lips toward the head, anxious to taste the rounded crown, the soft skin.

"*Stop.*" His hands grasped beneath her arms and threw her back to the bed. She bounced lightly before he landed hard and hot on top of her. "Another time. If you do that, I'll come before I get in you, love." His kiss branded her, burying the word she swore she heard.

No time to think. To ponder.

His hard cock brushed her inner thigh, smooth and probing against her tender flesh as it inched upward in time with the thrust of his tongue, the arch of his back. Her legs spread wider, opening to him. Begging for the next crest.

The soft head of his erection rubbed over her opening, teasing then retreating. She moaned and pulled on Damian's shoulders, a silent plea for what was so close.

He broke the kiss, sweat dripping from his forehead, his breathing haggard, quick. "It'll hurt some," he stated, regret edging the words.

It didn't matter. Pain was negligible at this point. "I'll be fine," she reassured him. "Right now I feel nothing but pleasure. I want this."

"Amber," he part growled, part moaned. "Too good for me."

"Never," she denied. "Just right for you."

He cursed under his breath, a small exclamation of submission, then shifted to run his fingers through her pussy once again. A quick swipe, followed by a slow circle over her sensitive clit. God. Could anything feel better?

He groaned again. "You're so wet. I need you. Now."

She spread her legs wider. "Please." She wasn't beneath begging. She just needed what he offered. Her entire body ached for the final peak. That final sensation that he was withholding.

Finally, she felt his erection edge into her opening. He paused. The significance burned in his eyes and was communicated in the trembling of his shoulders and the measured intrusion that tested his restraint. She wanted more. Instinctively, she knew there was more.

"Just do it," she insisted as she wrapped her legs around him. "I need more. I need all of you."

He reared his head back then jerked his hips and surged completely into her. Her muscles flexed, her arms and legs clutched him to her, holding him tight as the pain flared. It hurt, burned, but he felt so good. He held her close, his entire body bound to her. "You're incredible." His low words barely penetrated the fog of her brain. "Hot, tight...so fucking incredible."

It was incredible, full, intimate. She trembled, the feeling wracking through her as her muscles stretched to accept him. Amazing. God, it was so damn amazing.

Then he moved, shifted his hips and pulled out until just the tip remained within her. The feeling, the rioting sparks of sensation soothed away the pain. He thrust back into her, the sparks exploding into a full inferno of new stimulation. She gasped, her breath locked deep in her chest until he repeated the motion. The air returned on a throaty moan that sounded more animal than human.

Thinking stopped—all that mattered was the feeling. The mounting crests of excitement, of pleasure that grew with each thrust of his hips. Incredible wasn't good enough. It was so much more.

The energy pummeled through her. His, hers, the stone. All meshing and blending until it pulsed in a demanding rhythm of desire.

Of belonging.

Damian thrust into her in time with the throb of the energy. His body matched the ancient beat, uniting them with the power that swirled around them. Stroking over her skin like a physical brush until every nerve was aching for release.

"Come, Amber," Damian demanded, reaching between them to rub her clit. "Come now. With me."

And she did. In a shattering burst of light and feeling, Amber soared along with her bird. Her muscles clenched, her back arched into Damian's hard chest. Wave after wave of pleasure shattered over her.

A startled moan left her lips. He matched her groan and buried his head in her neck, then bound her to his chest in a tight grasp. He shuddered and came with her in a warm gush of energy. Power.

The golden light engulfed them. Binding them as it wrapped around their joined bodies in a blaze of pulsing heat that lifted her even higher, threw her over the edge and let her sail.

The light shattered, the energy parting then exploding outward in an atomic burst that pushed against her skin, electrified it until even the air excited her. Damian's arms tightened around her as the energy tightened its hold and cocooned them in safety. In that instant, she felt her energy alter. The stone pulsed, clamped tightly between their bodies, one side touching each of them. Like a channel, it pulled a part of her through the stone while simultaneously feeding part of Damian into her.

The siphoning of energy, a true blending of power, of essence, blasted through her and sent her on another ride of pure, undiluted pleasure. He was truly, unquestionably hers.

Vaguely, she registered the quick flash of fire followed by pain that seared the back of her hand before her world darkened.

"Damian," she whispered, her body wrapped around his as the golden light pulled her into unconsciousness.

Distantly, the angry roar of a beast registered through the fog of her brain. The feral tones broke through the energy, leaving a black streak of ice in its wake. The coldness pushed against the heat, driving frigid, hard rivets at the layer of warmth. Amber shivered, small bumps of trepidation stinging her heated flesh.

In warning or invitation?

# Chapter Nineteen

Damian shifted to the side, pulling Amber against his chest. The fog slowly cleared from his head. The darkness receded as his senses gradually returned to functioning. What in the hell just happened?

Amber moaned against his chest, the vibration raking down his side where her body pressed against his. The air cooled his skin and brought with it more clarity.

Something more than sex had just happened between them.

He rubbed a hand over his eyes and blinked away the last of the haze. Amber arched lazily against him, stretched like a satisfied cat, then cuddled up to rest her head on his shoulder. He winced, prepared for the pain, as she'd forgotten about his shoulder wound. But there was none. He looked down and saw that his skin was completely healed. Not even a hint of a scar remained.

Un-fucking-believable.

His head thumped against the pillow, his thoughts misfiring around the recent turn of events. Her fingers glided over the lingering moisture on his chest, sending an instant flash of pleasure straight to his cock. Damn thing should be down for the count after what just happened, but it instantly twitched in a valiant attempt at revival.

Cursing silently, Damian pulled away against her grumbled sigh of protest. He returned from the bathroom, a warm washcloth and towel in hand.

She looked up, then blushed from head to toe as she took in his intention.

"I can..." She trailed off as her voice faded, her gaze dropping to look at the bed. Her legs curled up, but his hand on her hip stopped her from turning away.

"So can I," he said gently. Just like with her hair, he wanted to take care of her. She kept her eyes adverted as he spread her legs. Her breath hitched and her blush deepened as he gently washed away the mix of blood and semen that stained her inner thighs.

Blood. The sight of it against her sex slammed home that he'd taken her virginity. Given freely, but still gone.

*A virgin bride by his side.*

Doubt tightened around the ache in his chest. There was no going back now. But had he done the right thing? Would she regret it later?

Returning to the bathroom, he cleaned off the remains of her virginity from his own body, proof positive that the deed had been committed by him. A deed he could not regret.

Truth—it didn't matter if she regretted it. He wasn't letting her go.

Discarding the soiled cloths, he returned to the bed and clicked off the small pool of light from the bedside lamp. He dragged back the covers then climbed in and pulled Amber to his side. She stiffened before she tentatively relaxed within his hold, one slow increment at a time. He pulled the duvet over them and brushed his lips across her forehead.

The quiet clashed around them. The ruffle of the sheets, her soft sigh, an errant drip of the faucet—each sound settled into the darkness that cloaked them. Between them, the stone glowed. A soft shimmer of violet, white and gold that emanated waves of warmth against his flesh.

"Is the day over?" she asked so quietly he barely heard her.

"What do you mean?"

Her fingers skimmed over his chest, her soft caress returning. "A lot has happened today," she said in the same low tone. "I was just wondering if the day was over or if I should expect something else."

He chuckled, unable to stop himself. His hand stroked through her hair, then brushed across her cheek. "Yes, the day is over," he reassured her. "I think we've both handled enough for one day."

She sighed and finally relaxed completely into him, curling around him in a link of belonging.

His dragon danced lightly in joy before it turned in a circle and settled down with a contented sigh. The wings fluttered, soft and light, before they curled in and rested.

"Damian?"

"Yes?"

She ducked her head. A pale streak of light from the bathroom provided just enough illumination for him to see the soft flesh of her bottom lip disappear between her teeth. "Is it always like that?"

He swallowed the chuckle this time. He tipped her head up until she was looking at him, her face once again tinged with a faint blush of red. "No, beauty. It's never been like that for me."

Her eyes widened before a soft smile curled over her lips.

"This was something special," he affirmed. "Something even I don't fully comprehend. But I wouldn't take it back."

He cupped her face, the possessiveness coursing through him in a tempestuous fury. He held her gaze, his fingers flexing on the tender skin of her cheek. "You're mine, Amber." Not a question in his mind on that. "There's no going back. I won't give you up. Not after that."

She sucked in a large gulp of air, fear and a slight mix of apprehension skidding across her face before she slowly released her breath. She lifted herself up and brushed her fingers over his lips. He held still and waited for her to process what he'd said and come to an understanding on her own terms.

"I'm not sure I like your choice of words." She tilted her head, her brows dropped in thought. "But I like the feeling they bring. I know I can't go back... I don't think I even want to anymore."

Relief flooded him as she peered into his eyes, searching for something before her face lightened, the spark of mischief returning to her golden eyes. "I'm okay belonging to you. Just as long as you know that you're also mine."

Quiet acceptance. So like her in so many ways. Yet there was more.

She wouldn't stand behind or before him. She would be at his side—equal. She'd just offered him a precious gift that no one had ever given him.

He pulled her in, holding her a breath away from his lips. "Deal," he agreed roughly, before lifting to meet her sweet, swollen lips.

She yielded under his mouth, accepting him. His heart beat hard and insistent as he surrendered to the energy. Relenting to the insistent push and allowing himself to trust in it—in her.

He drew back from her soft lips and the tempting warmth of her mouth "We need to rest," he told her as he tucked her head against his chest. "As much as I would love to finish that kiss, tomorrow is another day of unknown. We need to be prepared for whatever comes."

She gave a single nod of acceptance, her hair brushing like silk across his chest. "I'm not afraid. Not anymore. Not with you."

He pulled her tight, hugging her to him in a sudden, desperate need to be what she needed. His eyes clamped shut as he silently willed the energy to be right. Her faith and trust in him was a gift he would never betray.

The energy within him burned, hot and vibrant as if new fuel had been added to a dying flame. Fresh, young and full of expectation. It flowed through, humming a song of life. Of new beginnings.

Of second chances.

A chance he vowed to honor.


Warmth encased her, surrounding her with an essence of security that she'd never felt before. Amber didn't want it to end. It chased away the cold that always lingered just around the edge of her consciousness. Instinctively, she snuggled closer to the heat and reveled in the sun-baked feel that enveloped her.

Beneath her, the body she was wrapped around stirred under her wiggling. Her eyelids flew open, the movement instantly eliminating the just-waking-up haze. The events of the last day crashed into her respite, shattering the quiet of her mind with the clarity of light. Her head flipped up and her gaze locked with the Damian's dark eyes.

"Morning, beauty."

His deep voice rumbled in his chest and vibrated into hers, which was spread unabashedly across his strong, bare one. Her stomach knotted, the warm flush of embarrassment blooming across her cheeks. It was stupid to feel shy after what happened between them last night, but years of insecurities fostered by her sheltered existence could not be dropped overnight.

Swallowing, she forced herself to smile and hold his gaze. "Morning."

The back of his fingers brushed against her warm cheek. "Still the blush," he said, the slight note of humor matched the teasing spark in his eyes.

"I think it's much like the hair." She admitted with a shrug. "Just a part of me."

"And just as beautiful."

The heat deepened. "You did that on purpose," she accused with a smile. The pleasure at the light banter spread through her like a slow-moving river, drifting down her until she was immersed in the calm waters.

"Just speaking the truth," he defended.

Giving in to impulse, she leaned down and nipped him lightly on the chest, finding the play new and wonderful. Surprisingly, she felt no shame about what actually happened last night. Instead, she felt whole. Finally.

"Hey," he admonished, flinching away before he rubbed at the little bite mark. "Be careful what you start here, beauty. I can take you down faster than you can blink."

"That's what I'm counting on," she taunted, adding a suggestive lift of her eyebrows, unsure where the coyness was coming from, but going with it anyway. It was freeing and, for once, pure fun.

As quickly as the previous night, she was on her back with him looming above her. Only this time, it was minus the clothing. Every inch of his gorgeous body was pressed intimately to hers. Including the hard length of his erection pressed firmly against her stomach.

Damian looked down at her, intent clear in his smoky gaze. "You only had to ask."

She laughed, the happiness bubbling out of her. "But the other way was much more fun."

"You're a minx," he said through his own laughter.

"No," she denied, flipping her arm up to show him the back of her hand. "I'm a bird. Remember?"

"*Shit.*" Damian's exclamation snapped the levity out of the moment.

He dropped his smile, his face hardening as he grabbed her hand and yanked her with him into a sitting position. "When did this happen?"

"What?" she asked, quickly tucking the sheet under her arms to cover her naked breasts. "You saw that yesterday."

"No. *Look.*" He lifted her hand up so she could see the mark. "When did *this* happen?"

She gaped in disbelief at the bird that was now intimately entwined around a winged dragon.

Damian's dragon.

The two animals looked at each other, their heads almost touching. Their wings were spread behind them before their lower bodies twisted together, the long, scaled dragon's tail wrapping around the feathery tail of the bird. The spiked end of the dragon's tail looped in a circle around her wrist like a bracelet, locking them in place. The dominant color on both the dragon and the bird was still white, but both were now shot through with stark streaks of violet and gold.

Just like the colors of the stone.

Quickly, she grabbed Damian's hand and held it next to her own. His breath hissed as they both stared dumbstruck at the now matching marks on the backs of their hands.

"Shit." Damian mumbled, bemusement lightening the curse. His hand fisted, causing the mark to flex and ripple over his skin. The tattoo-style mark was perfectly blended, the two animals equal in strength and form. Unified.

"How?" she whispered, too in awe to speak any louder. Tentatively, she reached with her other hand to skim over the newly formed mark. Like before, her skin was still soft and smooth where the mark was.

"Hell if I know." He chuckled, then finally relaxed his fist and brushed his fingers over the mark on his hand. Instantly, she felt his touch as if he were stroking her hand, causing a wave of goose bumps to flow up her arm. The bird cooed softly and wrapped itself even tighter around the dragon. Even though the mark remained unmoving on her hand, Amber felt the movement and emotion through the energy that vibrated within her. The dragon tucked its head and gently rubbed its snout over the soft-feathered cheek of the bird.

"What do these mean?" It was a question she'd been meaning to ask for a while.

He looked at her, his brows lowering. "You don't know?" The doubt registered in his eyes.

"How would I know? The bird just appeared on my hand eight weeks ago when I touched this damn stone." She grabbed the stone and lifted it off her chest to let it twirl from the chain in front of her.

"I bet that was quite the surprise."

"Yeah, just a little." She let the stone fall back down to plunk against the sheets that stretched over her breasts. Missing the heat, needing the comfort it brought, she lifted the cloth away and slid the pendant under the material until it rested against her skin in the valley of her breasts.

Damian looked down at the marks and shook his head as if he was trying to figure them out as well. After a long period of quiet contemplation, he explained, "Everyone in the Energy races is born with a mark on their hand. Both Energen and Shifter. A mark of belonging. A statement of power. The mark appears as a two-dimensional, unchanging image. A standard, flat tattoo of sorts. But to the people of the Energy races, it is actually as much a part of us as the hand itself. As you probably know by now." He shot her a quick look. "I can assume that you've felt its response, the movement, the messages it sends to you. To us, the marks are living, breathing creatures that move and communicate with each individual through our own energy. Like us, they listen and respond to the energy, both within us and around us."

"How?" The whole concept seemed so foreign and impossible. She almost laughed out loud at the thought. As if everything else she'd experienced in the last twenty-four hours was normal and acceptable.

His eyes narrowed as he studied the new mark. "It just is and always has been. They are our friends, our anchors...a sort of energy barometer that lives beneath our skin."

"Do they have meaning? The different marks?"

"Generally, within the Energens, our marks align to our elemental ability. The Shifters are always a dragon of some sort."

Understanding dawned once again. "So when your mark changed to a dragon, it was assumed you'd changed to their side."

His shoulders slumped when he exhaled as if he was tired of defending that question. "Yes. But I didn't."

"I know," she assured him, rubbing a hand across the broad expanse of his shoulders, a touch of comfort she hoped he wouldn't reject. "Why do they change?"

He shrugged. "I don't know. Mine was the first. No one can remember it ever happening before. That mine changed to a dragon was what made it so condemning." He twisted his marked hand back and forth as he stared down at it. "Now it's changed twice in a day. To top it all off, I've never heard of someone having two animals on their hand."

"Really?" So what did it mean? Why would the two of them have the same mark, one that mixed both their animals? The questions assaulted her once again, but she refused to succumb to the niggling of fear that crept into her conscious and rubbed icily against the back of her mind.

"Really." He gave a light sniff of irritation before he pulled away and scooted off the bed, keeping his back to her.

"Damian." Her voice made him pause, but he didn't turn around. "Are you okay?"

His spine stiffened with his inhale, his muscles rigid and stiff. His voice, when he spoke, was low and coarse. "I'll be okay when this is done. When the questions have answers and mysteries are resolved. Now, we should get dressed and prepare for the day."

The warmth and intimacy of just moments before was gone, overpowered by the reality of what they still faced. Of the questions that had no answers and the unknown that loomed before them.

"And what can we expect today?" she asked without expecting a real answer.

He looked at her over his shoulder, his expression void of amusement. "I have no idea. But with luck, we will make it to the end."

# Chapter Twenty

Amber finished tying the laces on her boots, then straightened and stood. She slipped into Damian's coat—the black, wool trench coat that she'd worn most of yesterday. The weight of it hung heavy on her shoulders, but it was welcomed. Oddly, it provided comfort, as if the material itself offered her a shield against whatever they faced.

She took a deep breath and inhaled the light scent of pine that lingered in the thick weave. She barely resisted the urge to close her eyes and enjoy the images that flashed in her mind of what had happened between them last night.

She'd given him her virginity.

A fact she'd finally had the time to process and ponder while she'd showered and prepared for the day. The silence had extended between her and Damian, not exactly uncomfortable, but no longer easy and natural as it had been when they'd first woke. Apprehension had settled like a sharp-quilled porcupine filled with all the questions and doubts that threatened to stab them both.

Still, she had no regrets. She'd given him her virginity willingly and without question. It almost seemed like she'd been waiting just for him. For that moment. To give away what most women today gave away without real thought or care. It's not that she had thought of her virginity as a prize to be had or even that special of a thing. Truly, until last night, it had made her more of a pariah than anything. But now, she understood why she had waited. Why her aunt had kept her so sheltered.

For whatever reason, it had been meant for Damian.

Yeah, and when did she get so philosophical? Logic would say it just happened. But if she dug down and listened to the energy, as she was slowly allowing herself to do, and believed as she'd told Damian she did, then it was telling her it was important that Damian was the one she'd given it to. There was a reason.

But why? Yet another big question on the ever-growing list.

"Are you ready?" Damian's deep voice pulled her out of her thoughts. He stood waiting by the door they both assumed was an exit. She sucked in her breath and held down the flash of desire that hit her deep in her core. The ends of his hair were still wet from his recent shower, and the light beard shadow that lined his jaw only added to the dark, sexy look. Throw in the bare chest with the holey jacket and jeans, a barrage of weapons strapped to him and he had the bad boy image nailed.

And he was hers.

The realization warmed her. Gathering the coat around her, she brushed her hair over her shoulder, flattened the violet scarf against the wool and mentally prepared herself.

"So what's next?"

In answer, he turned to the door and twisted the knob. To her surprise, it clicked open.

"Really? We could have been out of here last night?"

"It looks like it. But where would we have gone? For whatever reason, we were safe here and we got the rest we needed."

"Ah, so right," came a voice from the other side of the door.

Damian whipped the door open to reveal the older man from the previous night. Instinctively, Amber placed her hand over the stone and took a step back. Damian, instantly in protector mode, shifted to place himself between her and the man.

The man was dressed much the same as he'd been last night in a white silk, Oriental-style jacket trimmed in embroidered, gold designs and loose matching pants. A welcoming smile curved his lips, but the intensity in his dark eyes remained.

"I hope you found things comfortable last night." The man gestured toward the room. "Breakfast is waiting if you will follow me." He turned and started down the hall without waiting for their response.

Damian looked back at her, a question in his eyes. Giving a small shrug, Amber stepped forward and set her hand in his offered one. His face softened just a touch before his hand gripped hers. Together, they exited the room and followed the man.

"Stay close to me," Damian murmured.

As if she would run away at that point. "Yeah. You don't have to worry about that."

The man led them to a small dining room that contained a low table made in another shade of dark wood and was appointed with Oriental-themed statues, pictures and pillows. Small lights were placed strategically around the room, shedding a soft glow on the table of food. The same dark red carpet from the bedroom cushioned the sounds of their shoes and added a hush to the surroundings that boarded on oppressive. Or maybe it was the absence of windows once again that made the room seem so close.

The lack of outside light was completely disorienting. She hadn't realized how much she relied on the light to gauge the time of day or night. Or even the location. She was assuming it was sometime in the morning, but without a watch or external reference, it was hard to be certain.

"Please, have a seat." The man knelt and took a seat on one of the pillows at the head of the long table. Delicious scents drifted up from the bowls and plates that covered the table, and Amber's stomach clenched in anticipation. But she waited for Damian to take the lead. Although the other man seemed friendly, she didn't trust that impression.

"Why are you helping us?" Damian demanded without taking a seat. "What do you want from us?"

The man tilted his head in a look of contemplation. "As doubting as your brother, I see. A trait that must run in the family."

"My brother?" Damian tensed, his hand tightening around Amber's. "What are you talking about? How did you know Khristos?"

The man smiled, then turned his attention to the table. He lifted a small teapot and gracefully poured the liquid into a tiny cup. "So quickly you assume it is Khristos I speak of. That says much." Small tendrils of steam curled up from the cup as he set the pot down without making a sound. "You do have other brothers, or do you forget them in your obsession over Khristos?"

Amber felt the tight shot of guilt and pain pierce through her as if it was her own. She gasped, the unaccustomed feeling of knowing so intimately what Damian felt was a complete shock. "What are you playing at, Ancient One?" The question shot out of Damian in a tight string of barely contained anger.

The man gestured to the table. "Join me and I will tell you want you need to know." He reached to a bowl that contained a tantalizing mixture of meat, eggs and rice. "Manners dictate that I should wait for you, but my stomach takes precedence over your indecision."

The casualness as he went about serving food onto his plate was so diametrically opposite to the strain that bound Damian and her, it was almost laughable. Making a decision, Amber took a step toward the table. She tugged on Damian's hand, a silent urge for him to follow. The man had answers and they had questions. Maybe they could find what they needed and, if nothing else, they would have a meal.

The man looked up, his eyebrows lifting. "So it is the phoenix who guides the dragon in this phase." He smiled then nodded once. "An equal with strength and courage to match the mighty dragon. Once again, I am humbled by the wisdom of the energy."

Amber paused, taken back by the strange words of the man. The phoenix? She should be used to such talk by now as that was all she'd heard of late. But it was still hard to hear herself referred to with such positive, strong adjectives.

"Please, have a seat." The man indicated a set of pillows next to him. "I promise I do not bite." A tint of mischief flashed in his eyes with the light teasing of his words.

Taking a steadying breath, Amber pulled deep and trusted what she felt. This man did not mean them harm. To date, he had not hurt her if she didn't count the giving of the stone to her as an act of injury. Damian still held back, the mistrust mingling with the residual guilt that had festered within him for so long she doubted he even recognized it as a separate emotion.

"Who are you?" Damian asked, his voice cool, but void of the accusations and confrontations of before. He allowed her to guide him forward and followed her lead as she knelt on a pillow and took a seat at the table. The fact that he let Amber take the seat between the two men attested to how distracted he was.

"I am one who has seen much, experienced more, and has lived far longer than expected," the man answered with a smile. "As you already sensed, Damianos, I am an Ancient. I have lived through thousands of cycles of life, death, and rebirth. I have witnessed the rise and fall of many great nations, participated in the wars, influenced great minds and silently cried as I watched the circle repeat itself again and again."

"Do you have a name?" Amber asked.

He reached over and handed her a large bowl of food, his silent offer accepted as she shifted a portion of the egg and meat mixture onto her plate. Only after she had passed the food to Damian did the man answer her.

"My name is not as important as what I have to tell you. You should focus on what is coming and worry less about the inconsequential details."

Damian set the bowl of food down and returned his attention to the Ancient. "If you do not refer to Khristos, then which brother did you mean?"

"Your restraint is admirable," the man said, acknowledging Damian's tight control on the anger she felt simmering within him. "It is your youngest brother, Loukianos, that I refer to. The brother you've never met."

Damian stilled beside her. "How do you know Louk?"

"It was he who started this path. He and his mate Airiana. The Two to start it all."

"His mate?" Surprise and doubt were heavy in the rise of the two words.

The man inclined his head. "Yes, his mate. A beautiful Shifter dragon who has brought great hope to the Energen world."

Damian's fist slammed on the table, causing Amber to jump along with the china dishes that clanked back in a chime of protest. "*You lie.*"

"Do I?" the Ancient calmly challenged. "It is she who brought back the beauty and power of the winged ones to the Energens. The joining of Airiana and Louk has once again procured the line of the winged dragons as our allies against Gog and the Shifters."

"No one in my family would ever join with a Shifter. They are all vile, evil creatures," Damian snarled, his face contorted in a mask of loathing and denial.

The Ancient glanced briefly at Amber then took a bite of food, evidently unphased by Damian's outburst. The ends of his long mustache bobbed up and down in a rhythmic dance as he slowly chewed his food. He swallowed, a leisurely act of time stretched out as a silent refute against the accusations.

Finally, he spoke. "Really? If I listen to the energy, if I observe the telling mark on your hands, I know that's exactly what you did last night."

"What?" Amber cried.

"Again you lie."

Their rebuttals overrode each other as they both scrambled to comprehend what the man just said. Reflexively, Amber covered the mark with her other hand, hiding the image that made the man say such a thing. The dragon responded with a sharp roar of anger while her bird screeched in a blatant cry of upset. Damian shot her a sharp look, and she realized he felt the same from the mark on his hand. Not only were the marks joined, but their emotions were joined within them as well.

What she felt, he felt.

The Ancient watched them, his deep brown eyes narrowing as he processed their reactions. "I only speak the truth, but it is nothing to be ashamed of. Things are not always as they appear—as you should well know, Damian."

The color dropped from Damian's face and Amber grasped his hand, projecting her support into him. He looked at her, confusion and questions fighting for dominance in his deep blue eyes before he pulled his hand from her grip.

She let him go even though the silent rebuke stung, sharp and painful as a dragon's bite. Cold immediately replaced his warmth, sinking to her bones and winding around her racing heart. But she held his gaze and kept her back stiff. She had no idea what the man meant or what Damian was thinking, but she did know that she was good. That she was not the possessor of evil. Never would she believe that.

And, most importantly, she would not cower under their judgments.

Damian ripped his gaze from her and shot an equally accusing glare at the man sitting calmly at the head of the table. "Explain yourself, Ancient. Is this some trick? Yet another ploy to disparage me? To make me an outcast in a world that already despises all that I am?"

"Of course not. You are the Chosen One. You and you alone hold the weight of many on your shoulders. Your choices, the decisions you make *right now* are more important than what is contained in this room." The man's voice rose in volume and tone as he continued. "Think, old one. *Feel* once again. *Trust* in what you know. If you do not, then we are all lost."

"How can I?" Damian challenged right back, leaning toward the man and forcing Amber to tilt away from the table. "All I know is distrust. All I know are lies and false accusations that have left me bloody and bare. How do I trust when it has slapped me in the face every time I have attempted to do so?

Tell me that, Ancient. Tell me why I should trust when it has never been given to me?"

"But it has, you fool. You have it right now if you do not throw it away."

"From a *Shifter*?" Damian spat out the word like it was a vile piece of poisonous food. "You just said that's what she was. Why would I want her trust when it is the Shifters who have taken everything from me?"

Amber winced, the angry, cruel words cutting her more sharply than one of his blades. She snapped her head around to stare at Damian in open disdain. How quickly he changed his tune on the words of one old man.

"You hypocrite," she fired at Damian, her anger burning over the pain, forcing her to fight back. "Last night you denied all accusations that I was a Shifter. You desired me and possessed my body without regrets. I slept with you in a bond of trust. But today, you willingly judge me with no more than his words." She stabbed a finger toward the Ancient. "Judge not lest ye be judged, Damian."

Amber fumed, her anger disguising the shock that reverberated through her at her own words. She had no idea where the Biblical verse came from, how it spouted from her mouth without thought when she was not a religious person by nature.

"Oh, I've been more than judged, Amber," Damian said with an icy calm that belied the fire of his energy. The energy that hissed within herself. "I've been tried, persecuted and punished for things I've never done. I've been tricked and fooled. I've lived a thousand years of pain that I was an idiot to ignore for you—someone who lied to me."

"Why do you think she lied?" the Ancient interceded, his sharp voice breaking through the hostility.

Damian's attention cut to the man. "If she is a Shifter, how could she not know?"

"It was you who wore the mark of a Shifter, not she," the man countered. "Yet you deny being one. Is it not possible that there are parts of her even she does not know about? That there is more at play than what is simply perceived?"

Strained silence followed his question. The food was forgotten as the three table occupants faced off in a battle of mute strength. Each of them struggled for what they believed in the face of strong opposition. The energy shifted around them in slow coils of tightening hostility. Mistrust disguised as anger pressed against Amber in a sickening hold that threatened to choke the air from her lungs.

After a long moment, Damian surged to his feet to pace the perimeter of the room. His hands were clenched on his hips in a pose that Amber now recognized as one filled with indecision and frustration.

Her bird sympathized with him and urged her to follow. However, she was just as angry and confused as he was. His actions hurt far worse than if he'd struck her across the face.

Amber closed her eyes and inhaled through her nose, seeking a clarity that had eluded her since that night in January when that man who sat so calmly at the end of the table gave her the stone. The object that started it all and led her to where she was at that moment. Opening her eyes, she returned to the beginning.

"Why did you give me the stone?"

In contrast to the atmosphere of the room, the man smiled. "Because you *are* the Marked One—the one in the world who can decide which way the battle will turn. The stone belongs to you. I was only holding it until it was needed. *Now* is that time."

She licked her lips. "Do I dare ask why?"

His face became serious, all pretense of joviality dropping with the curve of his lips and the stiffening of his spine. "Because the dragon is awake."

"I don't understand."

"With the coming together of The Two, he stirred within his cage, his thousand years of slumber completed. A multitude of elements have collided at this exact moment in time to make it happen. But those are irrelevant to what is next. The Year of the Dragon is far more important than any suspect—by its end, the dragon will be free. There is little we can do to stop that end, but there is much we can do to stop his rise."

The man's words only confused Amber more. "What dragon?"

The Ancient shifted his gaze to Damian, who still paced behind her. "Damian. Tell her what dragon I speak of."

Damian cursed under his breath before she felt his irritated movements grow still. She kept her back to him, unwilling to show him anything else.

"The dragon he refers to is the Shifter leader, Gog," Damian stiffly answered.

"Ah, so you do understand the importance of where we are," the Ancient said to him.

"If what you say is true, then of course I do."

"And why would I lie?" the man questioned. "If you let yourself feel, if you believed as I said, then you would know what I say is true, without me having to tell you. In fact, I think you do—only you refuse to accept it."

A low growl echoed through the room. A frustration that Amber could empathize with. "But how? The dragon has been trapped in his metal cage deep within the earth's crust for as long as I've been ostracized."

The Ancient tilted his head. "Did you hear what you just said? Think, old one."

She knew the instant understanding dawned within Damian. The energy exploded within her in a combustible mixture of disbelief, denial and rage. The emotions so potent her spine arched and her head snapped back as if she'd received a sharp kick between her shoulder blades. Even if she didn't get the importance of what was happening, it was clear that Damian did.

"No." The denial fired from Damian with a hot blast of sizzling energy. The angry waves rolled through the room in a fit of frustration. "It's not possible."

"Why not?" the man challenged. "Because you don't want it to be? Denial will not change the facts."

Another harsh curse, a sharp thump of a fist hitting the wall echoed around the small space. "All this time and no one bothered to tell me. A thousand years of opportunity and not once did anyone see fit to let me in on what was happening?" Bitterness tinged every word, every accusation that Damian hurled at the man.

"To tell you would have changed the necessary outcome. Knowledge would have changed you, and that could not be risked." The Ancient rose from his seat in a graceful lifting of weight. Amber shifted to follow his path as he made his way to stand before Damian, undeterred by the hostility that radiated from the taller man. "You have endured much so that you can understand much. Empathy built from experience is far more powerful than that gained from words. You are but one of the sacrifices we had to make in order to trap the dragon in the cage."

"So me being condemned and ostracized for a crime I didn't commit, that was all planned?"

The other man had the grace to look away before he once again met Damian's gaze. "The situation presented an opportunity that was seized upon. But it was you who had the grace to walk away despite what you knew to be true. You who forsook all that you were born into for the betterment of the race."

"How could my leaving hold such power?"

"To challenge the verdict and stay would have cause great strife and unrest within the Energen community. Sides would have formed, battles fought until the good energy was tainted with the very evil Gog fosters. In leaving, you let the good continue. You willingly sacrificed everything that was dear to you and in doing so saved the rest."

It was Damian's turn to look away. "How could you know I would react that way? Was that manipulated too?"

"Your actions are your own, Damian," the Ancient answered. "You know we are not powerful enough to influence that. It is time for you to let go of the guilt you've harbored since Khristos' death. Let his actions be his own."

Damian cringed, physically wincing away from the words. "And what about Khristos?" he bit out weakly. "Was he also a sacrifice?"

The Ancient gave a slow incline of his head. "Yes, unfortunately."

Pain—Damian's—ratcheted through Amber, starting in her chest and pounding outward until it blanketed her in weary misery. Damian stumbled backward until his back smacked the wall and he sagged into the solid mass. He stared blankly at the ceiling, his body a mix of tense nerves and sagging muscle.

The Ancient reached out and rested a hand on Damian's shoulder. Whether out of exhaustion or defeat, Damian did not pull away from the touch.

"It is much for one family to endure. To give up and sacrifice," the Ancient sympathized. "It was that sacrifice, one made out of pure honor and love, one given not out of obligation, but from a willingness to do right—to do good—that provided the energy required to bind the bars and hold the beast."

"Who knew?" Damian asked weakly. "Who else knows the truth?"

The Ancient pulled his touch away and clasped his hands before him. "There are only a few or else the power wouldn't have worked."

"My father?"

"No," the man said with a slow shake of his head.

Damian's eyes squeezed tightly closed, the pain rippling across his face with a constricting of muscles that traveled down his arms and pooled in the tight clench of his fists.

"Who was the girl?" The question was asked through the stiff hold of his lips. "Why did Khristos kill her?"

The Ancient stepped away from Damian and moved across the room until he was once again facing both of them. Amber pushed to her feet, her legs weak under the weight of the revelations, but she refused to be at a disadvantage. She stood separated from Damian by a few feet, but once again the deep chasm of doubt and mistrust gaped between them.

The man waited until they both looked at him before he finally spoke. "She was a possible Marked One, a descendant of the bloodline that holds the latent Energen gene and the same one from which Amber is birthed. The last bloodline of the ancient Moshup, an Energen who helped the natives after the Energen city was built in what is now called North America."

The repeated words of the shaman crashed into Amber, forcing her to accept them for what they might be. The truth. The latest disclosure numbed her body and mind until she no longer felt anything.

"Khristos made the right choice when he chose to sacrifice the woman instead of letting the Shifters take her," the man finished. "Her bloodline was too rich with power to allow the Shifters to gain control of it."

"But what does all this have to do with me?" Amber's weariness drifted unwanted into her voice.

"It's all about choice, young one," the Ancient said patiently. "We all make choices every day that impact the outcome of our lives. It just happens that the choice you make will affect the lives of many more than you can comprehend."

"Again, why me?" The sudden weight that pressed upon her shoulders was as physical as a fifty-pound bag of sand being strapped around her neck. Once again, she felt the darkness creeping in, the cold surging through to stoke the fear.

The man looked her over with eyes that held more knowledge and wisdom than existed on the physical plane. Eyes much like the tribal shaman's at home, only the Ancient's eyes contained ages of understanding that defied logic. Those eyes moved to Damian before he finally spoke to her.

"Because you, Amber, are blooded of both Energen and Shifter. A dual status held by no other. A power of positive and negative that can flow either way." He paused before continuing slowly. "Your father was a Shifter. A man who wooed your mother until she fell for his false words and charms. It was the Shifters' attempt to dilute the bloodline and end the threat of the Marked One. But their attempt backfired when you were born with the exact qualities the energy had been waiting for."

The answer stopped her thoughts and froze her heart as none other could. How could that be true?

"My entire life I have been raised under the perception that I am a normal human with just enough Native American blood to allow me to claim ancestry to the Wampanoag Indian Tribe. A distinction I didn't even relish." A small snort of derision left her nostrils. "As the outcast bastard of the tribe's disgrace, I was subjugated to ridicule and scorn for as long as I can remember. And now you're telling me that all the garbage about me being the harbinger of destruction that his people"—she pointed at Damian—"have accused me of is also true?"

Unwanted, undesired like always, the tears glistened on the edges of her eyes. She wished it was all false. That everything that had been said was a lie. But a part of her knew it wasn't. That denial would no longer help her.

"No, child," the Ancient soothed. "I am not accusing you of that. You alone contain a balance *within* you that has the power to change the equilibrium of the world. There is more to you than most know. Than you know. But you must accept that in order to use it. In order to do what is needed."

"And what do I need to do?"

"You will need to discover that on your own," he said kindly, his soft words floating across the room on a wind of patience. "Knowledge gained in discovery is a lesson not forgotten."

"And if I don't want to discover it?"

The Ancient's eyes softened in a look of understanding. "Sometimes discovery is forced upon us despite our wishes to remain clueless. Knowing does not always bring clarity. Likewise, understanding does not make a task easier."

She resisted the urge to scoff at the man's cryptic words, which provided more of a puzzle than a solid answer. She needed to think. Time to process everything. So much had been said and revealed that she no longer had any grip on what she felt or wanted. Her world was out of control, a feeling that tore at her orderly life and left her floundering. Even her connection to Damian was now in doubt.

"I want to go home," she demanded, surprised at the strength in her voice. But going home was exactly what she needed. Hard, even strides moved her until she stood directly before the Ancient. "You have the power. Send me home. That is the choice I am making. The one that is right for me. Send me home. Now."

The Ancient tilted his head, his long mustache swaying with the movement as he contemplated her demand. Behind her, Damian said nothing. Made no move to stop her.

"If you concentrate, you can do that yourself," the Ancient finally said.

"I don't want to concentrate," she fired back as she took another step closer. "I'm tired. I've heard enough of the wild stories and accusations about me and my life. About who *I* am. I did not choose this path. *You* forced it on me with that damn stone. What I do from now on is up to me." She took a deep breath, an attempt to temper her rising anger. "This is my choice. I am not your pawn to be wielded as you wish."

"Are you sure this is the choice you want to make, child? To leave is to forsake the protection I am providing."

She turned back to the man who had stood by her through it all and spoke one word filled with question and her last thread of hope. "Damian?"

His cold paralysis encircled her, the dark edges fighting to creep in around the cracks that extended and widened in her battered soul. The burn of rejection deepened as Damian remained immobile, his silence continuing.

She turned back to the Ancient. "Send me home."

After another long pause, the man finally consented. "As you wish."

Damian inhaled sharply, the slight hiss snaking through the air to wrap around her aching heart. The two marks cried out in unified denial as the dragon's tail slowly uncoiled its tight hold on the white bird. The separation burned against the sundering of two forces that should never be parted.

The energy rejected her decision; the stone fired in angry refusal against her chest, trying desperately to overpower her demand. But it didn't have the strength to change her will. To force a choice she didn't want to make. The energy could only respond to her desire, not manipulate or control it.

The clarity of that understanding only strengthened Amber's resolve until she felt the prickling sensation unfold from within her to encompass her.

*Remember, child, sacrifice is but an act of giving if done with the right intentions.* The parting words whispered in her mind before disappointment and loss descended as she dissipated away. To her surprise, the raging pain was still palpable despite her molecular state.

But it was a pain she would endure. One she had battled before and survived.

Only it had never burned as deep and all-consuming as it did right then.

# Chapter Twenty-One

In a move of instant decision, Damian thrust away from the wall and dove for Amber. His dragon roared in approval as he made a frantic grab for her disappearing form.

His arms closed around air.

He was too late. Amber was gone.

Pain raked through him from the sudden absence of a vital part of himself. The force of the impact of his shoulder hitting the ground was nothing compared to the internal agony.

He'd hurt her. Again. When he'd told her he wouldn't.

But she'd lied to him. Or had she? Was his own bitterness and history keeping him from seeing the truth? From accepting what was blatantly obvious?

The energy flushed hot and powerful through the emptiness. Amber's feelings—sorrow and betrayal—fought for equal ground against his own anger.

But the feelings were weakening. Growing fainter the farther she went from him. Need motivated him. Desperate, he faded out to follow her energy trail.

Despite what she was—part Shifter enemy—he couldn't let her go.

His molecular form slammed hard against the circle barrier. A barrier that prevented him from exiting and chasing after Amber. The reality of his entrapment sent out biting curls of frantic recklessness that consumed him with fury.

Solidifying back in the room with the Ancient, Damian turned his rage on the man. "Let me out of here," he roared as he stalked toward the man. "You let her go, but you keep me? What game are you playing? Her life is in danger."

"I didn't think you cared, old one."

Damian wanted desperately to hit the infuriating man. To knock him down and physically stop the games he played. But force wouldn't work, and his last thread of rational thought kicked in to remind him that although the Ancient appeared smaller and weaker, he was actually a hundred times more powerful than Damian.

Turning away, he stalked to the wall and braced his arms on it. Breathing deep, he tried to pull up the emotionless, icy void that he'd functioned within for the last millennium. The stark emptiness of existence that had allowed him to move on when his life had imploded so long ago.

But it was nowhere to be found.

His throat was raw, dry to the point that his attempted swallow felt like sharp edges of glass being forced down to pierce the lining of his esophagus. His arms buckled, his head falling to slam against the wall. Amber had ripped the door wide open on the emotion-free box he had perfected and now he couldn't go back. All the feelings he hid from and swore he didn't need—didn't want—were now fully exposed and waiting to be acknowledged.

"I shouldn't care," Damian finally rasped, his back still to the Ancient. "My head tells me to let her go. Not to care." He inhaled and closed his eyes in an attempt to black out the pain. It didn't work. "But I can't. Everything else in me tells me to go after her. To save her."

"And why is that?"

Damian pushed away from the wall and turned around. The Ancient stood rooted in the same spot, his hands clasped behind him. His face held no emotion. No hint of support or thought as he waited patiently for Damian's answer.

"Because she's mine," he finally admitted, the low words dragging from the depths of his soul to hit the air with the truth. His dragon roared his approval at the admission. Beside the dragon, the white bird cried.

The Ancient smiled. "She is safe, Chosen One. I sent someone to follow her and watch out for her until you can return. I would not put one so valuable at risk."

Damian stepped forward. "Then let me go after her. Let *me* protect her."

"You have your own demons to conquer before you can help her, Damian. You are the Chosen One for a reason. You have lived through much, endured much, so you can do much. But your first step must be to accept the past so you can go home. Your people are waiting for you, Damian."

He couldn't stop the scoffing sound of disagreement. "Wrong. My *people* tried to imprison me yesterday. Once again, they refused to believe me. Called me a liar. I owe them nothing." Bitterness twisted hard and tight in his gut.

The Ancient's eyes narrowed, a deep wrinkle creasing his brow. "Maybe. But you owe yourself more. You owe Amber everything."

"Which is why I need to go to her. To protect her." Even now, he felt the bond weakening, his strength waning as the distance between them grew.

"The king will rise, his virgin bride by his side..."

"What?" Damian gaped at the man, who was now spouting words of lunacy. "King? Don't think so." Hell no. He shook his head in adamant rejection.

"I know so."

"How?" He stepped forward until he was in the Ancient's face. "How could you possibly know all this? What gives you the right to dictate the future?"

The man did not back down or cower in the face of Damian's rage. Instead, his dark eyes held fast to Damian's as he leaned into the anger, meeting the challenge that was extended. "I know because I have lived. Because I listen. Because I believe." The steel in his voice held strong against the softness of the words. "Your future is your choice, not mine. I dictate nothing."

"Hell of a game you're playing, then."

"Wake up, Damian," the Ancient snapped, his sharp reprimand a solid slap. "Go do what's right. Go prove them wrong. Be who you know you are, and all will be right."

"And who am I?"

The man leaned back, his shoulders softening along with his face. "You are Damianos Aeros, Son of Kadmos and heir to the House of Air. You are no more or less than that unless you choose it to be so."

Damian spun away from the infuriating man. His fingers raked through his hair, pulling on the strands until it hurt. Desperate, he grabbed at the last morsel of doubt he could cling to.

"But she's not a virgin. Not anymore." The admission leaked out of him on a cringe. The sharing of something so private was a violation of an unspoken trust.

A low crinkle of laughter broke through the hostility that held the room in its tight grip. "But she was when it was needed."

Damian whipped around and pierced the man with a hard stare. "Explain yourself."

The Ancient's lips curled in an enigmatic smile, a light of mischief sparking his eyes. "You've been gone a long time, but even you must remember that a relationship consummated within the bounds of a sacred circle creates a binding connection stronger than any words."

Damian's knees buckled, his weight too much for the sudden enormity of responsibility the words represented. He crouched, his head resting in his palms as he processed the latest revelation.

"By the laws of the energy," the Ancient continued, unaffected by Damian's descent to the floor, "you two are bound. A mated pair. When she came to you, she was a virgin. Your virgin bride."

"You tricked us," Damian accused.

"No. You joined willingly. I had nothing to do with that."

Damian's head whipped up, a snarl curling his lip. "But you cast the circle. You made it what it was with the hope your plan would work."

The man had the decency to incline his head in admission. "I will not deny that. It was a necessary play in order to hasten the outcome. Time is running out. I only accelerated what would have happened eventually. At least be man enough to admit that to yourself."

The muscles in Damian's thighs tightened, prepared to spring. Denial rose in his chest and fought valiantly to rush forth and reject what the man was once again saying. But the bile stuck in his throat and burned a rancid path of refute as it fought against the truth.

Heaving a deep sigh, he pushed to his feet and once again faced off against the man who was both his nemesis and his ally. "You have manipulated my life, torn my family apart and forced endless years of pain and misunderstanding upon many who did not deserve it. For that, I despise you."

The man simply nodded, his acceptance a smooth ease of agreement.

"From now on, my life is mine."

"Of course," the Ancient agreed. "Your life was always yours. The choices you made belong to you and you alone. That is the power of a true sacrifice, one given in the belief of rightness—in truth and honor—in spite of the personal pain it inflicts."

Damian bit his tongue to hold back the retort. Instead he pushed forward. "Are you responsible for this?" He lifted his hand to show the intertwined dragon and bird. The two marks were now completely separated beneath his skin, each struggling against the pain that pulled them apart.

The man smiled again. "No, old one. That is the doing of the energy—of the two of you. A sign of dual power. Of a joining that will bring great strength to the coming war. Together, you will ascend and lead the Energen race in the battle that faces us all. It is your destiny. It is time you rise to it."

"And the wings on the dragon? What do they mean?"

"The winged ones were once our greatest strength, our allies, against the serpentine Shifter dragons." The Ancient narrowed his eyes. "You must recall the tales, the stories of the great winged giants of the West. The dragons that soared on positive energy until the Slander convinced the world they were the evil ones. He persuaded all who would listen to kill the winged ones into extinction and tricked them into honoring the eastern wingless dragons instead. The ones who are the true bearers of the negative energy and of all that is evil."

Damian stepped back and dropped his hand, trying once again to absorb and reconcile the words of the Ancient. "And Louk? What of him and his—" He stumbled over the word. "Mate?"

"What of them?" the man snipped, impatience finally filtering through his voice. "Listen to what I say and don't fight what you know to be true. Your own denial holds you back. Not your people or the energy. Only *you*."

Emotions warred with the logic, with all that Damian knew. His dragon paced, eager to rejoin its mate. The energy pushed at him to follow, to find Amber and keep her by his side.

Forever.

She was his bonded mate.

"Drop the barrier, Ancient," Damian demanded, his voice filled with the authority of a CEO controlling his destiny. Or a king commanding his right. "There is only *one* thing I need to do right now. The rest will play out as the energy determines. Now let me go to her."

As simple as that, the invisible barriers dropped. Damian felt the energy give way and then he was gone, his heart following his need. His life hinged on the unbreakable link that connected him to his future.

Amber.

# Chapter Twenty-Two

The cool brush of the late afternoon wind wound through Amber's hair, pulling the ends up in a taunting dance of defiance. She snapped her head back and inhaled the salty air. Closing her eyes, she absorbed the freshness and embraced the freedom that surrounded her.

The solitude that held no expectations or judgments.

She stood alone and confused, poised on the edge of the Aquinnah cliffs. The steep edge located at the western point of Martha's Vineyard was both rugged and beautiful. Dusk crept up behind her as the sun made its slow descent beyond the horizon, glimpses of it flashing through the solid bank of clouds that cloaked the sky.

She shuddered against another strike of the wind, the icy currents circling her neck and snaking under her clothes. Amber hugged the wool coat closer, a valiant attempt to retain what little warmth she had as she looked out over the crashing waves of Vineyard Sound.

Unwanted, Damian's scent drifted over her, embracing her in security while cutting her with betrayal. She gasped, releasing a huge gust of pain that tore from her chest and threatened to take her to her knees.

It hurt. A simple description that didn't come close to defining the ache that encased her in a numbing iciness steeped in rejection. Once again, she wasn't good enough. Tainted by association. By blood she didn't want. Didn't ask for.

But it was in her nonetheless.

Still, it didn't define her. Didn't make her who she was.

And who was she? The question echoed inside her, the answer edging close, but still so elusive. Her hands fisted in the deep pockets, her knuckles banging the forgotten collection of artifacts from the previous day. A simple if not subtle reminder of all that had changed.

A seagull screeched high and long in the distance, its wings spread wide as it caught a current and soared with the wind. Below her, the uniquely aqua-colored waves pounded the sand and rocks in a repeated cycle of abbreviated fury.

Crash and retreat, break and fall back.

Maybe that was what had brought her here. The simple reminder of the repeated circle of life. Of the continued beat of peaks and lulls that pulled you forward into the next event. Waves that let you ride high on the crest before they crashed against the cushioning grains of sand or the hard, cutting rocks.

But it didn't answer why she was there. She had wished to return home and instead she had solidified on the cliffs—the lands of the Wampanoag Indian Tribe and the very people she would love to disown. To her, home was back in Newport at the little antique shop where she'd spent over half her life caring for discarded objects and forgotten memories. Not here, among the very people who despised her simply because she was a by-product of her mother.

But she stayed because the beauty and peace of the spot soothed her. The energy brushed soothingly over her face and around her chest, easing the ache and promising an end to the pain.

That, and because she wasn't certain she could pull off the porting trick without the Ancient's help.

Glancing at the sky once again, she realized her internal clock was completely askew. The lateness of the day had taken her by surprise, but maybe the whole porting thing took longer to execute than she realized. And she had no idea how long they had slept.

Slept. With Damian. Another jolt of pain shot from her chest. Her bird cried in protest, a cry that was echoed in her own heart.

The pain was followed by another harsh gust of wind that beat at her body and forced her attention back to the elements. To her surroundings.

To the person approaching in the distance behind her.

Her hair lifted and twirled around her head, sending sharp snippets of sensation from the crown down her spine. The energy fueled her in warm bursts of heat that countered the chill of the wind and whispered of the presence.

Friend.

Her tightened muscles relaxed incrementally, the steps of the visitor unheard over the harsh cut of the wind. Testing, pulling deep, Amber called on the energy to tell her who it was. Could it do that? Could she?

Gentleness, authority, hard resilience, respect.

Kayla.

The certainty of the identification flowed through Amber with a confidence that broached no question. No doubt. She smiled, a soft acceptance of what the energy told her. An understanding of what she was capable of doing. She turned to watch her friend make her way up the ridge.

Maybe it was time for her to accept who she was. All of who she was.

She had been so quick to throw out accusations and judgments against Damian, yet she was just as guilty. *Judge not lest ye be judged.*

Over the years, had she unconsciously proclaimed a judgment on herself? One of unworthiness, of fault? Was that the cause of the subtle doubt buried deep in her subconscious that held her back and kept her from taking what was hers?

Her life had become a quiet state of acceptance, of what people said, of her station in life. Of her outcast place in a society that seemed to reject the very fiber of who she was.

Now, it was time to change.

Acceptance. The truth washed through her, burning a new path of understanding as she slowly straightened her spine.

She was Amber Morningstar—the blooded descendant of Moshup, the ancient leader of the Wampanoag people and an Energen. Her shoulders moved back.

She was Amber—the only daughter of a misguided and lost mother who gave away her body in the delusional hope of finding her soul in the arms of a man. Her chest expanded.

She was Amber—the prophesied bearer of destruction or salvation. Her chin came up.

She was Amber—blooded of both light and dark, positive and negative. Shifter and Energen, beings that fought for the fate of the world in their hidden battle over the energy. She inhaled.

She was all of that. And more.

The power surged in her chest and beat in hard time with her heart. The wind snapped and bit around her, little nips of approval. It lifted her hair, pulled on the hem of the coat and soothed her with long caresses against her cheeks.

Inspired, Amber lifted her arms and held her hands to the sky. Her entire body tingled, fizzy snippets of energy from the tips of her fingers, down her arms, through her torso and legs until each little toe felt the change.

She reached out for the power she knew was there and waiting for her. Her bird soared with her, flying high into the currents in the ecstasy that unleashed with the freedom. Left behind, the dragon paced and prowled, the need to be at its mate's side driving a fiery spike through the dragon's heart that smoldered and burned in misery.

In that moment, she became the energy. It bound to her like a second skin, adhering to cells, attaching to every nerve ending and lighting her soul with a newfound identity. The purity of the revelation was both quiet and explosive. It settled ever so gently in her heart while blasting a cannon-sized hole in her mind.

She was Amber Morningstar—who she became from that point on was completely up to her. No matter what everyone said or thought or judged or predicted or...it didn't matter. She was the one who decided how she felt about herself. And for once, she was proud of who she was. Proud of all she was and what she could become.

"The power becomes you." The soft voice drifted on the air and melded with the vitality that encircled them.

Kayla. Her friend had reached Amber's side and now stood beside her in quiet acceptance. For who and what Amber was. Approval vibrated from Kayla as strong as the crashing waves below.

Amber lowered her arms, the moment past but the power remained. She held out her palm and focused. Almost instantly, a ball of flame burst from the smooth skin. It held, twisting in mingling colors of white, yellow and violet as it danced in a formed sphere of sizzling heat.

"And this does not surprise you?" Amber's focus remained on the unnatural fire that burned in her palm.

"Yes," Kayla answered, her word clear in the sudden quiet that had settled around them, the wind now silent in an act of courtesy to their conversation. "And no. This is what you were born to do. Be. It's beyond common logic, but it is, nonetheless."

"So you knew? All along you knew?"

"Some. Most of it, yes."

"And that's why you were my friend when no one else would be?" The flame in her hand flickered, sputtering at that last hint of doubt.

"No, Amber," Kayla said as she rested a hand on Amber's forearm. Her firm grip added reinforcement to the words. "I was—*am*—your friend because of your gentle heart and quiet kindness. I am your friend because you are one to me."

"And now?"

"That doesn't change. Your life may lead you from here, but I will always be here for you. True friendship doesn't die with distance."

Amber squeezed her fist shut, cutting off the flame to end the little show. Her palm hummed with the receding energy, but her skin held no mark or indication that fire had just burned there.

Tucking her hair behind her ear, she turned her head to finally look at Kayla. Her friend met her gaze, strong eyes of deep brown that held nothing but warmth and kindness in them.

"Thank you," Amber whispered, her throat too tight for anything stronger. The simple statement expressing all that she felt. "How did you know I was here?"

Kayla smiled, a mystical expression reminiscent of her shaman grandfather. "The wind told me."

Yesterday, Amber would have laughed at that answer. Today, she understood and accepted. "Are you one of them?" Her brow wrinkled. "Us?"

"No," her friend denied with a slight shake of her head. "My role, the role that has been passed down through my family, is only to guard the one who is. But now that you know, you can do that yourself."

Amber looked back over the water and absorbed it all. The words, the view, the freshness that nipped in the cooling air. The sun had finally dipped below the horizon, allowing the darkness to follow like an obedient slave. Before them, the fading light still held the faint glow left from the sun. But behind her, she could feel the darkness approaching. A physical beast that stalked the light in the perpetual battle for supremacy.

"But who will protect you, human?"

The cold, silky words had both women whipping around to find the source. The dark coldness that was forever present around the edges of the energy expanded at the sight of her stalking nemesis. Kassandra.

The cocky woman stood about thirty feet back, strategically blocking any exits for Amber and Kayla, which were few given the steep cliff that plunged behind them. She was dressed much the same as the previous night only this time she wore a long leather coat that flipped and slapped her calves as the wind returned with its earlier gusto.

"What? No dragon tonight?" Amber taunted as she instinctively stepped in front of Kayla.

"The night is still young," Kassandra practically purred back, her throaty reply full of sultry confidence. "There's still plenty of time to kill you both."

"Didn't you try that before?" Amber's simple question was edged with barbs. "Without success, I might add." She let her lips curl up with confidence. Confidence that was felt, not feigned this time.

"But there are no circles to hide behind this time, pup." Kassandra flipped her curls over her shoulder and braced her feet farther apart as she leaned into the ever-increasing wind. "And I have more than a thousand years of experience and power behind me."

The truth of her words rippled over the energy. The woman before them was old, strong and powerful. Amber swallowed and took a step toward the enemy, pushed on by the wind at her back shoving her away from the edge, away from Kayla. Her hands hung loose and ready at her sides. The little dagger in her pocket wouldn't help her in the fight to come.

And there would be a fight.

"Why does Tubal want me?" Amber asked.

The woman's face contorted in an angry scowl at the mention of her mate. "He doesn't want you. He wants your power, you fool. Something you're too stupid to even realize you have."

"What will he do to you when he finds out you hurt his prize?" Amber prodded back.

"Who'll tell him?" Her nemesis made a big show of looking around the area. "It's just you, me and the useless human. I doubt if any of us will squeal to my mate."

Amber used Kassandra's distraction to inch further away from Kayla. It was a calculated risk between staying close to protect her friend or drawing the fire away from her. Literally.

"Won't the energy tell him?" She wasn't sure that was true, but from all she'd learned so quickly, it sounded plausible. The scowl that darkened Kassandra's face confirmed Amber's assumption.

"You think you're so smart," the Shifter sneered. "Let's see how far brains get you against this."

The fireball appeared and flew at them almost faster than Amber could react. Fortunately, reflexes kicked in, causing her hands to come up to deflect the deadly projectile. Like magic, the fireball bounced off the invisible shield of air and sailed over the cliff edge into the night.

Behind her, Kayla gasped—a sharp intake of shock—but that was all. So like Kayla to remain steady and strong in the face of the unbelievable.

Across from her, Kassandra snarled, the low, feral sound hinting at the animal that lived within her. The animal Amber really didn't care to see again.

Her heart thudded as adrenaline kicked in. She could do this. The ability was there—she only had to reach for it. Use it. Believe in what she could do.

Calling up her own fireball, Amber returned the assault, aiming the flaming ball directly at Kassandra's head. The woman ducked, a simple move that let the ball fly over her head to fizzle out in the damp grass behind her.

Kassandra straightened and laughed, the throaty vibration beating against the winds that carried the tint of manic evil to them. "You surprise me, pup." She strolled to the side, but her eyes remained on them, some of her cockiness pulled back. "This just became way more interesting. Let's see what else you can do."

The stone fired up, burning hot pulses of energy into Amber, vitalizing all her senses and honing her instincts in anticipation of what was coming. Her animals, the bird and the dragon, also responded; the two fighters bared their claws and circled in excitement. The ache of separation remained, hindering them, but did not stop them.

Instead of waiting for the other woman to attack, Amber went on the offensive. Stepping forward, she sent a volley of fireballs at her opponent. Calling a quick succession of the flaming gold and violet missiles into her hands, she propelled them forward as fast as she could. Kassandra shrieked while she dove to avoid the attack. She rolled gracefully across the high grass, a moving target that dodged all of Amber's fireballs.

"*Run!*" Amber shouted at Kayla before Kassandra sprung to her feet.

Keeping up the distractions, Amber remembered Damian's trick and raised her hand to call to the sky. Almost instantly, a lightning bolt shot from the clouds and cracked into the dirt a foot from where Kassandra stood. The woman launched herself backwards on an angry wail of frustration.

"You bitch," Kassandra cursed. "You shouldn't be able to do that. You can't control two elements."

Amber had no idea what the woman was talking about. It didn't matter, either. The energy had become a bonded entity within her, vitalizing every nerve ending until she felt as if she was glowing from within. It felt like she was finally whole, like the piece of her that had always been missing was finally, finally in place.

A smile lit her face in exhilaration, a feeling that vibrated through her and stoked her confidence. The wind pounded off the surf and followed her call to blast her enemy in a full frontal heave that lifted the woman off her feet and tossed her backwards a solid ten feet until she landed with a hard thud on her back.

With her enemy down, Amber risked a quick look to check on Kayla. Unfortunately, her friend hadn't listened to her and still remained near the edge of the cliff. The warrior in Kayla must have kept her there ready for the battle, not running in fright.

But even that brief distraction came at a price. A searing pain struck Amber's hip with the direct hit of a fireball. She stumbled backwards and quickly pounded the flames out of the coat. Fortunately, the flames hadn't penetrated the coat's thick weave, so her skin remained unscathed. She couldn't help a faint smile at the thought that the coat really had protected her.

A small cry brought her attention back to Kayla. Beside her stood Kassandra, a look of victory covering her face as she made a grab for Amber's friend. The woman must have ported in behind Amber to get to a weaker target. Kayla stumbled back, barely avoiding the grab. A flash of panic covered her face before she caught her footing and kicked out, catching her unprepared attacker in the thighs and stalling Kassandra's approach.

Amber took the opportunity and reacted. Pure instincts and a need to save her best friend propelled her legs forward. She ran at Kassandra, a full-out sprint bolstered by fear and anger.

Amber slammed into the woman's side, taking her by surprise. The impact knocked the air from Amber's chest, but she held tight to her hostage and kept running. The forward motion combined with the shock of her move allowed Amber to achieve her goal with little resistance from Kassandra.

A half second later, she sailed off the edge of the cliff, Kassandra tightly clasped in her arms.

Amber's heart stopped, terror clamping down on her brain as they plunged toward the hard rocks below. In her ears, a scream wailed. Briefly, she processed the wide-eyed fright and disbelief in Kassandra's eyes just inches from her own.

Then Amber let go.

She opened her arms and let the Shifter fall alone, shock and realization registering on Kassandra's face. Her mouth opened in a silent scream as she plummeted through the dark toward the rocks.

The air caught and coiled around Amber, heeding her request and slowing her fall until she hung horizontally suspended some fifty feet from the ground.

Kassandra slammed into the jagged outcropping of rocks at the base of the cliff, her body crumbling in a sickening smack of bone that drifted up over the wind. Her eyes remained wide open but sightless to the image of Amber hovering above her.

The wind roared, a sudden burst of approval that coated Amber in power. She'd believed. Trusted the energy and herself, and the element approved.

The darkness was almost complete now. The half-full moon was still cresting, but provided enough light to cast a glow through the breaks in the clouds. The small amount of light was soothing against the blackness.

Slowly, she righted herself in the air then called on the energy and lowered herself to the beach below. Her feet touched down in the soft sand next to the gray and red rocks that cradled Kassandra's limp and broken frame. Blood streaked down the rough stone, leaving bright red rivers behind before it was absorbed into the golden sand below.

Amber gulped and choked, her hand slamming over her mouth before she remembered to breathe. The close-up of the body was disgusting. The sickening stench of blood combined with the unnatural bend of arms and legs twisted in Amber's gut. She swallowed and forced down the bile that threatened to rise up her throat.

In the distance, the waves crashed against the shore and she focused on that. On the repetitive, soothing sound. The tide was out, providing a generous expanse of beach between the water's edge and the cliffs that allowed the sound to carry and echo softly over the distance.

Remembering Damian's words, she knew what she needed to do. Even if she didn't want to do it. Kassandra might look dead, but he'd said the only way to kill a Shifter was to remove the head.

Her throat burned with the suppressed acid that refused to go back down. How could she decapitate someone? But how could she walk away and let this woman live? This Shifter who was out to kill her? War wasn't pretty.

And this was war.

She glanced upward to the cliff edge. Kayla was gone, or at least Amber couldn't see her. She released the restrictions that gripped her mind and let the energy flow in. In a wave of embracing warmth, she absorbed the truth of her sight. Her friend was safe—for now.

Amber's stomach coiled in gruesome resolve. Taking a deep breath, she released her hand from her mouth and reached into her pocket, her fist clenching tightly around the hilt of the dagger. Her damp palm gripped the soft, leather-wrapped handle, her fingers spasming around the item in objection to the task.

Taking a shallow breath, she stepped forward, refusing to think. There was no room for contemplation or regrets. For weak stomachs or weaker will.

The wind swooped in to stroke her hair in an approving caress. She climbed over the rocks, her boot slipping on the blood, her knuckles scraping against the hard surface as she caught her fall. She cursed in frustration, but pushed on until she was positioned over Kassandra's broken form. The sightless eyes stared at Amber, pinning her in a guilt-laden hold.

Amber shivered, a violent rejection of her resolve. Could she do this?

And there, on the edges of the energy, was the help she needed. Her senses dulled with the infiltration of the coldness. Emptiness descended upon her, a blissfully blank darkness that took hold of her mind and emptied her conscience. The icy numbness descended from her head until her body and actions were detached from her mind until she felt nothing but the chill that erased her emotions and soothed away the pain.

How easy it was now. To lift the knife. To grip it with both hands over her head. To envision Kassandra's head separating from her body. By her hand.

Her bird screeched, a high-pitched wakeup call of warning.

The stone flared to life, an instant shot of heat that burned through her chest and flashed against the ice. Her chest contracted in shock; her head jerked back in a ripple effect as the fire burned through her limbs, evicting the cold.

Amber recoiled. What was she doing?

This wasn't her. No matter what, she couldn't kill in cold blood. She couldn't cross that line.

She let her arms drop, the knife dangling from her slackened grip. She couldn't kill the woman, but she could still neutralize her. Quickly, she exchanged the knife for the collar in the coat pocket, the one that had circled Damian's neck. Working the hinge open, she spread the metal wide and eased the open collar around the Shifter's neck. She snapped it closed then gave the metal collar a quick tug to ensure it was locked before she scrambled away from the gruesome task.

Swiftly, almost desperately, she wiped her hands on the coat in an attempt to remove the blood that had smeared on them. Kassandra's blood.

The enemy. Her enemy.

Turning away, Amber stumbled away from the body, needing air and distance to process everything once again.

The energy expanded, a ripple of disturbance on the beach to her left. Another presence.

"Going somewhere?"

Amber snapped her head up at the same time that her stomach twisted in dred. The energy flared and sparked from the stone while recognition hit.

Before her stood Tubal.

A very angry Tubal if the hard tilt of his brows and curl of his lip were any indication. His dark, hard eyes held hers, his features cut from crudely carved marble. Dressed in the black leather that seemed to be required for combat, the man was an intimidating presence of menace.

"Home would be nice," she managed to reply. Somehow she even succeeded in making her voice sound calm despite the fear that once again gripped her muscles in frozen tension.

The malicious croak of his laughter sounded hollow in the empty night air. "To my home. The only possibility open to you now."

The power of the evil was so close, tempting and taunting her to succumb. To fall into the lure and listen to that part of her that flowed within her.

The part she'd never acknowledged and would resist now.

Exhaling, Amber spread her stance and prepared. "There are always more possibilities if you know where to look for them."

Tubal lifted his mouth in a sinister leer then raised his hand into the air. The wind whipped across the beach, spitting sand at Amber's jeans and ripping her hair into tangled knots down her back.

Warning lights went off in Amber's head as the energy snapped at her skin. A quick glance at the circle traced in the sand and she knew what Tubal was doing. She had to stop it if she wanted any chance of surviving.

Her hand shot up, her defense launched.

The energy was advancing around the two of them, powered by Tubal and closing them off. The rippling wave of energy circled around Tubal and her, a visual arc led by flames as if to taunt her—frighten her—as it trapped her within the ring he was casting.

She couldn't let that happen.

The stone throbbed between her breasts, revolting against the entrapment. Amber pulled on the stone's energy, on her own powers and slammed up a wall in front of the enclosing wave. Tubal's energy crashed against her energy wall, the flames fanning and spitting outward from the invisible block she held. The force of the impact was like a physical blow to her body, causing her to stagger back, but she remained strong and refused to crumble. Sweat beaded on the back of her neck, her biceps quivering under the strain.

Tubal's eyes widened in surprise before his brows dropped and the evil scowl deepened. His lip curled up in a sneer.

"How?" His one-word question was filled with the deep anger of disbelief.

How what? Amber didn't have the mind space to figure out what he was asking.

She tried to brace herself for another attack, but there wasn't much she could do to defend herself. All her power and concentration were focused on holding off the closing of Tubal's circle.

Instinctively, she knew she had to act before he did. Flicking up her free hand, Amber shot a stream of flames directly at Tubal's chest with a speed she hoped would catch him unprepared.

Tubal dropped his arm to block the attack, the deadly fire clipping the edge of his forearm and burning a jagged line through the sleeve of his leather jacket. He roared, his anger blasting the air with its vile acidity.

Immediately, the half-formed circle dropped, the energy fading away with the Shifter's distraction.

Amber dropped her arm and sagged forward with relief. She'd done it. She'd stopped the circle from being completed. She still had a chance.

Swiping her hair out of her eyes, she sprinted down the beach. Her boots dug into the soft sand, the grains sucking them in and making her legs feel weighted. But she persisted. The need to escape pushed her forward despite the unlikeliness that running would work.

As if he read her thoughts, Tubal's evil voice drifted to her. "Running won't work."

Maybe not, but it was worth a try.

She made her way toward the water and harder sand where it would be easier to run. A fireball whizzed, snapping and hissing, by her head. *Damn.* Too close. Tubal was playing with her. She knew that, and the fact tore at her as his throaty laughter filtered across the beach. A foggy mist was settling on the lower portions of the beach, bringing with it a dampness that swiped against her cheeks in tandem with the bite of the wind.

Her breath was panting, short staccato puffs of air that bordered on panic. Before her, two more forms took shape in the mist, their images coming into focus through the disorientating wisp of fog.

Immediately, Amber stopped.

The tall blond male and equally imposing dark-haired female stood together, hands clasped in a united front before her, halting her escape and blocking her forward exit.

Amber turned her back to the water and looked behind her. Tubal stood just down the beach, his deadly focus on her before it shifted to the two down the beach. In front of her, the steep wall of cliffs loomed imposing and unscalable.

She was caught in the middle. Breathing deep, she fought down the panic that made her heart thunder and reached for the courage Damian believed she had.

This was her life and the choice she made here could very much determine if she survived to experience that life.

# Chapter Twenty-Three

"Airiana," Tubal's voice boomed down the beach. "Why are *you* here? With *him*?"

"Grandfather," the dark-haired woman answered. "I'm here to fight for what's right."

"And it's right to turn on your family?" Tubal growled. "On all that you were raised to believe?"

The woman lowered her chin. "When what I was raised to believe is evil and wrong? Then yes. It is right to turn on my family."

"I can't allow that, Airiana."

"You don't have a say, Grandfather." The woman raised her hand that was clasped tightly with the male's. "I have chosen my mate and my side."

Tubal roared, his anger radiating down the beach in a cold ripple of violence.

Amber's attention whipped between the two forces on opposite sides of her, grateful their personal conflict pulled the attention from her. A wave rolled in and washed over Amber's boots, pushing her forward just an inch. Heeding the subtle sign, she followed the flow of the energy and made a sprint toward the cliffs.

A long stream of fire blazed before Amber, cutting off her advance. She flailed back to avoid the heat of the flames, her boots catching in the sand and causing her to stumble before regaining her balance.

The loud roar that followed and echoed through the night made her freeze. Amber knew that sound. One she wished she'd never hear again.

A dragon.

Another flaming dragon.

In Tubal's place stood a large, red-and-black-scaled dragon.

The dragon dipped its head, lifted heavy lids and glared directly at her. Its deadly intent was clear. Amber was its prey.

Short, white horns sprouted between pointed ears and from under a tuft of fine, scarlet hair that spread along its jaw and down the ridge of spikes that ran along its back. The large beast tossed its head and let out another ear-shattering roar. Flames reached high into the sky, golden-red shimmers of heated death.

The sound was like a trumpet call to arms, all along the beach behind the dragon more shapes started to form within eerie, black clouds of wispy smoke.

More Shifters.

The dark energy that grew and crested from that direction assured Amber she was right. The cold increased with each form that solidified. The negative energy flowed down the beach like the putrid downdraft of a sewage plant.

Chills encased her and she shivered, unable to stop the visceral reaction. Unwanted, the coldness seeped in and called to her, urging her forward, toward the dark.

To surrender.

To follow.

To the answers it could provide. To the numbness that drifted through her, blanking her fear and soothing her worry. Her problems solved. All of them forgotten in the freedom offered by the cold.

She leaned toward Tubal but her boots held firm. The lure was stronger than before. It tugged at her until it seemed so right, so easy to go with Tubal.

The wind gusted off the open water, charging across the sand with a single-minded intent. It hit Amber in the chest then cut around her to push at her body from all sides. Her hair whipped around her head and over her face, blocking the view of the Shifters. In the brief moment of darkness, she snapped back.

Amber grabbed at the annoying mass of hair and held it tightly to keep it out of her face. In a bizarre way, it was like an anchor holding her grounded. A reminder of who she was.

What she was.

At her back, Amber felt the warmth soothe over her and slowly surround her until the cold was eliminated. Pivoting to one side, she looked down the beach toward the mysterious pair. Not at all surprised, Amber watched as a small army of men and women took form on the beach behind them. All armed and ready for battle.

The Energens had arrived.

The two sides established. An ancient battle ready to repeat. And in the middle was Amber Morningstar. The time had come.

Inhaling, Amber lifted her arms to the sky and believed, calling to the energy in a silent prayer of faith.

The wind buffeted Damian in the face, a hard slap of shame and reproach that stung clear to his soul. The energy tore at him, ripping him apart as he took in the scene below.

He had arrived high on the cliffs just seconds before. His vantage point provided an unbroken view of the battle forming on the beach below.

But right then, all was frozen as if the entire image were but a painting. A brushstroke in time.

The pale light of the half moon illuminated the scene in a stark visage of light and shadow. The glow shimmered off the expanse of water, reflecting back into the night and staging the show below.

Two sides ready for battle and in the middle stood his Amber, alone but strong.

Damian's urge to rush to her side was stayed by the image she projected. She was a physical force that radiated power from her as she stood between the two sides. The middle compass point with her legs braced apart, her hands spread wide as they reached into the sky. Her head was tilted back, her beautiful hair lifting and dancing behind her in a silent dance to the power.

She was glorious.

His dragon growled and paced, its claws drawn and scraping in its urgency to get to her. Back to its mate. Beside it, the bird soared, its spirit filled with belief and understanding as it scouted out the battle to come.

*Fool.* He'd been such a fool to doubt what he knew. To doubt her.

The energy circled, a slow-cycling twister that hovered over Amber. It was unseen but felt by all who were present. Through the ranks, both sides watched in stunned awe while simultaneously preparing.

Then she moved, one quick swipe of her arms to the side that brought with it the sharp crack of a lightning bolt. The blazing streak of energy was accompanied by a solid line of flames that shot from her palms, both attacks directed at the black and red dragon.

Her side chosen.

Instantly, the battle commenced in a smooth mesh of chaos and order.

The dragon roared and twisted to the side, his serpentine body moving out of the path of the lightning as he crouched and ducked under the flames.

Tubal. Damian knew the energy even if he'd never seen the man in dragon form.

The two sides of the battle charged, creating a distorted visual reminiscent of ancient battles. Swords drawn, battle cries raised, adrenaline raging. Mixed within the standard weapons was the volley of fireballs from the Shifters countered by the Energens with propelling boulders, air shields, lightning bolts, water spouts and their own return of fireballs.

Determined to save Amber, Damian started to port to her but stopped, his dash halted by the sudden appearance of a Shifter behind her. Damian immediately called to his power, sending a bolt of lightning at the man. The energy nailed its intended target in the chest and sent the enemy flying backwards.

Faster than he could port, more forms appeared around Amber. Tubal sent a round of dragon flames through the night sky that danced and hissed several feet above Amber's head. Damian fired down more bolts of lightning as other Energens converged on the attackers, swords rising and falling in bloody defense of Amber.

His mate. The glory of the rightness burst in his chest and sent his energy soaring with the beautiful white bird.

Behind Tubal, more Shifters transformed, the dragons emerging in a sinuous line of death and destruction. The dragons dispersed across the sand, beasts of fire and power that descended on their opponents with vicious intent. In dragon form, the Shifters were formidable beasts, but they still had weaknesses. They couldn't port in that form, and their fire abilities were limited to what they breathed.

The Energens countered with their own powers, the elements responding to the calls of the various wielders. Earth, water, fire and air—all were present and in use. Against the might and size of the dragons, the human form Energens appeared easily conquered. The Energen advantage was their ability to wield all of the elemental powers and from a great distance.

A sand funnel took shape and tore through the Shifter ranks, shooting boulders and pellets of sand at the enemy. Lightning bolts struck at the hard hides of the dragons while Energens from the House of Fire wielded swords that blazed with fire.

Behind him, Damian felt the energy shift and knew the battle had reached him. Turning, he unsheathed a sword from his back and swung in one motion. The enemy jumped away, spun and returned with his own strike of iron. The two swords clashed in a long-heard clang of metal, power and strength held in the hands of man.

The vibration of the swords echoed up his arms as his eyes narrowed on his attacker. Recognition hit and spiked the rage that burned deep within him.

"What? You're not running this time?" Damian taunted the man with the Native American features. The same man who'd disappeared from the alley that Amber had run from in Chinatown.

The man cursed. "I didn't run the first time." He jabbed and swung a broad arch with his sword in a juvenile move. "I was waiting to finish you now."

Damian easily dodged the swing and laughed. "And what will that gain you?"

"Glory," the man grunted. "Position. Recognition."

"And Amber?" Damian asked as he advanced. "What of her?"

The man grinned, a malicious leer filled with lust. "A great piece of ass that was supposed to be mine. The little slut wasn't as easy as her mother. I'm going to destroy her just like I did that fucking junk shop."

Fury raged within Damian. Breathing deep, he fought for the balance that would keep him focused on the battle before him. Each swing of the sword, dodge of a blow, strike of a blade was a challenge in concentration.

This kill would be for Amber.

His shoulder muscles ached, bringing back buried memories of battles fought long ago. Back to the time when their war was more open. When the battles were not as hidden and humans were openly recruited to sides, even if they didn't understand what they were really fighting for.

Back before the dragon was trapped and Damian was exiled.

Ancient times.

*Damian.* The word echoed in his head, a whisper of welcome that cleansed his mind and centered his power. *Amber.*

His sword struck out, a long swipe of death that lit in flames—a burning blend of white, gold and violet fire. Surprise shot through Damian, but he didn't pause or question. The power was fresh and heady, filled with a newness that itched to be used.

Fire. He, an Energen with the power of air, could control fire. The power of the Shifters, an element of the Energens.

*Amber.* Damian called back mentally—a Spirit power. Three powers—he could control three elemental powers. How? There was no time to question the facts or to doubt the energy. *I'm here. For you.*

The Shifter's eyes widened in surprise, his shoulder dropped and Damian's sword hit its mark, a clear strike through the neck of the Shifter. The energy pulled the flaming blade through the flesh in a cauterizing swipe of mercy. Instant death.

A death that was too quick for a man who had tormented Amber.

His opponent crumbled, his knees buckling as his arms twitched in a last flickering of flexing nerves. Damian turned away before the head hit the ground, his attention immediately back to Amber.

Below, the fight raged. Fire streamed from her hands as she held off a Shifter. Xander, flaming sword raised in combat, along with Ladon and Phelix surrounded her. Damian's two oldest friends and his brother protecting what had so quickly become the most precious thing in his life.

In fact, the entire Energen Guard was there fighting for Amber. Protecting and defending her from the Shifters. Keeping her safe.

Damian focused on getting to her. The beach below was a landmine of battling forms and energy. Constant movement and crossing energy patterns made it strategically hard to port into a position close to her.

*Hold on, Amber,* he called to her. *I'm coming.*

*To kill me or help me?* she snapped back, her spirit and strength clearly felt even through the non-verbal communication. Her doubt throbbed within him. It was his fault; his own actions had caused that pain. He'd been such a bastard to her. Once again, he'd turned on her. After he'd told her he would never hurt her again.

He couldn't—wouldn't—lose her now.

His heart burst at that thought. His chest ached with a sudden intensity that took him to his knees. *You're mine, Amber. All of you. I'm sorry I doubted you.*

Below, she turned, her eyes meeting his over the distance. The energy connected them across the space and within him, he felt her pain ease.

*Then fight with me and prove it.*

Her simple order had him surging to his feet, his determination solidified. He would die to protect her. Shifter blood and all, she belonged by his side. She was a fighter and now that she'd accepted her power, she was beyond gorgeous. *Shield yourself,* he commanded. *I can't get down there.*

She turned away and threw up a block against an incoming fireball. Panic fired in his gut as the dragon Tubal advanced on Amber. The long, serpentine dragon wound its way through the battle breathing fire and swinging its long, spiked tail at will.

*Around you,* he yelled, trying to keep the panic from his voice. *Erect a shield entirely around you. And hold it. It will protect you.*

Damian reached to the air and called another succession of lightning bolts down at Tubal. But the dragon swerved and dodged the blows, using his long body to twist around the attack. The dragon lifted its head, his eyes focusing up at Damian as another roar bellowed out of his mouth.

Damian swung his head, looking up and down the beach for an open place to port to. Desperation raced up his spine as the scent of fire, flesh and blood mingled with the wind that hit him in the face and slapped across his bare chest.

There was nowhere close for him to land. He reached out his senses to encompass the water only to find a crisscross of energy patterns blocking him there as well. As if to emphasize the point, a large wave was pulled from the ocean to careen across the beach and crash down on the back line of Shifter forces. The mass of water crushed the unsuspecting bodies, flattening them to the beach and sending sprays of mud and sand over the red clay of the cliffs.

From the corner of Damian's eye, a rush of movement pulled his attention to the depths of the Energen forces. Within the mix of Shifters and Energens battling, two more dragons took form. Two identical black dragons, the color so rich and deep the scales gleamed almost blue in the reflection of the moonlight.

He looked back to Amber to see that she'd completed the shield. *Hold it, Amber,* he told her. He could feel the effort it was costing her. The energy required to hold the shield against the oncoming attacks was taxing. It pulled her strength and tested her newfound powers.

Her arms and legs were spread wide as if bracing against the frame of a doorway. She lifted her head as his words reached her.

*It won't last long.* The words were strained.

Sweat trailed down his chest and back, heedless of the icy wind. Flames lit up the night, the battle intensifing with each second that passed. *Then port out of there. Now!*

*I can't,* she answered. *I'm not strong enough.*

Tubal was almost within striking distance of Amber, his breathy flames clearing a path as he stalked his prey. Around him, the Shifter army fought. The evil, dark energy cloaked the pristine beach in a rank, vile stench that sullied the sanctity of the place.

The evil bastard couldn't have her. Never. He'd already taken one person Damian loved. Tubal would not have another.

Damian pulled deep and called up a fireball. The white, gold and violet ball danced in his palm, taunting him with proof of his new power before he let it sail through the night at the fucking dragon.

On the other side, one of the black-blue dragons rose, taking flight into the night to float on the air. Its gossamer wings were spread wide to catch the wind before it paused and held mere feet away from Damian. He stumbled back, surprise catching him unprepared for the vision before him.

The dragon stared at him, its deep blue eyes nailing him with recognition. The energy pulsed around Damian, and he listened.

Loukianos. His brother.

How?

The large dragon blinked, a slow closing of eyelids as if to say he understood. The confusion, the denial, the doubt. All of it raced through Damian in an instant before he banished them all.

It simply was.

The matching dragon—Louk's twin, only smaller—soared over the battle, shooting angry flames down on the unsuspecting Shifters from above.

Winged dragons.

Understanding dawned in Damian.

He inclined his head at Louk, then stepped back. Louk turned and soared toward the matching dragon, his mate, to fight by her side for the Energens. It was a beautiful sight. One that caused many to stop, watching in both awe and confusion at the vision most had never witnessed.

The winged dragons had returned.

An angry roar of denial fired through the night. It was a call of rage and frustration from the dragon Tubal that bounced off the clay cliffs and vibrated down the beach. The sound was so fierce, so primed with evil that the fighting came to an instant halt.

A pause that echoed with the abrupt silence.

In that moment, Damian took two huge steps and soared off the cliff into the cool air of the night.

# Chapter Twenty-Four

Amber held strong, but her strength was waning. Under the heavy coat, her shirt was soaked with sweat. Perspiration beaded on her forehead and dripped unwanted down her face and into her eyes. The salt stung, and she blinked away the annoyance as she kept her arms braced wide to hold the invisible energy field in place.

The stone burned against her chest, hotter than ever before. But it didn't hurt or sear her skin. The warmth invaded her body and mind as if an inferno burned until she felt consumed with the power.

Around her, the energy pulsed, power unfurled and, newly tested, rippled over the mass of gathered fighters. She watched, caught in the awe like everyone else.

The raven-black dragons soared with a beautiful grace in the night sky, their long bodies held aloft by paper-thin wings. They were stunning in their magnificence. The simple fact that something so large could float so effortlessly in the air was mindboggling on its own.

The dragon Tubal let loose with an angry roar of pure menace. He tossed his head high, shooting flames in the direction of the two dragons that circled in the night just out of his reach. The frustration and unbridled fury of the beast radiated over the crowd on the wave of cold energy that blanketed the beach.

With a joy that felt both foreign and welcomed, her dragon reared its head, took a mighty leap and soared into the air.

Amber gasped, her heart stuttering as she watched Damian leap from the cliffs high above. Too stunned to think, she dropped her shield and cried out in denial before she remembered that he controlled the air.

In the next second, he shifted.

In a blur of man and beast, a stunning white dragon took form.

The large animal descended to the rocky beach at a frightening speed. Her breath caught, panic assaulting her as the dragon plunged down. Then, in a smooth unfurling of grace, wings extended from his sides, expanded, then caught the wind and lifted him into the night.

*Damian.*

Her muscles sagged, relief and amazement consuming her. A white dragon. Damian could shape-shift into a white dragon. And he was good. He was positively striking in his dragon form. Primarily white with hues of gold and violet shimmering on the scales, he appeared like a piece of the moon streaking through the dark. A dusting of fine, golden hair lined his long jaw, the soft strands catching and fluttering in the wind as he soared. She itched to touch that hair, to run her fingers through it and feel the texture against her skin.

"Awesome," she yelled to him. "You're amazing."

The joy pounded through her in time with her inner dragon. The white bird screeched with happiness to see its mate free and soaring by its side.

Lost in the moment, focus totally on Damian, Amber turned in the sand to watch the dragon coast on the wind, glorying in its freedom. Desperately, she wanted up there with him. She belonged with him. The energy told her that, but it was her heart that finally admitted the truth of the feelings.

She jumped and yelled with the joy that filled her. Battle forgotten, there was nothing but her and Damian on the beach. His long tail switched behind him as his wings flapped and his head turned to look down at her. She smiled a big, cheek-splitting grin as she watched him glide through the night.

*Amber.* Damian's sharp cry broke her thoughts. *Look out.*

Too late. Flames hit her, surrounding and engulfing her.

Pain. Hot. Smothering. Unbearable.

Amber dropped to the ground, instincts pulling her down and pushing her to roll away from the heat, away from the flames. Her coat smoked and smoldered on her back. The scorched scent of burnt hair reached her nose as her cheek burrowed into the refreshing coolness of the wet sand. Her thoughts sputtered as she realized one major fact.

She'd messed up.

*Amber.* The panic of Damian's voice thundered into her numb mind.

Forcing herself to move, she pushed on her arms, ignoring the pain until she was able to flop over on her back. Above her, Damian let loose with a streaming wall of flames that hit the dragon Tubal on the back.

Around her, she felt the battle closing in. The Shifters outnumbered the Energens. The coldness was getting closer, numbing her and chilling her to the bone.

She struggled to her knees, a need for survival forcing her up. The backs of her hands were red and tender with burns, the skin peeling away in spots. But the pain was distant, almost disconnected from her.

The scene around her was a mass of blood, beasts, swords, men and elemental gifts. Phenomenal and frightening.

"Damian," she whispered. Somehow the softness felt appropriate amidst the clamor of battle.

Within her, she felt Damian's panic. His anger and frustration at his inability to reach her. But more importantly, she felt his love.

For his people. His family.

For her.

The love had replaced the guilt that had hardened within him for a millennium. It freed him to claim what was rightfully his. More importantly, to claim himself.

*I love you, Damian.*

His attention snapped back to her. His wings flapped, a hard beat of rejection. *Don't give up on me, Amber.*

In front of her, Tubal stalked closer, his big, black eyes dancing in victory as his tail slammed against the sand, a plume of loose sand shooting up to emphasize his triumph. Around her, she felt his army closing in. They had her.

*I never did. Ever,* she told Damian. *I'm sorry I failed.*

*Port, Amber. Damn it. Get out of there.*

*I can't.*

Overhead, Damian roared, a fiery burst of denial.

Tubal shifted, moving seamlessly from dragon back to human form. His head dipped down, and his dark hair hung across his forehead shadowing the evil eyes that locked on her. His leather coat snapped in the wind as flames illuminated the air behind him. He was a vision of destruction. Using the last of her strength, Amber pushed to a stand, refusing to die like a sacrificial lamb at his feet.

"You're mine." The evil snarl cut at her.

At her sides, the Shifters had moved in to block the Energens. A steady stream of fireballs lit up the sky in their constant bombardment to hold off Damian and the two black dragons. Another set of Shifters battled the ground forces that fought to reach her. She knew the Energens were trying to protect her. The energy was clear on that.

"You're too late," she told Tubal. "I'm already Damian's."

The evil man laughed, a deep, chilling rumble that scraped against her nerves. "That can be changed."

"No. It can't," Amber insisted. "I belong to him."

Tubal scowled, his eyes widened then turned to evil slits. "He's *fucked* you." He cursed again, a foul string of expletives that hit the air in a sharp, hard beat. "But I still have time. You'll forget him as soon as you're with me tonight."

"That'll never happen." Amber lifted her hand to draw up a fireball, but got nothing. A flame sparked then fizzled, her energy exhausted.

Tubal laughed at her pathetic display. "Not so powerful now, are you?"

The stone still burned against her chest, but the energy seemed to be locked within it. As if it were preserving itself for something. The mystery of the stone frustrated her beyond thought. Why would it quit on her now when she needed it most? Was there a trick to it that she was missing?

She reached out to the sand, trying desperately to lift it into Tubal's face. Nothing. She had nothing. It was like the power had never existed within her.

Tubal took another step forward, and behind her the Shifters closed in. There was nowhere for her to go. No escape.

The wind gusted off the ocean, a long howl of denial as it funneled around her to beat at Tubal's chest. He leaned into the force and bared his teeth at the invisible element, meeting the challenge and plowing through it with ease.

Amber slipped her hand into her pocket to clench the handle of the dagger. Her last defense, as measly as it was. Useless, really. She wasn't going to kid herself. Reality was just ten steps in front of her.

The icy coldness crept into her bones, extinguishing the fire that had burned there just moments before. The energy felt malicious and evil as it surrounded her. It smoothed over the tender flesh of her cheek in a blatant attempt to seduce her. Her pulse slowed, her eyes felt heavy, the alluring call of the dark power whispered to her.

Wanted her.

It coiled around her neck, a serpentine caress that snaked under her collar and slithered down her spine as it whispered sweet words of enticement.

And she was tempted to follow. To believe what it promised.

"That's right," Tubal encouraged. "Listen to the energy. Hear its call. You want it, Marked One."

Marked One.

She *was* the Marked One. The bringer of destruction. Of death.

*No. Never.*

Amber blinked and shook off the hold of the evil energy. Fear lodged in her throat at how close she'd come to succumbing. To following what she knew was wrong. She could not let that happen.

*Do it, Damian,* she called to her man. *You have to. You can't let him take me.*

*No,* he roared back. *I can't.*

*You must.*
*Never.*
*Trust me,* she urged. *You must do this.*
Tubal stepped forward—Amber stumbled back.
*I can't,* Damian insisted. *I won't.*
*You must or I will. It's the only choice.*
A calm washed over her at the words, an acceptance of the inevitable. A sacrifice she would make for the future. She would not be responsible for the end of the world.

She withdrew the dagger from her pocket, determination setting in. To hell with the prophecies.

As the Marked One, she would prove them wrong.

The air rushed over his face, cooling fingers that chilled his scales and urged him to follow through. To finish what Amber demanded of him.

The impossible.

Damian roared, letting go of the anger and frustration that boiled within him. He flapped his wings and dodged a series of fireballs before he fired back a long breath of flames at the attackers.

Despite the distractions, his primary focus remained on Amber.

*Don't do it, Amber,* he ordered. The hilt of the dagger she clutched gleamed in the firelight, her intent clear to him. Failure burned in his chest. The same pathetic uselessness that was so fresh in his memory assaulted him and burned deeper than any superficial fireball wound. He was a big fucking dragon and still he couldn't stop the events.

Couldn't protect someone he loved.

He circled, then dove, determined to reach her.

The air split around his snout, coursed over his scales as he tucked his wings and stretched out his long body into a streamlined missle. Pain laced through his chest as fireballs hit the tender underside of his belly and seared the hair on his spine.

He ignored it all. He was close.

He could save her.

The force slammed into his side out of nowhere, twisting him sideways to tumble through the air. Claws dug into his shoulders and held tight.

*No.* Denial raged in his mind as he looked into the deep blue eyes of his brother. Louk's snout was pressed close, almost touching Damian's as they wrestled in the air.

*Why?* Damian twisted, frantic to break free of his brother's hold, but he couldn't shake him loose. When he finally stilled, Louk's hot breath streamed over Damian's face in an exhale of understanding. Slowly his brother blinked as his claws tightened and squeezed on Damian's shoulders.

*Submit.* The energy pulsed the command.

*No. Never.* Pulling on his rage, Damian lifted his rear feet and shoved with all his strength into his brother's unprotected belly. A guttural growl left Damian's throat, but Louk refused to let go and eight sharp streaks of pain slashed through muscle as Louk's claws cut through Damian's scales. The wounds were inconsequential compared to the freedom he won.

*Amber.*

Turning quickly, Damian dove back toward his mate.

His heart froze, and his wings came out, breaking backwards as he came to a sudden halt in the air. Around him, flames flew by, water pelted the beach and fire danced on long arcs of swords.

Hell on earth. A battle for the all-important, long prophesied Marked One.

*Don't, Amber,* Damian roared, panic cutting off the oxygen to his lungs. *Don't you dare.*

She stood poised, the edge of the dagger placed against her throat. Tubal was just feet away, a flame burning hot and ready in his palm.

*I must,* she answered. Not a hint of fear lingered in her voice. *If you won't. I trust the energy. I believe as you told me to do. Now I will listen to what it says.*

Damian scrambled, looking for other answers. Another way out. He twitched his tail madly in the weightless air, his gaze cutting across the field looking for alternatives. But he found none.

The circle of Shifters tightened around Amber. Soon, one of them would reach her and then she'd be gone. His instincts screamed to save her.

The energy told him otherwise.

Why?

Why her? Him?

Damian let the pain go in an ear-splitting bellow. Then he dove, his world centered and focused on Amber. The rest of the battle, the assault on his dragon body, was forgotten. Nothing mattered but her.

The energy slammed into him before splitting and slicing around him as he flew toward her. Belief. Trust. Honor. Sacrifice. The words repeated and vibrated with the rush of the air.

Then, when he was just feet away, Tubal lunged.

The knife gleamed against Amber's throat; a trickle of blood streamed down her neck.

*No,* Damian thundered. *No.*

It was her strength that made him succumb. The total calm that flowed through her and into him. Acceptance.

She was willing to sacrifice her life for the betterment of the world.

Tears fell from Damian's eyes, big drops of water that sizzled against his scales as he finally heeded to Amber's demands.

She looked up as if she'd felt his surrender. Her golden eyes held his, a small curve of a smile lifting her lips. Understanding and forgiveness offered in a shortened heartbeat.

*Thank you.*

Her voice caressed his heart even as the flames burned his throat and scarred his soul. He let the fire burst from his chest and descend on his love.

*Amber.*

Rejection, primal animal denial encompassed him even as he held the flames on the two forms directly below him.

Tubal and Amber.

A deep roar of frustration lifted from the inferno as both bodies succumbed to the blaze. Their clothes burst into flames, the fire adding to Damian's flames.

*No.* What had he done? The unthinkable. The impossible.

His breath ran out. The flames died from his mouth. But the bodies still burned.

In an instant, Tubal's form disappeared, the Shifter porting away.

Amber dropped to her knees and crumbled, her body completely engulfed in flames. But she didn't scream or fight the fire.

*What have I done?* his mind repeated, the question an infinite loop in his head as the tears continued to fall from his eyes.

*No.* The injustice tormented him as he rallied against the fates. *Why?*

Again. Again, he had to suffer.

A low, keening moan of despair left his throat as the scent of cinnamon curled within his nostrils. Amber's scent. It lifted in the smoke, from the heat of the flames as she burned.

He'd killed her. He'd killed his mate. His love. His life.

For what?

# Chapter Twenty-Five

Damian's dragon body plunged from the sky, a dead weight of pain that no longer cared if it survived. His life had been too long, too much.

He slammed into the sand, a jarring plunge of force that pummeled his side and head with rivets of sharp pain.

Death. That was what he wanted.

He should be dead. Not her.

He let go of the energy and felt his body change back to his human form. The dragon—a fucking curse he never wanted to see or feel again. Never wanted to be again.

The heat from the blaze kissed his skin and taunted Damian with what he'd done. The unusual white, gold and violet flames reached into the night advertising his deed, the colors proclaiming his actions to everyone on the beach.

He needed to get to her.

Slowly, he moved. He forced his limbs to function, to crawl toward her. To what he'd done. The sand squished between his fingers, bit into his palms as he pulled himself to the fire. The tiny grains stuck to his wet cheeks and sliced at his eyes.

Nothing mattered but getting to her. Joining her.

Cinnamon—the scent rolled over him as he got closer. It seemed to blanket the entire beach with its distinctive, rich fragrance. It washed away the smell of the ocean, the salt and seaweed aroma disappearing under the powerful spice.

Fuck the energy. Fuck the world. He was done bearing the pain for nothing.

He pulled on his strength and lunged toward the fire. Toward the flames that danced and hissed at the night in a mocking waltz of accusation.

Xander stepped into his path. A hand pulled on Damian's shoulder.

"*No.*" Damian fought the hold, tried to fight his way around the imposing bulk of his one-time friend.

"Damian, stop," Louk ordered, his voice strong but gentle.

"No." He twisted and tried to punch his brother. To hit the man who'd stopped him from saving Amber. Ladon and Phelix joined in the struggle and together the four men finally wrestled Damian to the sand. The men pinned Damian, his chest buried in the cold sand, his arms pulled behind his back. A knee jabbed into his spine, grinding the sand into the bare skin of his chest. But Damian kept his head lifted, his eyes still focused on Amber's burning form and the unearthly flames still reaching high into the dark sky.

"Wait, Damian," Louk whispered in his ear as he held him tight from behind. "Trust me."

Around him, the fighting had stopped. The Shifter forces were gone, having left after Tubal exited and they realized the Marked One was dead.

"Why?" Damian snarled, the anger rising to bury the misery. "Why should I trust?"

"Because of who you are," his brother answered. His youngest brother, who knew nothing of Damian's past. Of what he'd endured and suffered.

"You know nothing, brother," Damian bit out.

"I know more that you think," Louk replied, his voice silk against Damian's anger.

Louk pulled on his arms, the force lifting Damian's torso off the sand until he knelt. Louk kept a tight hold on his arms, but now Damian had a clear view of what he'd done.

The Energen forces had gathered to form a wide circle around his destruction. The faces of the men and women who'd fought for Amber now flickered in and out of the light and shadow of the fire that consumed her. The very person they had battled to save.

Damian dropped his head in shame, unable to meet the eyes of those who had finally believed.

Bitterness ate at the tattered remains of his heart. Cold, empty and hollow. His dragon wailed in fury at the injustice and the aching loss of his mate. Beside it, the white bird lay still and motionless. Silenced by death.

"*Damian.*" Louk spoke sharp and commanding into his ear. A tug on his arms brought Damian out of his blackened misery. "Watch."

Louk was right. He should watch what he'd done. Suffer for his actions. That was justice.

Damian lifted his head, the weight of it straining his muscles with the effort. The flames sparked and snapped as they shifted and grew, reaching higher into the night. His gaze held, mesmerized by the shifting colors and changing form.

Around them, the wind died. An unnatural silence and stillness settled on the beach. An almost inappropriate peacefulness rippled through the night and reached out to him. Gently, it pulled at him, begging him to understand.

To accept and trust.

How could he?

*Damian.* The soft word swept through his mind, the purring voice of Amber jerking him upright in disbelief.

A torturous wail of denial ripped from his chest and echoed off the blood-red rock of the cliffs. He pulled on his held arms, desperate to break free. To get to her.

In the next moment, a sweeping wave of energy rolled out of the flames and blasted the surrounding gawkers with a shuddering jolt of pure power. Of silken strength that brushed at Damian with familiarity.

He stilled. Within him, his dragon circled and paced around its downed mate, its agitation and impatience rising with each broad sweep of its tail.

Damian's breath stopped. Hope flared.

Could it be possible?

Then, out of the flames it rose. A collective gasp went up before silence fell.

The large bird, wings spread wide, lifted from the flames in a slow ascension of mystical power. Stunning in its grace and beauty, the apparition held everyone in its grasp as it continued to rise into the night. The bird was mostly white with gold and violet hues glinting through the feathers in a taunting illusion of color.

How? Impossible. Unbelievable.

But real.

Damian struggled free from Louk's slackening hold and stepped forward. The bird tipped its head and held his gaze, the golden eyes snagging his heart and stealing his breath.

*Amber.*

The bird tossed its head back and opened its beak to release a piercing call of joy before it shot off into the sky, gold and violet flames streaking behind it. A single flap of its large wings had it lifting higher before it turned and coasted over the beach.

Stunning.

Joy leapt through Damian as he gloried in the gift.

Laughter tilted through his head in unison with the high, lilting call of the bird from above. Freedom. The feeling radiated through him as Amber continued to soar above the stunned occupants of the beach. For yet another time that night, everyone watched in awe and amazement as a legendary animal coasted over them.

A white phoenix, the bird so easy to identify now.

In three large running steps, Damian leapt, shifted, and soared into the night to meet her.

Laughter bubbled in her throat, the freedom exhilarating. The night air stroked through her feathers, light touches of love and welcome. Of belonging. Amber laughed, the sound coming out as the high, tilting cry of a bird.

Her. A phoenix.

She tilted her wings, gave a flap and soared in a low, graceful glide over the beach below. Her eyes sought out Damian, the man who had sacrificed so much for her. She'd felt his pain, the complete anguish that had consumed him when he'd accepted what he needed to do.

What he did do.

Ultimately, his sacrifice had saved her. But he hadn't known that.

Her keen eyes searched the beach; she needed to find Damian. To explain. But he wasn't down there.

*Damian?* She called out to him, doubt creeping into her voice.

*Here*, he answered, strong and steady. *Beside you.*

A harsh flap of wings cut through the air, and Amber turned her head to see Damian soaring next to her. He was power and grace blended into one stunning form.

*Always*, she answered, positive that would forever be true.

In unison, the connection so strong it was like there was a literal bond holding them together, they gave one more flap of their wings before they turned, circled, then coasted back to the beach.

They landed in the middle of the ring of Energens, exactly where she had burned just minutes before. Only now, not even the sand was darkened to mark the event. Her talons touched down in the sand as she curled her wings to her sides. She didn't shift immediately, but instead waited for Damian, pulling from his energy.

Next to him, she was still small, her head barely reaching his shoulders. Around them, the people watched and waited.

Damian dropped his head and shuffled his feet. His gaze scanned the circle, seeking what, she didn't know. Then his wings expanded to tuck around her, pulling her close to his warm scales.

He lifted his head, a regal declaration as he lifted one of his five-toed claws into the air and let out a mighty, flaming roar. A chill of possessiveness and pride ruffled her feathers and expanded her chest.

This man, this dragon, was hers.

How? She didn't know. But she wasn't going to question it anymore.

Slowly, the men before them bowed their heads and dropped to a knee in a formal bow of reverence. She recognized one of them as the man who had met them at the door of the farmhouse, which now seemed like eons ago. She watched, stunned and overwhelmed as their actions were copied and repeated in a successive wave of deference until the entire circle was kneeling in supplication to them.

The dragon and the phoenix.

Damian's amazement matched her own. But within him, she felt a quiet thread of homecoming, understanding and forgiveness.

He turned to her and together, they shifted. The second her body formed, she was in Damian's arms. His embrace crushed her to his chest, then his mouth was on hers. Hot, claiming and more than welcomed.

His hands laced into her hair before he slowly pulled back to stare into her eyes.

"How?" he whispered, the wonder expressed on his face as he absorbed her features.

She understood what he was feeling because it matched her own. "I don't know," she answered. "The energy encompassed me when your flames hit. I could feel the heat, the sizzle of the fire as it joined with me, but there was no pain. And inside me, the energy flared, ignited by the flames. The stone came to life and for a time, I became one with the fire." She caressed his cheek, the stubble rough and comforting under her fingertips. "Then I found the bird. And I understood what I could do. What I could be."

He touched her as his eyes followed, skimming over her as if he was checking to see if she was whole, real. Somehow, she was completely unhurt. Not even her hair was singed. The fire had rejuvenated her instead of killing her. Even her clothing had returned, unmarked, when she'd shifted back.

His hands slid to her hair, and he tipped his head to rest his forehead against hers. "Don't *ever* scare me like that again." His breath brushed warm across her cheeks and lips.

She smiled. "Never."

She felt his sigh of relief under her hands as they caressed his chest and in her heart where his energy was joined with hers. It was then that their animals rejoiced, the dragon once again curling around the phoenix in a jubilant embrace for the return of its mate.

The energy settled around them, a contented exhale at what should be.

Damian grasped her hand and together they turned to face the men who'd first knelt down to them. His energy flowed openly through their joined hands, a vital piece of who she now was.

The stone was warm against her chest, but for the first time ever, it was absorbing the energy—their united energy—instead of giving energy. She could feel the difference even if she didn't understand the reason. Like so many things now, understanding wasn't a qualification for accepting.

"Look," Damian said, tugging lightly on her hand as he tipped his chin upward. "On the cliffs."

She lifted her gaze, her hand clenching around Damian's, astonished at the sight that met her. There, high on the Aquinnah Cliffs that overlooked Moshup Beach, the moonlight shone down on a long line of people as they stood silently watching the events below.

Her people.

Recognition drummed withinin her even if the faces were hidden in shadow.

In the middle, holding a long staff topped with feathers, was the Wampanoag shaman, Joseph. Flanking him on each side were Kayla and Aunt Beverly.

"How?" Amber whispered, knowing the answer would not come. Her free hand shook as she lifted it to rest against her lips. "Did they know?"

"Does it matter?" Damian asked.

Slowly, in virtual duplication of the Energen forces just moments ago, Joseph, Kayla and her aunt dropped to a knee and bowed their heads. In a rippled domino effect, the people down both sides of the line followed until the entire mass of people on the cliffs were kneeling in respect to them as well.

"Wow," she said under her breath. Her heart beat hard and demanding at the impact of the simple show of respect. She now understood what Damian had felt.

Finally, after years of ridicule and scorn, she was accepted by her people for who she was. Even though it shouldn't matter, it meant so much.

Tears formed, blurring the image before her even as her shoulders pulled back and her chin lifted in pride. "Now what?"

In apparent answer to her question, Joseph rose, raised his staff high, then turned and walked away. Her aunt rose next, lifted her hand in a silent wave, then followed Joseph away from the cliff's edge. All down the line, the people of the Wampanoag tribe stood and followed suit until once again, the cliffs were empty.

At that moment, the wind gusted off the water to blow across the beach and over the cliffs, the long grass that edged the top waving silently in the emptiness.

"Rise," Damian commanded to the men before them, the authority in his voice leaving no doubt of his position. The four men in front rose, each one lifting their heads to meet Damian's gaze. All of them were covered in blood from the battle, their clothing torn and battered from their efforts to protect her.

The man in middle, the one from the house, stepped forward. His voice was deep and full of respect when he spoke.

"Damian, it is time for you to come home."

# Chapter Twenty-Six

Damian inhaled, his chest expanding with warm air and pride. But more, it was filled with the long-awaited relief of coming home.

The scent of jasmine and honeysuckle blended in the night air and settled into the warm spring breeze that drifted inside the walls of the Energen compound. The constant temperature that persisted within the city was a benefit of the race's abilities to control the energy and elements. It was a benefit that he'd missed along with so many other things.

In the open courtyard where they'd been brought stood the formidable line of Energen elders. The Heads of the Houses of Air, Fire, Water, Earth and Spirit. The same people who had accused and crucified Amber and him so recently.

Amber gripped his hand, a lifeline he would never let go. It was because of her that he was now home.

"You good?" she asked softly, even though she was the one who was completely out of her element.

He gave a tight smile and a short nod. "With you, yes."

Cronus, the Ancient of the enclave, stepped forward, his hands spread wide and open, a large smile of welcome lighting his lined face. "Damian. Amber. Welcome home."

Damian stiffened, but held his features placid. He wanted to believe the welcome was true and heartfelt. "That is quite a change from yesterday."

*I am sorry for all that you had to endure, Damian.* Cronus's words drifted into his mind.

Giving away nothing, Damian responded in kind. *And you knew all along? You were in on it all?*

The elder dropped his hands, his eyes narrowing slightly. *The new power sits well on you.* He turned to Amber. "I apologize for my actions yesterday. Unfortunately, it was a necessary move to test your path. The Marked One has chosen the light and for that, we are forever grateful. Welcome to our world, Amber."

Amber lifted her chin and gave a tight smile in response. Damian squeezed her hand, a private signal of approval. She was so beautiful standing there, proud and regal after all she'd been through. All she'd accepted and overcome so quickly with a grace that stunned him to his soul.

*Your strength amazes me,* he told her silently.

*As does yours,* she replied.

Cronus stepped forward and stared pointedly at Damian's hand, the one that bore their mark—the intertwined white dragon and phoenix. "It is as the saying goes: when the dragon soars with the phoenix at his side, the people will enjoy happiness for years, bringing peace and tranquility to all in the energy."

"I've never heard that saying," Damian mused, his eyes narrowing at the truth of what Cronus was saying.

The Ancient looked up, the countless years of knowledge and wisdom sparking in his eyes. "It is a very old Chinese saying that has long been twisted to mean something different than its original intent. Like so many things, Gog persuaded and enflamed a belief that was far from the truth. But that is his gift, his deadly skill that has incited strife and war for more years than we can comprehend. The Slanderer, The Oppressor—names for Gog that fit because that is what he does."

"But we can change that?" Amber asked, her voice a solid cord in the thread of doubt that wound around Damian.

Cronus smiled, a gentle easing of respect and understanding. "The two of you are our best hope of finding peace once again. The balance is tipping. Too much in either direction will cause an imbalance that can never be righted. The dragon and phoenix united in our lead will correct the course and keep us steady."

The elder's face sobered before he continued. "The time has come for you to ascend, Damian." Cronus turned and pointed to the long set of stairs that rose majestically into the night sky. "Last night, these rose from the ground when you joined with Amber. A sign to us that our king is ready to rise."

The elder turned back to face them. "Your sacrifice has been for a reason. You have proven yourself loyal and strong. And now, with your mate by your side, you must rise to lead our battle against The Oppressor. For soon, Gog will be free."

"Why?" Damian's question echoed through the courtyard, the small group of people cringing at the hardness of his voice. "After all I have been forced to endure, why?"

"Louk and Airiana were the catalyst," Cronus explained. "The Two that came together despite the odds against it. With them, the dragon woke, but they also brought proof that the mighty winged dragons still existed." Cronus crooked his fingers, and Louk stepped forward from his position behind them. At Louk's side was a tall woman with a striking blend of Asian and Caucasian features. Damian assumed she was the Shifter the other Ancient had referred to and thus Louk's mate.

"They were the first in the series of steps that must be executed over this year, the Year of the Dragon." Cronus looked at Damian and Amber. "You two are the key to the second. The most vital step that you must complete, or all the rest will fail. Our very survival is dependent upon you accepting who you are and your role in the coming war. You must ascend, Damian, with Amber at your side, or all your suffering will be for naught."

"Why us?" Damian had to ask. "Of all the Energens in the world, why me? Why her?"

Cronus looked to the sky then turned to Amber. "Tomorrow, you will turn twenty-four."

She smiled, a slight flush rising on her cheeks. "Yes. Tomorrow's my birthday."

Cronus returned her smiled. "Born on the vernal equinox in the Year of the Dragon, conceived by both Energen and Shifter. She who straddles light and dark, born of both positive and negative, will define the course of the Great War. Like your namesake—amber—you are the true connector: the balance that harmonizes yin and yang, as well as the past, present and future."

"But it is only with Damian that I have that balance."

"Yes." Cronus nodded then addressed Damian. "You are the stabilizer. The rare one with a strength of character strong enough to endure a thousand years of pain and wrongful exile without losing himself in misery and self-pity. The second son and heir to the House of Air, you, Damianos Aeros, are the Chosen One for what you bring our world. It is through the Air bloodline that the winged dragons have returned. You are a descendant of the Royal House of the Winged Dragons and thus heir to the throne. I know this because a five-toed dragon is the mark of royalty reserved solely for the king."

Damian's gaze dropped to the dragon mark on his hand where one foot visibly displayed five toes. His focus snapped back to Cronus. "Did you know this when you played your game a thousand years ago? Did you know this about me?"

A spark of sadness flashed in the Ancient's eyes. "There was never a certainty, only a hope. And it was never a game. Not when so many lives were—are—affected. We can only listen to the energy and trust that it will yield the results we need. There was no way to know that the winged ones would return. The energy picked you as being strong enough to carry the burden of the sacrifice required to trap Gog...now, we know why."

"If that is true, then why did it take until now to manifest?" Damian could feel the truth in what Cronus was saying, but the doubt was still there. The turnaround in his position within the Energen world had happened too fast for him to just believe.

"The stone is the key," Cronus answered as he tipped his head at Amber. "It is the key that unlocked the latent Energen gene in Amber and the dragon gene in you. Its power was forged when the earth was young, when the energy was purest."

"So why didn't you tell us this yesterday?" Amber spoke up, her eyes narrowed in thought. "Why did we have to play this game of lies and mystery for the last two days?"

Damian let a small smile show. Leave it to Amber to poke at the heart of the matter, and to identify the most important detail and seek the answer.

"Because each move had to be made by your own free will," Cronus said. "Each decision on your path to this moment had to be made by you alone in order to obtain this end."

"What end?" Damian asked.

"Louk and Airiana's joining brought them the gift of dual power, the ability for both of them to wield his power of air and her power of fire, both in human and dragon form. Your joining has gifted the two of you with everything. The ability to shift shapes *and* to wield all five powers—air, water, earth, fire and spirit. This is a gift of true supremacy given only to ones who have the inner fortitude to withstand the lure of the evil that can come with holding so much power. A power the energy has never given to anyone—until now."

Damian resisted the urge to stumble backwards at the impact of the Ancient's words. It was only Amber's strong grip on his hand that held him steady.

He closed his eyes and digested all that had been revealed. There was so much to understand, but little time to do so. The energy was pushing, the urgency building to accept his—their—fate and blindly follow. But could he?

"And you, Father?" Damian opened his eyes and held the steady glare of his father, who stood behind Cronus. "What do *you* think of this?" For the first time since arriving at the compound, sweat gathered down his back. His stomach muscles clenched as he waited for his father's response, the man who had despised and blamed him for the death of Khristos.

The man whose opinion mattered the most.

His father, Kadmos, moved forward, each step aging his features until he stood before Damian looking old beyond his years. His blue eyes were dull, his cheeks sunken, his lips thinned in a grim line. Damian remained still and held his tongue as his father slowly regarded him, then Amber.

His father looked to Louk, blinked, then back to them. Slowly, as if the very movement would break his bones, his father bent to one knee before them.

The impact was instantaneous. Damian lost his breath and with it, the last of his resentment and doubt.

"I owe you much, Damian," his father said, his voice low and filled with pain. "But mostly, I owe you my love. Something I stripped unjustly from you years ago. Now, I can only hope my actions don't keep you from being who you were meant to be."

Damian dropped to his knees, humbled by his father's admission. The strong, formidable leader of the House of Air was admitting to his mistakes when he had been wronged just as fiercely as Damian himself. He reached out to grip his father's shoulder. It was his first contact in over a thousand years with the man he had once admired and aspired to emulate.

Kadmos flinched, an almost imperceptible movement of muscles under Damian's palm. Cautiously, the man lifted his gaze to meet his son's. Unbelievably, tears shimmered in those eyes. Tears Damian hadn't seen him shed even at Khristos's death.

Damian cleared his throat, his words suddenly lodged behind the ball of humility that was stuck there. "It is you, Father, who has endured more than any one man should be expected to shoulder. The loss of two sons, the betrayal of so many. The weight is heavy for one man to carry alone. It is time you let it go and let the past remain where it is. I have."

His father blinked, swallowed and then lifted his hand to grip Damian's shoulder. A sharp squeeze, a nod, and they both stood. An understanding reached in a way only men can achieve.

Damian took Amber's hand and spoke to the assembled group. "There is much for Amber and I to discuss. Much that has been thrust upon us in a very short amount of time. I hope you will understand if we take some time to ourselves."

"You are welcome to your old room at our house," his father said. "Your mother will want to see you."

Damian's heart twisted at the thought of his mother. "Thank you, Father. But right now, we need our own space."

"You know what is next," Cronus said solemnly. "I know the energy has told you what needs to be done to protect the city." He gave a sharp, assessing look to both of them. "We will expect you back here in time to complete your ascension."

Damian gave a nod then tugged Amber to his side and dissipated out. The break was as much for him as her. He needed to hold her, to ensure that she was okay. She was his first priority and all that mattered in his world.

Right now, the rest of the world could wait.

# Chapter Twenty-Seven

They solidified in the living room of Damian's safe house, the comfortable surroundings instantly relaxing him. But it was the warmth of the woman in his arms that gave solace to his soul and peace to his heart.

Somehow, at a rate too fast to comprehend, she had broken past every barrier he'd erected around his emotions and exposed them to the glaring light of reality. He could hide no more, nor did he want to.

"Amber," he breathed against her hair. The long, silky mass drove him mad with a desire to feel it wrapped around them, caressing their bare skin as he made love to her.

"Damian," she answered just as softly, her warm breath stroking the skin of his neck, igniting a burning craving to touch her, to feel her heated skin beneath his hands, against his body.

Pulling back, he tugged her hand to follow him as he moved to the bedroom. The energy was thick with anticipation as they walked past the large bed that beckoned and into the master bathroom. He felt her question, her emotions so tied to his that little could remain hidden between them.

Instead of terrifying him, the sensation was one of rightness. Of what he had been waiting to find only he never realized it until it was there.

He dropped her hand and started the water in the shower, the pattering sound of the spray filling the space and echoing off the marble. Turning back to her, he had to laugh at the unsuppressed delight that covered her face.

"Shower first," he said around the deep chuckle that lingered. "Then we'll talk."

A coy smile curved over her lips as she began to unbutton his big coat, the one she'd worn for almost two days now. The one that now belonged to her more than him. He stepped up to help slip it off her shoulders, the scent of cinnamon surrounding and drugging him with its intoxicating lure to her.

"Maybe we could shower and talk," she said, shooting a shy but calculated look over her shoulder as he hung the coat along with his ruined leather jacket on a hook.

He turned and pulled her back to his chest, the soft strands of her hair rubbing against his skin in a taunting slide of seduction. Her head settled on his shoulder, a low moan escaping her lips. He ran his hands under her shirt, the smooth skin of her stomach burning hot embers of desire into his flesh.

"That is the best suggestion I've heard all day," he murmured into her ear.

She laughed, a throaty sound that notched up his need. "It wasn't hard to top the offers we've been given today." She turned, her hands sliding around his neck as his palms skimmed across her stomach to rest at the small of her back. A spot he fully intended to explore with his lips in the very near future.

She looked into his eyes, the golden tones of her own eyes darkening to the color of deep, aged amber found in ancient trees. "Do you question this?" she asked, the snippet of doubt and fear threading through her energy.

"No," he answered honestly, pouring all his conviction into his energy, his voice. "Not you. I can't question such a gift after so many years of emptiness."

She looked down, her lip disappearing between her teeth. "Not even the speed of it all?" Her gaze met his again. "Is there a chance it's all wrong?"

"No. Not a chance," he insisted, tugging her against his length. "There's no way this is wrong."

He bent his head, descending upon her with a heated kiss of affirmation. She opened her mouth in acceptance and met his passion with an urgency that matched his own. The desperation of the connection speared him deep in his chest and almost dropped him to his knees.

She dug her hands into his hair, pulling his head down tighter into her embrace as she sucked longingly on his lip. The steam from the shower billowed out of the stall, banking the space in a moist, heated cloak of seduction.

His erection rubbed tauntingly against her lower stomach, aching for release from his jeans. A demand he needed to heed.

Pulling back from her lips, Damian slipped her shirt over her head to drop it carelessly on the floor. He disposed of her bra just as quickly so she stood before him naked from the waist up, the stone shimmering seductively between her breasts. His breath left his chest, one big exhale of disbelief at his fortune.

Her breasts were round, fuller underneath and tipped with coral nipples that begged him to take them. Touch and suck them until she moaned in bliss.

"Gorgeous doesn't even begin to describe you."

Her cheeks darkened to a deep tint of red, a beautiful part of her that only complemented the midnight hues of her hair and made her even more alluring. But she didn't look down or shy away from him or his words. Instead, she reached for the waistband of his jeans, the brush of her fingers against his stomach his undoing.

He groaned and stepped away, jerking a hand through his hair. "Shower." He pointed. "Now or we'll never make it there."

She laughed, her head tossing back in levity, causing her hair to shimmer and dance down her back. "Right, shower."

He turned away. It was either that or take her on the cold tile floor, and she deserved better than that. He stepped into the closet and stripped away the rest of his clothes. He took a deep breath and waited until he heard the click of the shower door closing.

His erection bobbed hard and insistent against his stomach as he walked to the shower. The blurred outline of her naked body taunted him behind the glass as she tipped her head back into the water, her beautiful chest thrusting upward with the action. The smoky tendrils of heat curled around her, weaving a dance his hands itched to follow.

He bit his cheek and cursed. How did he deserve her?

Whatever the case, he wasn't letting her go. Their future was still up in the air, but he knew without doubt that his would be with her, whatever she decided.

Opening the door, Damian stepped through the steam and into her arms. His dragon growled and tightened possessively around the phoenix, a deep sense of connection rippling over his nerves and into his heart.

She slid her arms around Damian's neck, pulling him down for another soul-searing kiss. The hot water streamed down Amber's back, heating her skin as Damian heated her soul.

She belonged in his arms. This she knew even without the energy telling her so. Her CEO. He was what she'd waited for, what the energy had been pushing for her to recognize for the last three years. He was her other half that now blended smoothly within her. Complemented her and washed away all the doubts and insecurities she'd held for so long.

Her phoenix cooed softly within the tight embrace of its dragon. Contentment settled gently within its heart as it tucked its feathered head against the warm scales of its mate.

Damian gave one last caress of his tongue over hers before he lifted his head. His eyes had deepened to the dark, taunting shimmer of early dawn. He skimmed his hands down her back, her breasts pressed erotically against his chest, the hard length of his erection trapped between them.

"Turn," he ordered as he grabbed her hips and flipped her around. She grinned and tipped her head back, letting the water caress over her neck and down her chest.

"I told you before you were going to kill me," he growled into her ear. He massaged her scalp, rubbing shampoo through the long mass of her hair. His touch sent sharp, fiery snaps of need down her body to settle low and hot in her core. Combine that with the gentle way in which he took care of her, and she was lost.

She let the small moan of satisfaction release from her throat before she responded. "I believe it was you who killed me," she teased as she leaned into his hands. Hands that stilled and clenched at her words.

"An act that did kill me," he said softly before he restarted his tender care of her hair.

"But you trusted the energy and me. That act of sacrifice is what kept me from Tubal and brought me back to you." She hoped he understood that.

He smoothed his hands over her shoulders and down her arms, the scent of pine and the outdoors teasing her nose. He washed her body using long, lazy strokes of tenderness that set her cells on fire while easing her tired muscles.

"I'm done with sacrifices," he bit out a bit harshly. "Someone else is going to have to step up and fill that need because the only sacrifice I'll make is for you and you alone."

She turned in his arms and cupped his face in her hands. "No more sacrifices needed. I have everything I want, everything I need right here."

His gaze held her; his hands moved back to her hair as he threaded his fingers through it to rinse away the shampoo. "And the future? What does that hold?"

She pondered her next words, wanting to ensure that they came out right. Her thumbs grazed over his jaw, the rough stubble scraping against her pads, the sensation snaking down her arms to further tighten her already aching nipples.

"Is it a sacrifice to be who you were meant to be?" His hands hesitated in her hair, a flash of doubt sparking in his eyes. "Do you still question who you are? Do you not know the strength and power you carry within you? They are the same qualities that allowed you to found and lead a corporation that has a fundamental impact on the earth's energy. It is your solid belief in doing what is right despite what others say that makes you who you are. Those qualities have *always* been within you. It's what your people need right now. They need you."

"*Our* people," he said. "Our people need *us* right now. Are you up for all that it means? For all of the changes it will make on your life?"

"Have you not listened to anything that's been told to us the last two days?" she chided. "This *is* my life. Evidently, this is why I was born. To be with you, at your side. Where I want to be."

"Really? No hesitation? No doubt?"

She smiled. "I didn't say that. Of course there's hesitation and doubt. But not about you. Us. What we're supposed to do. Walking away feels safe, less daunting. However, it's also the weaker path, the one chosen by those who can close their hearts and minds to the pain and suffering their actions will inflict on others." She searched his eyes, reached into herself and felt his energy, the swirling turmoil of emotions that pulled at him. "I don't think that's something either of us can live with. We may be many things, but selfish has never been one of them."

His hands rubbed down her back, over the rounded humps of her bottom, up her sides until they cupped the tender sides of her breasts, leaving a trail of blazing heat in their wake.

"Selfish, no," he agreed. "Except where you're concerned. If you're not all right with all of it, I'd walk away and not look back." He swallowed, looked away then back into her eyes. "Trust is hard for me. It will take a while before I can fully extend that emotion—if ever. But I trust what the energy is telling us to do. Most of all, I trust you."

"So we're good on this?" She licked her lips, her stomach knotting in a quick tug of finality. The impact of what they were discussing settled in with the leaden weight of responsibility it held. "Are we to rise, Damian? Will you be the leader they need now?"

He tipped his head to rest his forehead against hers in that intimate way of his. He cupped her face, his touch so gentle and possessive that it melted away the tension, loosened her stomach muscles until she exhaled and relaxed into his hold.

"I can only be that person with you by my side." A roughened edge of vulnerability lined his words, a trait he allowed only her to see.

"Always," she assured him.

He exhaled, the stress leaving his body just as hers had done moments ago. "It won't be easy," he challenged, one last wall of defense going up.

"Where's the fun in easy?"

He kissed her, a hard, sharp burst of happiness. He pulled back, his voice husky with emotion as he spoke. "I love you, Amber. I swore I'd never say that. Feel that. But you crashed through the walls so fast, I couldn't stop it. Couldn't stop you." He eased his hand under her hair to grip the back of her neck. "You're mine, and I'm never letting you go."

Her heart raced even as it melted. The security that came with belonging settled into her like the warm water and hot steam that encased them in its soothing cloud of protection.

"Mine," she assured him, reinforcing the word with a sharp tug on his hair to pull his lips closer to hers. "You're mine. My love. My heart. And you are so not getting away."

She reached her lips to his in an all-out crush of possession. All that mattered at that moment was the man in her arms. Her phoenix arched its head and let out a long, lilting song of joy. The dragon released a fiery breath of agreement as it coiled its long body closer to its mate.

The energy pulsed hotter and brighter with each caress of his hands and thrust of his tongue. The stone throbbed and burned, his hard, water-slicked chest pressing it into hers. And once again, she felt the stone absorbing their combined energy as it flowed between them in an unfiltered blending of power and strength.

The knowledge slipped into her like the soft flutter of settling wings.

The Chosen One and Marked One—together they would rise.

# Epilogue

They stood poised at the base of the long rise of white, stone stairs that stretched into the early morning sky. Damian looked down at Amber, his chest expanding in pride and love.

Her long, midnight hair shimmered and glowed in the soft light of the breaking dawn, subtle hues of red and yellow dancing over the silken mass from the line of torches that lit the courtyard. She lifted her golden eyes to meet his.

"Ready?" he asked.

She nodded. "It's almost time."

He looked around at the gathered group, meeting the eyes of Cronus first then his father's. His mother stood regally next to his father. Even with the distance, he could see the tears that shimmered in the firelight before she blinked them back. He would ease those tears soon.

Flanking them were his brothers.

Phelix stood tall and somber next their father, his face a mask of hardened pain that was lightened slightly by the gentle depths of his eyes. Phelix had been but a boy when the events had started a millennium ago, having to endure the fallout and live with the burden for as long as Damian. There was much they needed to work through, but he hoped one day they could reconnect that bond that held brothers close.

One he'd had with Khristos and finally wished to establish with his other brothers.

Loukianos stood strong and assured next to their mother, his arm around Airiana. They were another surprise in the list of revelations that Damian would need to unravel. They would be powerful weapons in the war to come. But first, Louk was his brother, one he wanted to know.

The families from each of the Houses were also gathered within the courtyard. He quickly caught the gaze of Xander as he stood with his family, the House of Fire and then Ladon with his family, the House of Water. Two friendships he hoped to reestablish.

"When this city was built thousands of years ago," Cronus said, his deep voice vibrating through the dark and ringing with authority, "measures were put in place to secure its safety. The shields have held strong, forged with ancient power and pure energy. But the threat that looms before us will be greater than what we have ever had to face. Gog will come for us, and the people of earth are primed and ready to follow him." Cronus looked solemnly around at the gathered group. "Damian and Amber hold the key that will unlock the last level of defense that we can erect to protect this city. The Sacred City."

Cronus looked to them. In unspoken unity, Amber lifted the hem of the long, white robe and placed her foot on the step in time with Damian's. He kept his back straight, his eyes locked on the small platform one hundred and forty-four steps above them. He knew the number without counting.

A light breeze swirled around them, pushing at his hair, tugging at the silk of the robe. On its wings, it brought the warm scents of spring and the hint of new beginnings.

Of forgiveness and blessings to come.

They reached the top and stepped up on the small dais as the earth slowly revolved into place, the incremental movements indiscernible to man, but so significant in the daily passage of life. In the center of the platform rose a stand, its top the size of a large platter with a sculpted design that was divided into four quadrants, each section separated by long channels that ran from the center opening to the outer ring. The etchings within each quadrant represent the blending of elements as they merged with each other and aligned to the four navigational directions.

Damian looked up from the center compass point and took a second to absorb the sight before him.

"Home," he murmured, warmth blanketing him in an open presence of welcome.

"Tell me about it," Amber encouraged as she followed his gaze to the shadowed outlines of the city that lay quiet in the pre-dawn light. "Share your world with me."

"The Energen lands stretch five miles in each direction," he told her. "The compound built within a protective circle when man was just beginning to inhabit the continent. This is the exact geographic center of what is now North America. A centering of navigational energy and a source of the very power we pull our strength from."

He turned and pointed. "To the East resides the House of Air, in the South is the House of Fire, West is the House of Water, to the North lies the House of Earth, and here, in the middle, is the House of Spirit. Each direction pulls on an elemental power and every Energen possesses one of these powers."

"Some of us more," Amber said. The light danced in her eyes and he almost laughed despite the seriousness of the moment. She turned away and pointed to the east. "That's where we entered last time? You had said we were at the eastern entrance to the enclave."

Of course she would remember that. "Yes. There is a gate in each direction that allows entrance to the enclave. The energy shield allows for Energens to port in and out, but I had been exiled, my permission to enter revoked. Xander had to verbally sanction our entry into the city in order for us to cross the shield gate and enter the enclave through the house."

Damian exhaled as he looked to the direction of the rising sun—a symbol of new beginnings and reawakening. A long worshipped entity of life and rebirth.

It was also the object they waited for.

For its alignment with the earth. The exact time when day equals night, light equals dark and the energy is balanced as it can only be twice each year. And in the center of the city, the center of the power, the compass awaited its key.

"Soon," he said with a tip of his head towards the lightening eastern sky. "The vernal equinox is almost here."

Amber inhaled a deep breath of freshness and renewal with the rising sun. It seemed so appropriate for the vernal equinox to occur at this time, just before the sun made its appearance on the land.

"The people of the first light," she said quietly. "That's what Wampanoag means. This time of day has always been sacred to my people." She smiled. "I spent my whole life wanting to belong somewhere and now I find I belong in more places than I could ever imagine. It's rather ironic."

The energy hummed around them. Not an auditory sound, but a physical vibration that pressed against her. The air around them felt thick and humid with anticipation for the coming moment.

Releasing her tight hold on his hand, Amber slipped the long pendant chain over her head. The stone slid against her skin, a streak of heat slicking a path across her chest as she pulled it from under the white robe. The loss was profound, but it had served her well, protected her while awakening the latent genes within her. It had opened the door to her Energen powers and guided her as she discovered the power of the energy.

Now, it had a larger purpose.

She laid the stone in her palm and admired its beauty one last time. Within her, she felt the earth shift. She looked to Damian. "Ready?"

"Yes. You?"

"There's no going back after this."

"And now even more so." He smiled placing one hand over hers and the other over her stomach. "There's been no going back since we started."

"So you know?"

"About the new life growing within you?" He smiled, his love flowing into her. "Yes, I know."

"Right." She inclined her head and inhaled again, this time a deep breath of preparation and fortification. Of course he'd feel the energy of the new life just like she did.

Damian let go of her hand, and she stepped forward to stand beside the ornate carving in the center of the platform, shifting until she was aligned with the quadrant that depicted the blending of air and fire. Damian moved to stand across from her, aligning with the quadrant of water and earth.

Power pulsed from the stone, the life within it aching to serve the purpose it was created for. Dropping the chain to the floor, she extended the ringed stone until it was positioned over the center of the sculpture. Damian clasped the other side of the ring then he lifted his head and held her gaze.

The energy pulsed, the earth shifted—the time had arrived.

Together, they lowered the stone into the center of the sculpture, the diamond shape fitting perfectly into the hollow opening in the middle, each corner aligning with the open channels that headed in each direction.

They each released the small clasps on the corners of the stone holding the ring in place, then Amber lifted the ring away.

The stone shimmered in perfection, the colors flashing and lighting as the power grew. Sparks of electricity danced upward from the stone, the small show a visual display of what she could feel. The energy was building within the stone, firing up as if it was pulling power from the pedestal itself.

Without warning, light shot out of the four channels, visual beams fired in violet, gold and white that extended into the waning dark, piercing the South, West, North and East with its light and power.

Instinctively, she reached across the pedestal to clasp Damian's hand over the stone. At their touch, a last beam of light shot straight up to meld around their hands and infuse them with one last boost of power and knowledge.

With it came clarity, revelations of old and visions of new. The images flashed through her mind quick and hot to linger within her subconscious for later dissection. In the far distance, at each gate, towers rose, reaching into the sky in replication of the one they stood on. The image appeared in her mind, the distance too great to for her to see all that happened.

The foundations of the pillars were layered in precious stones: jasper, sapphire, chalcedony, emerald, sardonyx, ruby, peridot, beryl, topaz, chrysoprase, jacinth and amethyst. The twelve levels rose in color from the base along a staircase that wrapped around the towers allowing access to the top.

She met Damian's gaze, the blue of his eyes matching perfectly with the skyline behind him. With the towers raised, the beams of light extending from the center stone faded away. The center stone, her stone, still glowed with power. There it would remain, the conduit for what was to come.

Damian walked around the pedestal until he stood beside her. Together, they turned to face the city below. With the lightening of the sky, Amber could see the thousands of people gathered in each direction.

Hands still linked, Damian used the element of spirit to communicate to all within the compound. The words flowed smoothly into the minds of all.

*The time has come for us to rise. To protect the humans whose energy keeps the world in balance. It is our call, our duty. My thousand years of exile have ended, and so have Gog's. This is the Year of the Dragon. By its end, the dragon will be free.* The crowd shuffled below, but the silence hung heavy and still across the air. Damian inhaled, then called out to the city, his voice carrying far and wide.

"Our city is sacred in the war to come. We must defend these walls and hold the gates, for within these walls is the power Gog needs. The four towers have risen—now their keys must be found."

He looked to her, then as one, they jumped, shifting in mid-air to fly over the crowd below.

The words of Cronus drifted through Amber's mind: *When the dragon soars with the phoenix at his side, the people will enjoy happiness for years, bringing peace and tranquility to all in the energy.*

She could only hope that would be true.
But only time would tell.

# About the Author

Lynda Aicher has always loved to read. It's a simple fact that has been true since she discovered the words of Judy Blume at the age of ten. After years of weekly travel as a consultant implementing computer software into global companies, she ended her nomadic lifestyle to raise her two children. Now, her imagination is her only limitation on where she can go and her writing lets her escape from the daily duties of being a mom, wife, chauffer, scheduler, cook, teacher, volunteer, cleaner and mediator. If writing wasn't a priority, it wouldn't get done.

To learn more about Lynda, please visit her:
Website: http://lyndaaicher.com
Facebook: http://facebook.com/lyndaaicherauthor
Twitter: @lyndaaicher

# SAMHAIN
PUBLISHING

*It's all about the story...*

# Romance

# HORROR

# Retro
ROMANCE

www.samhainpublishing.com

CPSIA information can be obtained at www.ICGtesting.com
Printed in the USA
BVOW031025100713

325586BV00006B/19/P

9 781619 213661